Drawing a deep breath, Lilly let her troubled gaze roam the room's faded elegance once more.

What she saw was neglect, not destruction. Was it possible that the townsfolk were too frightened of the haint rumored to occupy the house to rob it? Strange, since even she knew the furnishings were worth a small fortune.

Recalling what she'd told William about preachers being unable to afford such costly things, her lips twisted into a bitter smile. The grand lifestyle suggested by Heaven's Gate and its furnishings would have been easily attainable if the reverend routinely fleeced his flocks.

Leaving, she crossed the hall and found herself in a bedroom. A mahogany chest with cabriole legs, claw and ball feet, and decorated with carved shells and scrollwork sat on the far wall. A tin bathtub peeked from behind a carved dressing screen.

Animals had helped themselves to some of the feathers from the rotting feather tick, and the tangle of sheets was stained with rust.

Her breathing hitched. Not rust. Blood.

Lots and lots of blood.

An
UNTIMELY FROST

PENNY RICHARDS

KENSINGTON BOOKS
www.kensingtonbooks.com

KENSINGTON BOOKS are published by

Kensington Publishing Corp.
119 West 40th Street
New York, NY 10018

All Kensington titles, imprints, and distributed lines are available at special quantity discounts for bulk purchases for sales promotion, premiums, fundraising, educational, or institutional use.

Special book excerpts or customized printings can also be created to fit specific needs. For details, write or phone the office of the Kensington Sales Manager: Kensington Publishing Corp., 119 West 40th Street, New York, NY 10018. Attn. Sales Department. Phone: 1-800-221-2647.

Kensington and the K logo Reg. U.S. Pat. & TM Off.

eISBN-13: 978-1-4967-0603-4
eISBN-10: 1-4967-0603-X
First Kensington Electronic Edition: August 2016

ISBN-13: 978-1-4967-0602-7
ISBN-10: 1-4967-0602-1
First Kensington Trade Paperback Printing: August 2016

10 9 8 7 6 5 4 3 2 1

Printed in the United States of America

This book is for my friend Linda Card, who, many years ago, when I was looking for a jumping-off place for this book, gave me an idea I'd never have thought of. At long last, here are the results.

Acknowledgments

This book couldn't have been written without the efforts of many people: Linda Hanabarger, with the Fayette County Genealogical and Historical Society, for the pictures, information, and street map of old Vandalia; Curtis Mann, with the Lincoln Library, in Springfield, Illinois, for the invaluable information about Springfield and especially Chatterton's Opera House; and Sandy and LaRee as usual, for reading and rereading and keeping me straight. Thanks to everyone at Kensington Publishing for taking a chance on me and working with me on my ideas and giving me such an awesome cover, and lastly to my editor, Tara Gavin, whose belief in me and my writing gave me another "first" and whose spot-on editing always makes the book better.

Death lies on her like an untimely frost.

—William Shakespeare, *Romeo and Juliet,* act 4, scene 5

CHAPTER 1

Chicago, 1881
Peacock Opera House

Blast it, he'd promised!

Lilly Warner's rising fury battled with an all-too-familiar disappointment. Pierce Wainwright, the cast's manager and the man who had raised her from the age of eleven, had finally given her a major role in the troupe's new play, *Society's Daughter*. Tim had promised to come and see her debut performance, but he hadn't shown up. Another of her husband's lies, offered for the sole purpose of momentary appeasement.

Too angry to be fearful, she jerked up the hood of her red woolen cape and stepped through the door at the rear of the theater into the darkness of the narrow backstreet. In less than a minute, she entered the main thoroughfare. Tendrils of fog writhed in the flickering glow of the gaslights, turning the few stalwart souls braving the chilly night into wraithlike phantoms.

Annoyance rose with every step as she navigated the four blocks to the boardinghouse where the members of the Pierced Rose Theater Troupe were staying during their brief stay in Chicago. She pushed through the doorway and was greeted by a rush of heat from the foyer fireplace. Pushing back the hood, she marched down the hall, mentally framing a series of questions for her absent husband.

Nearing Pierce and Rose's room, Lilly noticed their door standing ajar. That was odd; the worldly-wise Rose was generally more careful about such things. Lilly placed her gloved hand on the doorknob, wondering if she should stick her head in and mention the oversight.

While she stood torn between the need to confront her husband and check on her friend, she heard the sound of a man's voice from inside the room. Sudden uneasiness caused her heart to beat faster. Who could it be? She'd left Pierce at the opera house.

The man spoke again, menace in his low tone. Before she could do more than acknowledge that something was terribly wrong, Lilly heard the sickening, somehow familiar, sound of flesh meeting flesh. She slumped against the wall, squeezing her eyes shut and covering her ears, attempting to block out the memories that sought freedom from where she'd banished them eleven years ago. She fought the craven desire to escape into the dark vortex of unconsciousness.

"Please, God, make him stop. Make him go away."

The words echoing through her mind were chanted by a child's voice. Her voice.

Do something!

Lilly whimpered. What could she do? She was only eleven, and someone was hurting her mama. . . .

Another cry, this one laced with an unmistakable pain, scattered the distressing fragments of memory. She opened her eyes. She wasn't eleven, the sounds she heard were not memories from her past, and the man in the other room was not her mother's killer, but whoever he was, he was hurting Rose. Lilly couldn't stand by and do nothing. Not again.

Taking tight hold on the doorknob, she shoved away from

the wall and burst into the room, gauging the situation in a single glance. Rose lay across the bed, blood trickling from her mouth, a mark that would become a bruise on her cheekbone, and tears seeping from her eyes into the graying hair at her temples. A man stood over her, a leather pouch clutched in one fist, a small revolver in the other. Lilly's eyes widened and her footsteps faltered.

"Tim?" Her voice was an agonized whisper. "What are you doing?"

"What do you think I'm doing, you stupid cow?" He held the money bag aloft. "I came for the money."

Money? Her heart began an agonized throbbing. "But . . . I gave you money this morning."

"Barely enough to get my shoes shined."

Hearing the mockery in his voice, she urged sternness to hers and held out her hand. "Give me my money, Tim. You have no right to it."

His beautiful lips twisted into a taunting smile. "Your money? You seem to forget that when you said 'I do' everything of yours became mine."

He spoke the truth. The law favored men in every way. Rose lifted herself to one elbow and swiped the blood from her mouth with the back of her hand. "Let him have it, Lil. It's not worth it."

Perhaps Rose was right, but it was money Lilly had been setting aside since she was old enough to do small tasks for the cast. Money she was saving to buy a little house somewhere . . . someday. Money she'd told him she'd given to Rose for safe-keeping. A surge of guilt washed through her at the idea that her own naïve trust had brought about this betrayal.

"It's mine," she repeated. "I've worked hard for it."

Timothy's handsome face contorted with disgust. His burst of laughter was short and hate filled. "So have I. I've listened to your pious preaching about taking a salesman's job until I want to puke. Well, I'm not a damned peddler," he all but growled. "And I might also mention that the thrill of bedding an innocent lost its appeal weeks ago."

Both Rose and Lilly sucked in sharp breaths. Old insecurities flooded her. Being beautiful, confident Kate Long's plain bastard daughter had never been an easy role.

"I'm done with it all," Tim was saying, "including you." His lips twisted into a parody of a smile and he shook his head. "What an easy mark you were."

Stealing her life savings and hurting Rose were hard enough to take, but when Lilly realized that he had taken advantage of her inexperience in the most dreadful way possible, rage overcame her shock. Without considering the consequences, she launched herself across the room at him.

Rose gave a shriek of fear. Not the least threatened, Tim stood his ground. When Lilly was within reach, he simply swung the arm with the pouch and hit her with a backhanded blow that sent her reeling against the fireplace.

Her head hit the mantel with a sickening *crack*. Pain sent her to her knees and darkness threatened once again. She heard the sound of boots thudding on the planks of the floor, heard a door slam and voices coming from somewhere far away.

Then someone lifted her, and a gentle voice asked, "Lilly, are you all right?"

She wanted to answer, but instead, she slipped deeper into the dark emptiness that held no pain, no frightening memories, and no hateful, lying words or acts of deception.

CHAPTER 2

"C'mon, luv, open your eyes."

The familiar sound of Pierce's voice nudged aside the comforting shadows. Lilly moaned at the intrusion. She wanted nothing more than to stay wrapped in the cocoon of oblivion that kept away the memories threatening her self-worth and her peace of mind . . . perhaps even her sanity.

"Lilly. Come, my sweet girl. Open your eyes for me."

The coolness of a damp cloth dabbing at a place on the side of her head accompanied the voice. Rose. The woman who had taken a young, damaged girl into her home and her heart when her mother was murdered. The woman Timothy might have killed if not for Lilly's intervention.

She reached out in a frantic gesture. "Rose!" Lilly had trouble making her lips form the whispered word.

"Thank God!" *Pierce.*

"I'm here." Rose sobbed and dabbed harder at the aching place on Lilly's head.

"Stop!" she said crossly, making another aimless grab. "That hurts."

Pierce's laughter sent her eyelids fluttering open. She glared at him. He only laughed again. "You'd best stop, Rose. We don't want to get her all in a pucker."

"I am not angry," Lilly managed to mumble in a sulky voice.

"No? What would you call it?"

"Enraged." She didn't sound enraged; she sounded exhausted. Recalling the events that had brought her to this point, she struggled to her elbows, an act that sent the room spinning and another wave of pain through her skull.

"Be still," Pierce commanded. "You may have a concussion—or worse."

"I'm fine," she grumbled, gingerly probing the knot on her head. "Just bloody furious. Did he get away?"

Rose gave a disdainful sniff. "Took out of here like a scalded cat," she said. "He almost knocked Roxie over as she came in from the theater. She's sent for the police and a doctor."

"I don't need a doctor," Lilly insisted, struggling to sit up. "It's just a bump."

"Maybe so, but I'll feel better if you're checked out," Rose insisted, propping her up with a couple of pillows behind her back.

"So will I," Pierce added. "As for the police . . . I don't know how much good they'll be. I have a feeling your Tim's done this sort of thing before."

Before Lilly had time to consider that, a knock sounded at the door. It was the physician, a middle-aged man with rounded shoulders and thick spectacles, who spent the next several moments asking questions about what had happened, poking and prodding, checking her pupils, and even pricking her hands and feet with a pin.

"Well," he said, removing his stethoscope from his ears and hooking it around his neck. "You're a fortunate young lady. It appears you have nothing wrong except a very nasty bump on your head."

"Thank God," Rose said.

"Of course, there is no way to completely rule out the possibility of a concussion or even a skull fracture, but in light of your responses and state of awareness, I'm not inclined to think the injury is that severe." He offered a dry smile. "You'll probably have the devil of a headache for a few days, so I advise that you stay in bed and get as much rest as possible."

"I'd like to return to my own room if that would be all right," Lilly said, the expression in her brown eyes pleading. Though she feared it was a fool's errand, she wanted to check on the small stash of money she kept there.

"Fine, fine," the physician agreed with a nod. "But I insist that someone stay with you for at least one night. Mrs. Wainwright?" he queried, looking at Rose.

"You couldn't keep me away," Rose assured him.

Several minutes later, Lilly was settled into the room she'd shared with Timothy. While Pierce walked the doctor out, Lilly allowed Rose to continue her motherly fussing. It seemed the least she could do. She was about to ask Rose for details about the robbery when Pierce poked his head in and announced that the policeman had arrived and wanted to speak with Rose.

"And I want to speak with him!"

Rose gave the quilts a final pat. "The doctor gave me a wee bit of laudanum to ease your pain and help you sleep, but I left it in my room. I'll be back with it just as soon as I talk to the copper and get my night things."

Lilly whispered her thanks and gave a compliant nod. As soon as the door shut behind Rose, Lilly opened her eyes and let her troubled gaze roam the bed chamber. Tim's straight razor and soap mug were gone from the shaving stand. The carpetbag that held his clothes was no longer in the corner where he'd left it. No trace of his presence lingered except the faintest scent of bay rum that clung to the sheets. She ran her palm over the place where he'd slept and blinked back the threat of angry tears.

Tim had belittled the most precious gift she'd had to offer— her purity. His cruel words hurt far more than the physical pain he'd inflicted. Did the innocence she'd brought to their marriage bed truly mean so little to him? Why had he thrown away everything over the silly argument about money they'd had earlier that morning?

When he'd asked for more money, she had braced herself for yet another battle and reminded him that she'd given him money the day before. To her surprise, he hadn't come back with his usual snide remarks. Instead, he'd looked at her with a tortured expression on his handsome face and told her that he wouldn't ask if it weren't important.

He'd seemed so pitiful that she felt churlish for denying him. Wanting everything to be right between them, she'd given him more money from the bag she kept in her trunk. Grateful, smiling, and incredibly attractive in his victory, he'd kissed her and apologized and taken her to bed. No doubt he'd been plotting to steal her money even then. How could he claim to love her one minute and do such a terrible thing hours later?

"You should know that a man will say anything to get what he wants."

Ice-cold and laced with contempt, the scornful words were so vivid that the man who'd spoken them might have been standing next to her. Somehow she knew the words were those of her mother's killer, a man who'd lied to get what he wanted from Kate just as Timothy had lied to get what he wanted from Lilly.

With an angry murmur, Lilly sat up, an action that set off a fresh wave of pain. Moving with care, she eased to the side of the bed and slid the few inches to the cold floorboards. Crossing to the trunk, she yanked open a small drawer, scraping aside the rose-scented garments and tumbling the contents of the other drawers in a frenzied, futile search for the pouch.

Gone. Every cent.

For the first time, she took a hard, objective look at her husband and herself. Tim was an opportunist, plain and simple. And though the live-and-let-live, nomadic lifestyle of the theater was liberating in many ways, that way of life had shielded her from much of society's ugliness, which left her inexperienced when it came to many of the world's workings.

Tim had no doubt taken one glance into her eyes and known that she was as green as grass, and he'd played to that naiveté every step of the way. She'd fallen for an inveterate schemer, following in Kate's footsteps despite every effort not to. What was the old saw? Oh, yes. Fool me once, shame on you; fool me twice, shame on me.

She'd been a child when her mother was murdered, bound by a child's limitations. As a woman grown, she was free of those constraints. She wasn't certain what tomorrow might bring, but she knew exactly what she had to do tonight, and she swore that she would never again be taken in by any man.

Lilly dressed as quickly as possible. She was anxious to be gone before her plan to go looking for Tim was thwarted by Rose's or Pierce's return. Assuming Tim had not yet left the area, narrowing down his whereabouts was simple. He was probably at MacGregor's, a combination drinking establishment, restaurant, and hotel within walking distance of both the boardinghouse and the theater.

Dressed and bundled in her red cape, she left her room, sidling furtively down the hall and out into the cold night once again. She grimaced against the icy wind that blew clouds as insubstantial as her marriage across the face of the quarter moon. Rain clouds. Weather typical of early March in Chicago.

It took just two blocks for her to realize that wrath and righteous indignation could carry one only so far. Her head ached dreadfully, her stomach churned, and for the first time since conceiving her impulsive plan, she became aware of the unfamiliar darkness surrounding her, taunting her with its dangers.

Buildings bordered either side of the street, their storefronts indistinguishable beyond the glow of the flickering gaslights. Raucous, masculine laughter mingled with a shrill female giggle. Raw wind tugged at her cape, carrying the scent of approaching rain and the faint, ever-present stench of rotting flesh and burning hair from the Union Stock Yards in the distance. Faint though it was, the revolting odor robbed her of her tenuous hold on her nausea and she doubled over, emptying the contents of her stomach into the gutter.

Drawing a handkerchief from her reticule, she wiped her streaming eyes and mouth and leaned against a brick building until the pain and dizziness subsided, rousing only when an owl's chilling *whoo hoo* echoed from somewhere in the inky blackness. A frisson of unease slithered down her spine. People disappeared at an alarming rate in Chicago. Reminded again of the dangers of the desolate streets and shadow-shrouded alleys, she quickened her pace.

She was wondering if she would make it when she saw light spilling from the windows of a brick-fronted establishment, illuminating a sign beside the door in the shape of a crest. Red letters outlined with white spelled out MACGREGOR'S. She paused, wondering at the best way to proceed. When she'd left the boardinghouse in a vengeful snit, she'd had no plan beyond finding Timothy.

A sudden memory of her newest character, the irrepressible Priscilla Dunlap, sprang to mind. With no fear of what others thought of her or her actions, that incorrigible miss would march into the tavern as if she frequented such places every day. She would belly up to the bar and demand answers. She would not act uncertain or afraid. As an actress, Lilly could do the same.

Taking a breath, she lifted her chin and stepped inside. Assorted impressions assaulted her senses: welcome heat from a nearby potbelly stove. The clink of glassware and dozens of individual conversations. There was so much smoke her eyes and nostrils burned. Rough male voices overwhelmed the backdrop of feminine laughter and the tinny tinkle of a piano in dire need of a tuning.

She hesitated in the doorway, fighting another round of queasiness and allowing her gaze to move around the alien world.

In keeping with many Irish-owned saloons, MacGregor's boasted a standup bar. Tim had done his best to convince her that taverns were not necessarily dens of iniquity. Besides offering drinks, they were places laborers learned of employment opportunities, paychecks were cashed, and the latest gossip could be overheard. Some establishments offered free lunches, usually something cold, though the more fashionable taverns offered fancier fare. A few even boasted restrooms and safes for items too precious to leave at home, a notion Lilly now realized held considerable worth.

Though hard-used, MacGregor's was relatively clean, and its patrons looked prosperous enough. Several men knocked back shots of whisky while squinting through a fog of smoke at a skimpily clothed chanteuse belting out a naughty song in a liquor-roughened alto.

Most of the women, whose painted faces were less pretty than pathetic, wore nothing but undergarments that pinched their waists to unnatural smallness and pushed their bosoms scandalously upward. They moved from table to table, bleakness in their eyes, forced smiles on their painted lips as they leaned suggestively over men who sat with one hand clutching a spread of cards, the other toying with a pile of chips or grasping a drink or cheroot.

And to think that much of society looked down on actresses! More than a bit scandalized, and seeing no sign of Timothy, she was about to cross to the bar to question the bartender when she felt a tap on her shoulder. She whirled, an action that caused the room to dip.

A very large man, with biceps the size of her thighs and a handlebar mustache that nearly hid his mouth, stood before her. His narrowed eyes were dark with menace beneath heavy eyebrows that were drawn together so that they looked like a single bushy ledge.

"I'm sorry, ma'am, but if you want service, you'll have to come in through the rear door."

Accustomed to the more impartial treatment women of the theater received from their male peers, Lilly had little patience for the silly customs the male-dominated world sought to impose on women. A knock on the head was not about to change that. She bit back a reply unsuitable to a lady and responded in an arrogant tone that would have done Priscilla proud. "I am not here to be served, sir. I'm looking for my husband."

The brute crossed his arms across his massive chest. "Rules is rules, ma'am."

Lilly met his gaze head-on and schooled her tone to one reeking with calculated patience. "As you can see, sir, I am already inside, so what good is it for me to go out and come in another door? Now," she said, as if the matter were settled, "would you kindly point out the owner?"

Uncertain how to handle the situation without resorting to force, the bouncer jerked his head toward the bar.

"Thank you."

She stepped around him and marched across the tavern to the long span of mahogany scarred with cigar and cigarette burns and dulled by years of spilled alcohol. The splotched, hazy surface of a mirror hanging crookedly behind the bar reflected the happenings in the smoke-filled room as well as the back of a stout man in a white apron who was drawing a mug of foaming beer. His fleshy face sported at least two days' stubble of beard below a thick, untidy mustache that drooped at the corners, giving him a frowning appearance. When Lilly plopped her beaded handbag down next to a bowl marked CHARITABLE CONTRIBUTIONS, he looked up in feigned surprise—as if, she thought crossly, he had not witnessed her encounter with the ape guarding the door.

With that innate sense that something unpleasant was about to transpire, the men standing nearest her glanced from her to the bartender and back, snatched up their drinks, and headed toward the gaming tables.

"Mr. MacGregor?"

"Aye," he said with a cautious nod. "I'm Danny MacGregor. And you might be?"

"Lilly Long. Timothy's wife. I was wondering if you'd seen him tonight."

"I'm sorry, ma'am, but I know na Timothy Long." MacGregor's Irish brogue was as thick as the head of foam on the mug. Shifting his gaze, he lifted the flagon toward someone behind her to let him know his drink was ready.

"I'm sorry," Lilly said, realizing her error. "My husband is Timothy Warner."

Was that a flicker of sympathy in MacGregor's eyes? With a disgruntled laugh, he leaned his hairy forearms on the bar. Lilly took an involuntary step back. He reeked of cigar smoke and sweat.

"I've no' seen Tim Warner tonight, or any night fer more than a week, and I'm no' holdin' my breath in the hope of it since the lad's run up quite a bar tab as well as owing Boatwright a bundle he lost in a game of Monte."

Lilly's stomach took a sickening dive. So *that's* why Tim needed the money. Still, despite disappointment, humiliation, and anger, dreams and love die hard. Before she could stop herself, she'd blurted a very un-Priscilla-like question. "Are you certain you have the right man in mind?"

MacGregor's laughter held no mirth. "I'm sure. Even in a city the size of Chicago how many Timothy Warners can there be come wanderin' through my door? I've got the right man. He told Boatwright he'd get the money from his wife the very next day, and we've not seen him since. The boy has a silver tongue, don't ya know?"

Lilly felt her face drain of what bit of color it might still possess. More lies. Lies to her, lies to MacGregor, lies to this Boatwright person.

"You do na look so good, Missus," MacGregor said, genuine concern in his voice. "I shouldna ha' been so blunt."

Lilly attempted a smile. "No apology necessary, Mr. MacGregor. Tell me, did he frequent any other taverns that you know of?"

With a thoughtful frown, MacGregor rubbed a palm against his whiskery face. "I canna' imagine him not lookin' fer a friendly game, but he never mentioned anyplace to me."

He glanced around, leaned across the counter, and spoke out of the corner of his mouth, with barely a movement of his lips. "The coppers were in here a day er two ago lookin' fer him, so I expect yer Timmy boy is off to greener pastures."

The finality of that possibility settled over her like a wet gunny sack, and her bold persona slipped. Faced at every turn with proof of Tim's perfidy, it was becoming harder and harder to convince herself that the incident at the boardinghouse was some sort of terrible mistake. Ignorance truly was bliss, and she wished with all her heart that she had not embarked on this fool's journey and heard these terrible things about him. She thanked MacGregor for his time and turned to go.

"Missus!" She looked over her shoulder at him. "It's not yer fault he's a liar and a cheat. I doubt you're the first pretty lady to be taken in by Tim Warner, and I can promise you won't be the last. Why, he even duped Colleen, and she's not one easily gummed."

"That he did, Danny boy."

The statement came from behind Lilly, who turned to see the woman who'd been staring at her earlier. The scantily clad, henna-haired creature squinted at Lilly through the smoke curling from the cigarillo she lifted to her lips. At first, Lilly took the floozy to be near her own age; closer inspection noted a furrowed forehead, a fine network of crow's feet at the corners of the woman's eyes, and a softness of the jawline that even her painted features failed to disguise.

Her makeup was every bit as heavy as what Lilly wore onstage. Garish red lip paint bled into the fine lines around a mouth whose left corner was adorned with a beauty patch. Rouged cheekbones stood out against a heavy dusting of powder. The kohl lining her jaded blue eyes was smudged. The sweet, cloying scent of cheap toilet water mingled with the smoke wreathing her head.

Lilly's stomach lurched once more. "Who are you?" she demanded.

"Colleen McKenna." She propped one hand on a plump hip and drew deeply on the cigarillo. "Boatwright and Daniel aren't the only ones Tim Warner owes."

Shock coursed through Lilly. Sheltered as she might have been, she didn't have to ask what the woman meant. Once more, her acting skills stood her in good stead. She summoned an imperious tone. "Are you suggesting . . . ?"

Colleen dropped the butt of her smoke onto the floor and ground it out with the scuffed toe of a red satin slipper. "I'm not suggesting anything. I'm tellin' ya that yer husband owes me for three nights."

". . . the thrill of bedding an innocent lost its appeal weeks ago."

Lilly wanted to scream that Colleen McKenna was lying, but the truth was in the woman's eyes and the memory of Tim's taunt. Unable to keep up the charade of sophistication any longer, she gathered the remnants of her composure and crossed the room, half blinded by tears of loss and degradation. As she passed the bouncer, she thought she saw a hint of sympathy in his eyes.

Fighting the urge to cry—more because she was so mortified than because she was hurt—she jerked open the door, slammed it shut behind her, and leaned against it, gulping in deep drafts of the cold, cleansing air. A picture of Tim's body pressed against Colleen's flickered through her mind. Lilly uttered a mild curse and swiped angrily at the moisture in her eyes, as if doing so would wipe away the image.

Tim Warner had dealt her a lot of misery the past four months, and she'd forgiven him time and again. This newest betrayal was impossible to comprehend much less reconcile, yet one thing was certain. He had exhausted every possible means of hurting her.

Drawing on her stubborn will, she straightened her shoulders and stepped from beneath the shelter of the broad porch. She lifted her face up, letting the chill drizzle that had begun to fall wash away the lingering traces of cheap cigars, cheap perfume, cheap lives.

With no thought to the shadows or what might be hiding there and even less to the pain pounding inside her skull, she ran through the rain toward the boardinghouse.

Just when she thought she could go no farther, she saw the lights of her lodging place glowing feebly through the mist, no more than a block away. In moments, she stumbled through the door and down the hallway to Pierce and Rose's room. Her barely audible knock was answered in seconds. Reeling with pain, she fell into Pierce's arms.

CHAPTER 3

With Pierce steadying her, Lilly was helped into the room. Rose told him to run along, while Lilly apologized over and over for worrying them. Once she was warm and cozy beneath a mound of blankets and cradled a cup of hot chamomile tea in her hands, Pierce was allowed to return. As usual, he got right to the point.

"I know something happened while you were gone. Tell me where you went." He pinned her with the look that had always made her tell the truth.

"I went to a place called MacGregor's."

"MacGregor's!" Rose echoed in a scandalized voice.

"MacGregor's is a tavern, Lilly!" Pierce said, as if she didn't know. "What in blazes were you thinking?"

"I'm not sure I was," she admitted, sinking back against the pillows. "I just wanted to try to find Tim and force him to give back the money."

He only cocked a dark eyebrow at her. "And you really thought he'd return to his favorite haunt and wait for you to come looking for him?"

"It wasn't very smart of me, I know." She drew a deep breath. Needing their comforting words, she launched into a detailed account of her visit to the saloon, letting the tale unwind in all its ugliness, omitting nothing, not even the run-in with the horrid Colleen.

"She was so coarse," she whispered, disgust and shame in her eyes. "I . . . I cannot fathom what Tim saw in her, or imagine him w-with her. I thought he loved me."

"What transpired between them has nothing to do with love, Lilly. There are some women and some men who aren't satisfied with . . ." His voice trailed away as he searched for a phrase that would not be offensive to her feminine ears. ". . . just one person. They prefer . . . variety."

Lilly understood that only too well. Her mother had been one of those women. She took a sip of her tea. "Tim's no good, Pierce," she said at last.

He shrugged, an elegant, yet totally masculine lift of his shoulders. "Most of us knew that from the start."

"Why didn't you say something?" she asked in an anguished whisper.

"You were innocent and totally besotted with a man for the first time. Would you have listened?"

Recalling the way her heart seemed to stumble the day she'd first met Tim and how, only that morning, she had reveled in his love making, she admitted, "Probably not. It seems that I'm as big a fool as my mother when it comes to men."

"I hardly think one mistake qualifies you as a fool," Pierce told her. "But chasing after a crook in the middle of the night . . . well, that's another story."

A crook. The man she'd promised to love forever was a thief, and worse. "I know, and I'm so very sorry for worrying you both." She looked from him to the silent Rose.

"I might forgive you if you promise to stay in bed a couple of days," the older woman said with a stern expression.

Knowing it was the least she could do to make amends, Lilly nodded. "I will, I promise."

"Good, then."

"So what do you plan to do about Timothy?" Pierce asked. "Will you divorce him?"

"Divorce?" Tim had stolen her life savings, had hurt her and Rose, and might have killed them but for the grace of God. He'd been exposed as a liar and a cheat and had defiled their marriage bed, striking a killing blow to her self-esteem in the process. Her intellect told her that her marriage was over, but divorce? A troubled expression darkened her eyes. "What would everyone think?"

"Most of us have been expecting something like this to happen since the first day you brought Tim to the theater."

"We don't stay in any one place long enough for the world to know or care," Rose added. "And believe me, Tim isn't the kind to let marriage vows stop him from finding his next victim, so why should you be tied to the rotter?"

Lilly gave a sorrowful sigh. "I'm sure everyone thinks I'm a fool for even imagining myself in love with him."

"They think no such thing. No one can fault another for loving, even if they love unwisely," Pierce said. "No matter how closely we may guard our hearts, love sneaks up on us when we least expect it, often against our will." His smile held a hint of deprecation. "We've all done it at one time or another."

Lilly longed to ask him if he was speaking of her mother, but now wasn't the time, not with Rose standing right there. She had no idea if Rose knew about Kate and Pierce, and she would never say or do anything to hurt the woman who had become her substitute mother. She knew she might never learn who killed her mother, or if Pierce was her father, but she did know two important things: All decisions—right or wrong—affected not only the person making them, but every life that person touched. She also knew with a gut-deep certainty that her mother's killer and Timothy Warner were cut from the same cloth.

"I'll give it some thought," she said after a few moments of silence.

Pierce smiled his approval. "Good."

"It's time for you to try to sleep," Rose said. "I'll be on that cot next to you in case you need me." She waggled a finger at Lilly. "And I'm holding you to your promise. I expect you to spend at least two days in that bed no matter how bored you may get."

"I understand," Lilly said in a meek tone.

Moments later, the lamp had been blown out and she was listening to the soft sounds of Rose's snoring.

Lilly felt as if she should cry. A normal woman would cry, wouldn't she? But the truth was that even though she'd tried to build a life with Tim, she really hadn't known him. If any tears were shed, they would be in anger and for her own stupidity, not the loss of a man who had used her so sorely.

Common sense told her that divorce was the right thing to do, but even freed from the vows they'd taken, it would be a long time before she was willing to trust another man with her body or her heart.

CHAPTER 4

By the evening of the second day, Lilly was convinced that she would go mad if she had to stay in bed another moment. She'd caught up on her reading, focusing on the happenings that were chronicled in the daily newspapers: a new play was opening at McVicker's; a modiste, recently arrived from France and specializing in all the latest Parisian fashions, was opening a shop just down the way; and the prestigious Pinkerton Agency was seeking suitable women to hire as female detectives.

When her eyes grew gritty from too much reading, she occupied her time by thinking about the changes the past few days had wrought in her life. She'd spent hours soul-searching, examining her feelings and devising suitably gruesome means of retribution for Tim if ever their paths crossed.

Learning of his true character had eradicated the last lingering traces of love—or whatever it had been—that she'd felt for him, and she vowed that no man would ever take advantage of her again. It was time to make a change, though what that might be, she wasn't sure. All she knew was that there was a big world out there, and she wanted to see more of it than the insides of trains, theaters, and boardinghouses.

She was entertaining a particularly dreadful end for Tim when a sudden idea leaped full-blown into her mind. It was perfect. She began a frenzied shuffling through the stack of newspapers on the coverlet, skimming the pages until she found the Pinkerton Agency's advertisement.

Always a great fan of Allan Pinkerton's dime novels, she applauded his methods as well as the skill his agents employed to bring about justice, especially when they took on roles, much like actors, to apprehend criminals. There were those who might deplore his tactics, but they could not deny his successes. The great detective lived by the simple tenet that so long as justice prevailed, the ends justified the means, which turned her thoughts back to Tim. Lilly read and reread the public notice, contemplating something that would change her life utterly.

Before leaving for the theater, Pierce stopped by with Rose to check on Lilly. That was good. They both needed to hear what she had to say. She had dressed in a no-nonsense skirt and shirtwaist, and coiled her dark red hair into its customary knot at the nape of her neck. There were circles beneath her eyes, and she still looked pale, but then, her complexion was naturally fair. She was nervous about the upcoming conversation, but at least fully clothed she felt more in control.

Without giving him time to open the conversation, she blurted out, "I was wondering how you think Allan Pinkerton would go about locating Tim and getting back my money."

Pierce turned to her with a baffled frown. "Allan Pinkerton? I haven't a clue, luv. Why do you ask?" He offered her an indulgent smile. "Are you thinking of hiring him?"

"Allan Pinkerton, the detective?" Rose chimed in.

"Yes, Rose. That one. Look at this." She picked up the newspaper she'd been reading and pointed to the pertinent piece.

Pierce scanned the print and pinned her with a hard look, while Rose tried to read over his shoulder. "What's this?"

"It's an advertisement for a female Pinkerton agent."

"I can see that," Pierce growled. "What in blazes does that have to do with you?"

Lilly looked from one to the other. "Mr. Pinkerton is seeking women to work for his agency. I mean to set up an appointment tomorrow to see if he'll take me on."

"Take you on?" Pierce echoed, aghast. "You mean *hire* you to be a detective?"

"That is precisely what I mean. And before you begin your nay saying, I want you to hear me out."

"B-But you're not qualified," the usually composed Pierce stammered in tandem with Rose's "You can't be serious."

"And why not?"

"It says here that the woman should be about thirty-five, and—"

"You're only twenty-two," Rose interrupted.

Lilly gave a dismissive wave of her hand. "Other than my age, I have the qualifications they require. I'm the right height, and my hair is fine, since they'll accept any hair color except blond."

"You don't have a"—Pierce looked at the notice again, searching for the right printed words—" 'large and massive forehead.' "

"Thank the Lord!" Rose chimed in with a shudder.

"I believe that specification may be based on Mr. Pinkerton's interest in phrenology," Lilly mused, giving a thoughtful shrug. "I've read that he is a devotee."

"Phrenology!" Pierce scoffed. Rose wrung her hands. "Isn't that the hocus-pocus nonsense that claims a person's character can be determined by the lumps and bumps on his head?"

Lilly frowned. "I believe so." She gave another unconcerned shrug. "Perhaps he equates large foreheads with more brains and thus superior intelligence."

Rose was shocked to silence. As if he were in a daze, Pierce shook his head. "You're quite serious about this nonsense, aren't you?"

"It isn't nonsense," she said, snatching the paper from him. "And yes, I am. Quite serious." She looked at Rose. "Did you know that he hired the first female detective in the country? Kate Warne? Isn't that exciting, Rose?"

"You are an actress, Lilly, not a detective," Rose said.

"Right," Pierce said, struggling on. "Acting is in your blood."

Lilly met his gaze, her eyes glittering with resolve. "You're right. I'm an actress. That's what made it all fall into place. Mr. Pinkerton has hired more than one female operative with a theater background. The ad says that the woman will be playing various roles, so I won't be bored at all."

"This whole cockamamie idea is ludicrous!"

"Why?"

"Because you've little experience with things outside the theater, that's why," Pierce said, his voice rising with irritation. "The real world will make mincemeat of you inside a month. I know you, Lilly," he said, shaking his finger at her. "You want to find Tim, and I think you believe you can somehow look for him at the same time you're chasing criminals. If so, you've completely lost your mind."

"For heaven's sake, Pierce! Don't be ridiculous! It's a huge country. I know my chances of ever seeing Tim again are slim. Furthermore, it may surprise you to know that I agree with everything else you said. I *do* have little experience outside the theater and our group of actors, which is why I was unprepared for someone like Timothy. I don't intend to let that happen again. No man will ever again seduce me with a handsome face or pretty words."

There was urgency in her voice. "I've given this a lot of thought, and I keep asking myself how many men are out there doing to other women what Tim did to me—or worse. I want to help them find justice."

The expression in her eyes begged for understanding. "I can use a gun and sword. I speak and read French and Italian. We've studied everything from astronomy to politics, agriculture to zombies and, if I recall aright, we've even discussed ladies' undergarments.

"You've taught me well," she continued. "Let me use that knowledge to help other women. If I don't know what to do in a situation, I'll just *act* as if I do until I figure it out, the way I did at MacGregor's."

Pierce sighed, and she recognized it as a sign of his weakening. "You are a hardheaded little chit."

"I won't argue with that," Lilly told him.

He shook his head. "You can't save all the women in the world from devious men, Lilly."

"I know," she said, her face a study in seriousness, "but perhaps I can save a few."

CHAPTER 5

The Pinkerton Offices
89 Washington Street / Corner of Dearborn

William Pinkerton sat at his desk in the Pinkerton Agency's Chicago office, weighted down with dread. His ailing father was still adamant that women could be of value in their investigations, which created an ongoing source of strife within the agency. Now the stubborn old man had placed an advertisement in the newspaper, determined to hire even more of the dratted creatures.

William had to admit that the accomplishments of Kate Warne, the first woman Allan had hired, had far exceeded his father's expectations, and there had been other undeniable successes since. However, William still had reservations, and his brother, Robert, was of the firm opinion that the general nature of women left much to be desired if the work became stressful or dangerous. Besides, it was unseemly for any respectable woman to travel in the circles often necessary to capture a lawbreaker.

So strong was his feeling on the matter that after Mrs. Warne's death, Robert, along with George Bangs, Allan's right-hand man, and Benjamin Franklin, the former chief of detectives of the Philadelphia Police Department who headed up the Philadelphia office, had tried to dissuade Allan from hiring more women. Allan had responded by sending the pretty former actress, Mrs. Angela Austin, to Philadelphia in a blatant exhibition of his power.

Robert had fired off an angry missive to his father stating that he wanted no women under his jurisdiction. Allan promptly shot back a letter of his own, pointing out that until he died, neither Robert nor William had any say in matters other than in the areas where they'd been given authority.

William sighed. And now, his father had put him in the hot seat by placing the advertisement in the paper. Already, seven hopefuls had arranged interviews. God alone knew how many more might respond.

Part of William's discomfort lay in the fact that Robert was in town for a visit and insisted on being part of the hiring process. William feared his brother would antagonize or terrorize the unsuspecting applicants so badly that they would run screaming from the interview.

He rubbed at his temples. Oh, if only he could go back to working in the field. Being in the thick of things was far more satisfying than sitting behind a desk. He sighed. He wasn't looking forward to the next few days, but he was in the business of solving problems, and he was good at it.

He only hoped Robert truly understood just how questionable Allan's health had been since the shock that had left him paralyzed and barely able to speak twelve years earlier. William knew that it was far better to indulge his father than raise his ire. After all, as Allan had pointed out, it was his agency, and one day William and Robert would be put to the test to see if they could maintain the quality of service he had established. Until that time, they would have to muddle through these last difficult years with as little strife as possible.

CHAPTER 6

For her interview with Mr. William Pinkerton, Lilly decided to be as truthful as possible without revealing details of her background. In general, she despised mendacity, but a bit of sophistry never hurt, and there was no sense giving him any information that might be used against her. She salved her conscience with the thought that if she became a Pinkerton operative, deception would be commonplace.

Hoping to portray a sensible young woman, she'd chosen to wear a tailored walking dress of forest green with a small bustle. Her hair was swept back at the sides and up into a knot atop her head, upon which perched a small veiled hat. If not the height of fashion, she was at least neat and professional.

As she and the clerk neared the door of William Pinkerton's offices, she drew a deep breath. Performing onstage before hundreds of people had never been this frightening. She had to remind herself that this was no different, except she would be performing for an audience of one.

"Mrs. Warner is here."

Lilly thanked the clerk and approached the man who had risen and stood regarding her as she neared a massive oak desk.

William Pinkerton, she thought, was the elder brother. She was halfway there before she saw a movement from the corner of her eye. Pausing, she saw another man standing next to a settee. Recalling a newspaper picture she'd seen, she decided this was Robert Pinkerton.

Before she could do more than ask herself what his presence meant, William rounded the corner of the desk, a smile on his face and his beefy hand outstretched. His handshake was firm, his palm dry and warm. His face was broad, and his hair was parted just off center left. Deep grooves ran from his nose and disappeared into the heavy mustache that nearly hid his upper lip.

"William Pinkerton, Mrs. Warner," he said. "Thank you for coming in." He gestured toward the other man. "This is my brother, Robert, who will be helping me make the best choice possible for the agency."

"Mrs. Warner," Robert said, crossing to her and emulating his brother's greeting. More slender than William, with hair that had a definite left part, and the corners of his mustache extended past his mouth toward a rather unremarkable chin.

Robert's hand was as cool as the appraisal in his eyes. Lilly fought to keep a sudden twinge of discomfort from registering on her face. Robert Pinkerton did not want her there. Instinct told her that he would make a formidable adversary. She was grateful his brother would be conducting the interview.

"Please be seated," William said, gesturing toward the chair in front of his desk. He settled himself behind its shiny expanse, glancing at what she supposed to be the résumé she'd left earlier.

At last he lifted his inquisitive gaze to hers. "Why, of all the positions a young woman of your age might aspire, do you wish to leave your family to travel around the country, possibly putting your life in danger?"

"I have no immediate family, sir. I never knew my father, and my mother was killed when I was eleven." That at least was the truth, as far as it went. "As for my reason for wanting to be a part of your agency, it is to seek justice, especially for women, because of something that happened to me recently."

"Please explain," Robert urged.

Looking from one brother to the other, she gave them a brief overview of her marriage, Tim's abandonment, and what she'd learned at MacGregor's. "It seems he is nothing but an opportunistic scoundrel who used me for his own ends."

"But that's terrible!" William exclaimed.

"Indeed."

"If you think to use our agency as a means to locate this man, you are here for the wrong reasons, madam," Robert stated in a cold voice.

Lilly responded with a bitter smile. "I am not that naïve, sir. I realize I'll probably never lay eyes on him again. In fact, I plan to divorce him and take back my maiden name," she said, making the momentous decision at just that moment.

She leaned forward, earnest entreaty on her face. "I'm sure you'll agree that many of your cases are crimes perpetrated by men against women. You know as well as I that society refuses to take women seriously or look at them as anything more than breeding vessels to be used to secure heirs. Relegating us to places of inferiority and weakness makes us easy prey for unscrupulous men."

"Your empathy is admirable, Mrs. Warner, but I fear your attitude does a grave disservice to the masculine gender." Robert's voice was silky smooth, his smile condescending. "Men only desire to see that women, who as we all know *are* the weaker sex, are protected."

What a pile of horse manure! Lilly schooled her features into impassivity and held her tongue. Voicing this opinion to her prospective employers would kill any chance she might have of being hired.

"That may well be, sir, but it is this very attitude that places women at a disadvantage. Taught to depend on men, we are unable to recognize and safeguard ourselves from those un-principled individuals who would use us for their own ends. Because of this and my own experience, which it seems I can do nothing to correct, it is my strongest desire to help bring about justice for other women who have suffered similar fates. *That* is what brings me here, gentlemen."

Lilly wasn't certain where the words had come from, but she felt they were apt and well delivered, if she did say so her-self.

William nodded. "I see," he said again. He shuffled the pa-pers on his desk, cleared his throat, and said, "And you are . . . uh . . . currently an actress."

"Yes," she said, nodding. "With the Pierced Rose Troupe. I've grown up in the theater, which is one reason I feel I would be an asset to your agency."

"Yes . . . well . . . your acting background is one of the reasons we called you in," William said, rubbing his mustache with a thick forefinger. "We often use disguises and infiltration in our quests, and other of our female operatives have been ac-tresses with much success to their credit."

"I'm aware of that, sir. My greatest hope is to follow in the footsteps of Mrs. Warne, Mrs. Austin, and the others. I'm a quick study. You may not be aware that traveling actors have a grueling show schedule that allows the production to change as often as every two days. Utility actors often know more than a hundred parts."

Both men looked taken aback by that little-known tidbit. "I see. And how long will you be here?"

"Another week," Lilly told him, pleased with the way the interview was going. "We're currently playing at the Peacock. Perhaps you're familiar with it."

"I am," William said. "It's a small opera house. Not as prestigious as McVicker's or Hooley's, but I understand its popularity is on the rise."

"You neglected to write down your age, Mrs. Warner." The intrusive observation came from Robert, who lounged on the settee.

Lilly bit back a sigh. Drat the man! She had deliberately left her age out of her list of qualifications, knowing it was going to be a thorny subject.

"Really?" She combined the surprised question with a troubled look. "I hadn't realized. Well, sir, I will be twenty and three in July."

"Ah." Robert Pinkerton managed to put a wealth of emotion in the single short word. "I'm sure you realize you are much younger than the requirements stated in the advertisement, yet you decided to apply anyway. Why?"

"I felt my other qualifications outweighed that one small detail. Besides the fact that women who tread the boards are quite self-sufficient, I've received a better education than most young men in this country. Mr. Wainwright, who took me in after my mother was killed, has given me an education equal to that of the son of an English aristocrat. I speak two languages besides English, and I am an avid reader, which enables me to converse on a variety of subjects."

"Very impressive, I'm sure, Mrs. Warner, but assignments are often quite dangerous," Robert pointed out.

"I understand the dangers, Mr. Pinkerton, but you should know that I have also been trained in swordsmanship and the use of pistols. I am a better-than-average shot and sit a horse quite well."

Lilly saw surprise and a grudging respect in both pairs of

eyes. The men posed a few more questions and asked her to wait in the outer office while they had a discussion on her background for the position. She was barely seated in the uncomfortable straight-backed chair when she overheard William say something she couldn't make out.

"Are you daft, man?" Robert's voice carried through the closed door.

The clerk looked up from his task and met Lilly's shocked gaze with a horrified one of his own. Dark red stained his narrow face, and without a word, he returned to his work.

Another mumble from William.

Robert's voice was angry and argumentative. Lilly heard comments like "far too young," "revenge," and "lack of experience." Her heart sank. If she didn't know better she'd think he'd been talking to Pierce.

Finally, the discomfited clerk had enough. Scraping back his chair, he leaped to his feet and knocked on the door, entered, and returned in a matter of seconds, a shamefaced expression on his face. Without a word to her, he went back to work.

There was a final murmured comment from William, and the door opened. He wore an expression of chagrin. Robert's gloating manner did not escape her. "Please come in and be seated, Mrs. Warner," William said. He cleared his throat and began a long dissertation contrasting the worthiness of her goals to her lack of worldly experience. He finished by saying, "I hope you understand that we must decline."

It took every bit of Lilly's acting skill to maintain a composed air and keep her disappointment from showing. She would not give them the satisfaction of seeing how crushed she was. Knowing she was beaten for the moment, she held her tongue and shook both men's hands in parting. "Thank you for your time, gentlemen, but be warned. You have not seen the last of me."

"Yes," William said. "Perhaps in a few years . . ."

She offered them an innocent smile. "Yes, perhaps. Good day."

She left the offices fuming. She felt that if it were left up to William, she would have been given the position, and if Robert Pinkerton thought he'd seen the last of her, he'd better think again!

Chapter 7

The Pinkerton Offices

Two days later, William awaited his second applicant of the day. After three days and more than half a dozen hopefuls, the too-young, somewhat militant Mrs. Warner had been by far the best candidate for the position, a fact that Robert, too, was well aware, though he wanted none of the lot. Nevertheless, William was determined that by week's end, there would be at least one female Pinkerton employed by the Chicago office, though pickings thus far were slim. One applicant was downright flighty; most had been visibly shaken by Robert's silent disapproval.

Lilly Warner had pluck, he thought, recalling the forewarning that they had not seen the last of her. He fully expected to look up in ten or so years and find her across the desk once again. Though he was not a proponent of feminism per se, Mrs. Warner was to be admired for her desire to help the cause of naïve and inexperienced women. William himself knew of many ladies who had been misused by the men in their lives.

A decisive knock sounded. The clerk swung the oak door wide, and intoned, "Mrs. Warren Partridge."

"Thank you, Harris."

William stood as Mrs. Partridge entered the room. She was tall enough, at least five foot six or seven. Her hair, dark with several strands of gray, was pulled back into a severe knot at the nape of her neck. She wore white gloves and a hat of chipped straw even though it was still a bit early in the season. Whether by choice or financial limitations, Mrs. Partridge was clearly no slave to fashion. Disdaining the popular slim-fitting skirt and bustle, she wore instead a plain white blouse buttoned to her throat and closed with a cameo brooch above a dark navy skirt.

She was quite buxom for such a slender woman, and she looked a bit broad across the beam, as his father might say. Wire-rimmed spectacles sat on the tip of her straight nose, giving her a scholarly appearance. Compared to the applicants who'd gone before her, she looked to be a down-to-earth, no-nonsense sort. Perhaps they were making progress at last.

He turned to Robert, who had risen, and saw an expression of interest on his brother's face.

"Come in, Mrs. Partridge, and have a seat," William said, extending his hand. "I'm William Pinkerton, and this is my brother, Robert."

Shoulders square, chin up, Mrs. Partridge crossed the room to give them both a firm handshake. Niceties satisfied, she accepted the chair across the desk and folded her hands in her lap.

"I assume you've read my résumé," she said, initiating the conversation, much to William's surprise. Her voice was high, a bit reedy, and more than a bit discordant to the ear.

"I have."

William called the information to mind. She was a widow, age thirty-seven, a former schoolteacher until her marriage, which, were there a God in heaven, should indicate intelligence, William thought wryly. There were no children to make demands on her. She had spent the past three years on an army outpost in Texas, where her husband, a sergeant in charge of new recruits, had been killed when his horse was frightened by a rattler and threw him.

"I'm a hard worker," she said in a clipped, precise tone. "And able to follow instructions. I've always enjoyed travel and research of any kind. My acquaintances tell me that I'm very observant, which would be an asset in the detecting business."

Before William could react to the way she'd shanghaied the interview, she continued to rattle off information about the family and the agency. Both William and Robert were a bit discombobulated by her knowledge of the family and even more disconcerted by her take-charge attitude. They questioned her on a few topics to see if she really was knowledgeable in several fields and found that she was. After thanking her for her time they told her they would let her know their decision in a day or two.

When she was gone, William and Robert sighed in unison. "You have to give her credit," William said. "She's intelligent enough."

"That is a plus," Robert mused. "She definitely fulfills most of the other requirements, but I'm not certain she could move in certain circles without drawing undue attention to herself. For all her qualifications, she comes across as a bit . . . abrasive, don't you think?"

"She needs to listen more and talk less," was William's take on the situation.

"As should all women," was Robert's dour reply.

The following day, the clerk ushered in a Mrs. Stephen Cartwright, a slender woman with blond hair swept up beneath a turban hat. Curls nestled at her nape and across her forehead. Too frivolous, was William's initial assessment. Good heavens! Was that a hint of color on her lips? Her slim dress was of baby-blue brocaded silk with the popular shelf bustle. Sapphire stones sparkled at her ears when she turned her head. She carried a frilly parasol and moved with undisguised grace, seeming to glide across the room.

"Good mornin'," she said, dropping a slight curtsy to him and Robert in turn. Her voice held a breathless quality.

"Please be seated, Mrs. Cartwright," William invited.

"You're William, did you say?" she asked, fluttering her eyelashes unashamedly. "And you're Robert. My. Such handsome men."

William cleared his throat and shuffled her résumé, anxious to get on with it. "It says here that you lost your husband in the war, Mrs. Cartwright."

"That is correct, sir."

"You seem terribly young to have been married some . . . let's see . . . fifteen years ago, at least."

She gave a little trill of laughter that sent a tingling awareness through William. "I was terribly young. Just sixteen when Stephen and I wed. We do marry young in the South, you know. Why, I'll be thirty-three my next birthday."

"You certainly don't look it." This from Robert, whose eyes had a glazed expression quite unlike him.

"Why, thank you, sir." She beamed at him.

"Was your husband in the military when you married?" William asked.

"No, sir. He joined up in December before General Lee surrendered the following April. I hated for him to go, but he was simply adamant about doing his part." A reminiscent smile curved her lips. "Why, even I did what I could."

She sat forward on the chair and glanced from William to Robert, a conspiratorial look in her sparkling brown eyes. "One time I managed to wangle a bit of important information from a Union captain who was quite smitten with m—"

She stopped abruptly, her smile vanishing, and sat up

straighter, placing a gloved hand against her cheek. Again her gaze moved from William to Robert and back again. "But you don't want to hear about that, now do you?"

William and Robert spent another fifteen minutes questioning the widow Cartwright, who explained why she felt she was qualified for the position, mentioning that she was well-read and was accepted in social situations. With a demure flutter of eyelashes, she stated that she believed she possessed particular skills to obtain information from certain gentlemen who might bear watching.

Resisting the impulse to whip his handkerchief from his breast pocket and mop at his perspiring face, William could only imagine what those skills might be. He already felt a twinge of envy for the poor fools who would fall under her spell. Satisfied that they had gleaned all the necessary information, William told her that she would be notified of their decision in a day or two.

Lilly left the interview with a feeling of smug satisfaction. She'd gone to three separate interviews as three different women, as well as accosting William outside the building to try to sell him milk. There had been no sign that he or his brother suspected any sort of foolery. It would be interesting to see whom they chose. If she didn't get the position, it wouldn't be for lack of trying.

CHAPTER 8

The day following her interview as Mrs. Cartwright, Lilly approached the law office of Simon Linedecker with a growing feeling that divorcing Timothy was not to be. Now that she'd made the spur-of-the-moment decision during her interview with the Pinkertons to rid herself of him, she was anxious to get the whole ordeal under way. Since she hadn't a penny to her name, Pierce and Rose had been happy to lend her the money to hire an attorney, and here she was, midafternoon and no further along than she had been when she set out.

She could not believe it was so hard to rid oneself of a thieving, fornicating husband. Though she knew society frowned upon divorce, she had not supposed that lawyers, who generally would do anything to put money in their pockets, would hold such negative viewpoints about a growing trend. Nevertheless, it seemed that reputable attorneys did not deal in "that sort of thing." One even went so far as to say that he had no desire for that kind of "notoriety." Her spirits had deteriorated with each legal representative she visited.

She had obtained Linedecker's name from the last lawyer

she'd spoken with—the fourth who had refused to even hear her reasons for seeking a divorce. With an excess of disdain, he'd informed her that Mr. Linedecker was not as discriminating as he and his colleagues.

Taking a deep breath, Lilly stepped into what she assumed was the outer office. The cramped room held bookshelves sagging with weighty law tomes and a scarred desk where a not unattractive, square-jawed young man sat chewing on the nub of his pen while examining some figures set before him. A lock of fair hair—devoid of pomade—fell over his forehead, which was wrinkled in a frown.

He looked up when she entered, myopic brown eyes blinking from behind wire-rimmed spectacles. A pleasant smile replaced the frown, and he stood, almost knocking over the chair in his haste.

"Good afternoon."

"Good afternoon. I was wondering if Mr. Linedecker might have an opening today. The matter is rather urgent."

"I'm Simon Linedecker," the young man said, extending his hand.

She accepted his handshake. "Lilly Warner."

"Please have a seat, Miss Warner. How may I be of assistance?" he asked, donning his most professional mien.

"It's Mrs. Warner," she corrected, as her mind sifted through the facts and came to some conclusions about the young attorney. His small office was not in the most fashionable part of town, and he had no office clerk, no pressing cases. Lilly felt certain she'd found a lawyer who would not be scandalized by her request. "I'm here to inquire if you accept divorce cases."

A self-deprecating smile revealed an attractive crease in his right cheek. "Not only do I accept them, I welcome them, Mrs. Warner. It is not easy to establish oneself fresh out of law school without the right family connections."

Lilly murmured an appropriate reply. For the most part, only the sons of the wealthy were able to obtain a law degree, but if she were to hazard a guess to the reason for his lack of clients, she would have to say that it was at least in part due to his boyish looks and his definite lack of polish. His rumpled tweed suit was out of mode, and the knot of his cravat was dated. His sandy hair, worn a bit too long for smartness, was rumpled, as if he made a habit of running his fingers through it. Instead of looking professional, he gave the appearance of an untidy schoolboy.

Lilly couldn't have cared less what he looked like. His law diploma hung on the wall, and he was not averse to helping her.

"Tell me about your marriage and why you wish to dissolve it."

Starting at the moment she'd literally run into him at the train station, Lilly recounted her meeting with Tim, the problems during the marriage, and ended with the tale of his thievery and assault on her and Rose. She also told him of her visit to MacGregor's and what she'd learned there, including her run-in with the loathsome Colleen. Linedecker made notes throughout her testimony.

"It sounds as though you have quite a case," he said when she finished. "How long did you say you've been married?"

"Just over four months." She opened her reticule, plucked out a folded paper, and placed it on the desk. "I brought my marriage license."

"Very good," he told her, taking the document from her and placing it on the one spot on his desk not covered in clutter. They talked a bit longer, and Lilly gave him the other information he asked for, stating that she would like to take back her maiden name. She wanted nothing to remind her of Timothy Warner and his lies.

"I'll be glad to help you, Mrs. Warner," he said at last. "It's troubling how easily women fall prey to unscrupulous men. My own sister married a scoundrel who kept her with child and then wouldn't provide for her and the children."

Lilly felt an instant connection with the unknown woman. "What happened to her?"

"She died giving birth to her fifth child," he said in a flat, emotionless voice. Then he seemed to shake off the melancholy. "I'm sorry. I'm not usually so forthcoming with my personal woes, but when I hear of others who are suffering from similar fates, it brings it all back. Unfortunately, there's little I can do about it but assist those who come to me for help."

"I'm very glad you feel that way," Lilly told him. "I was beginning to think I'd have to stay married to the man." They discussed Linedecker's fee, and she paid him a portion to get the proceedings started. As he walked her to the door, he asked, "How can I reach you?"

"I'm not sure where I'll be after this week," she told him, taking the business card he offered and handing him one of her *cartes de visite,* one of the popular calling cards most actors carried, listing their qualifications. If she left with the troupe, they would be going to Springfield; if the Pinkertons hired "Mrs. Cartwright" or "Mrs. Partridge," Lilly had no idea where she would be sent. "Once I know something, I'll be in touch."

"Good enough. I'll get started right away."

CHAPTER 9

Lilly rose each day and went about her usual business, practicing her lines, going to rehearsal, and giving a performance each night, but the Pinkerton brothers were never far from her mind. Mrs. Cartwright had received a letter from the agency stating that she did not fit the criteria. Lilly had expected as much. The Southern belle was far too flighty and flashy for serious undercover work.

"Mrs. Partridge" had yet to hear from the agency, and the troupe was scheduled to leave in less than a week. If she hadn't heard from William Pinkerton by then, Lilly had no choice but to get on the train bound for Springfield.

On Tuesday afternoon, she was preparing to study her lines—Pierce had given her yet another lead role in a new comedy—when there was a knock at her door. To her surprise, Pierce stood there, an envelope in his hand.

"Some young man brought this a few minutes ago," he said. "It's from Mr. William Pinkerton to Mrs. Warren Partridge."

Lilly snatched it from him and, hurrying to the desk, she

slipped the letter opener beneath the flap and slit open the envelope. Her hands trembled as she pulled the paper free and unfolded it.

"Well, what does the bloody thing say?" Pierce grumbled after a moment.

She stared in disbelief at the letter. "They want me—Mrs. Partridge—to come back for a second interview at two o'clock this afternoon." She looked from the note to Pierce. "That's encouraging, don't you think?"

"Very." Pierce summoned a thin smile. "And won't the brothers Pinkerton be surprised when they do hire Mrs. Partridge and find out she's Lilly Long?"

"I'm not telling them that!"

"Of course you are."

"Are you mad? They'll be furious and boot me out the door."

"Lilly. Luv." Pierce placed his hands on her shoulders and gave her a little shake. "You have no choice but to tell them the truth."

She shook her head and stared into his resolute eyes. The idea that had seemed so smart just days ago now seemed impulsive, and worse, foolish.

"Don't look so down in the mouth. It will be fine."

"How can you say that? I deliberately set out to bamboozle the most respected law enforcement agency in the country."

"No, no, you haven't."

"What would you call it?"

"What was our purpose when we concocted the plan for you to go back as two different people if they turned you down?"

"You said it would make them see how good I was at acting. At becoming another person."

"Correct. And did they recognize either of your other personalities?"

Lilly grew thoughtful. "No," she said at last. "They didn't seem to at the time, and from their response, it would appear that they believe we are three distinct people."

"And what does that tell you?"

Lilly thought about it a moment and her discomfort eased somewhat. Leave it to Pierce to put things into perspective. She lifted her chin in triumph. "That I did a bang-up job of bamboozling the most respected law enforcement agency in the country?" she asked with a cheeky smile.

"Well, yes," Pierce said with his own smile. "You did do that. But what it says is that you did a bang-up job of what you set out to do. You played your roles to perfection. Even if they are a bit miffed, they'll be forced to admit that your acting ability is unsurpassed. You tell them that you came back to interview as different women to prove to them that you can do the job, and do it convincingly. And that, my dear," Pierce said with a smile, "is how you play this hand."

CHAPTER 10

For the fourth time, Lilly took a carriage to the Pinkerton offices. Though she'd been to Chicago several times, the speed of its growth never ceased to amaze her. The ten years since the fire that had destroyed more than three square miles of the city had in some ways been a blessing. Narrow streets had been replaced with thoroughfares that were at least eighty feet wide, many of them paved with brick or cinder. Some were even macadamized, and gaslight illumination was common. Even the gutters seemed cleaner, she thought as her cab pulled to a stop at her destination.

She entered the agency's office and offered Harris a prim nod. He told her to be seated. She searched his eyes for any signs of recognition and found none. The knowledge gave her scant comfort. Did she really believe the Pinkerton men would be impressed with the fact that they had been tricked by a chit of a woman?

"Mrs. Partridge? The Misters Pinkerton will see you now."

Lilly rose, smoothed her palm over her graying wig and

drab olive-colored skirt, and followed him to the inner office door.

"Thank you, Harris," William said. Turning to Lilly, he said, "Please come in, Mrs. Partridge."

As she entered the room, Lilly noticed another man seated on the sofa next to Robert. She clamped her mouth shut lest her jaw drop open in surprise and did her best not to stare. Unless she was mistaken, the third man in the room was the celebrated Allan Pinkerton himself. Though he had come far since his stroke, the once-vigorous investigator was clearly not the robust man he once was. He had aged beyond his sixty-one years.

"Mrs. Partridge, I'd like you to meet my father, Allan Pinkerton, the founder of the Pinkerton National Detective Agency," William said, gesturing toward his father.

"Forgive me for not standing, Mrs. Partridge," the legendary detective said, "but I've walked more than ten miles today and am a bit weary."

Allan's Scots accent was still thick, and his speech was somewhat slurred, but his shrewd gaze missed little. As silly as it was, Lilly's first inclination was to curtsy. Instead, she crossed the room, leaned forward, and offered her hand. "Mr. Pinkerton," she said in Mrs. Partridge's grating voice. "What a pleasure to meet you. I've been a fan of your detective stories for some time, and my copy of your memoirs is quite dog-eared from so much reading."

"Thank you for your kind words, Mrs. Partridge. My sons tell me that you have many qualities that might be useful in our line of business."

It didn't escape Lilly's notice that Robert's mouth had drawn into a flat line of disapproval.

"I believe so, sir."

William gestured for Lilly to take a seat, which she did, her back ramrod straight.

"We understand that you have no family to make demands on you," he said, steering the conversation back to the task at hand, "and we wondered what your commitment might be to your current position."

"I haven't taken a teaching post since coming from Texas," Mrs. Partridge told them.

They questioned her at length and in more depth about her schooling and the subjects she had studied, and asked her about her ideas on how to go about "detecting." Appearing satisfied with the answers she gave, William said, "Of all the applicants, you appear to be the most qualified, except for one other whose credentials were impeccable but was far too young for our purposes."

"Oh?"

Allan Pinkerton laughed, a rusty, hardly used sound. "I'd like to have met the lass," he said. "William was quite taken with her."

Lilly hadn't expected that such an opportune time to reveal the truth would be dropped into her lap. "Really?" she said, in a slightly shaking voice. "Perhaps that can be arranged."

Without pausing long enough to lose her courage, she reached up with trembling hands and removed Mrs. Partridge's wire-rimmed glasses from her nose and then pulled the wig from her head to reveal her own glossy red hair.

"Good heaven above!" William cried. "Mrs. Warner!"

He was definitely shocked, Lilly thought. In fact, his face looked so red she feared he might succumb to a fit of apoplexy as his father had. Well, the fat was in the fire now, so there was nothing to do but see if she could pull it out.

"Yes," she said in her normal voice, a voice that was tinged with a hint of asperity. "And I must admit I was disappointed that you let my age stop you from at least giving me the position on a trial basis, since Kate Warne was hired when she was but twenty-three. Mrs. Cartwright was disappointed as well."

"Mrs. Cartwright?" William repeated, frowning. Robert tilted his head back and groaned.

Without a word, Lilly reached into her reticule. Allan's face wore a considering expression, and the brothers could only watch with open mouths as she withdrew the lace-edged fan and proceeded to flutter it in front of her face. Rising and dropping into a deep curtsy, she gave William a coy look. "I was so disappointed when you turned me down. Why, I had a sick headache and had to take to my bed for a full day."

Returning to her normal tone, Lilly said, "Of course, Mrs. Cartwright did not really expect to be hired. She is a rather flighty creature."

"By all that is holy," Robert shouted, leaping to his feet to shake his finger in her face. "You, madam, have attempted to play us the fool."

"That was not my intention, sir," Lilly told him in an even tone. "I only—"

"Bah! You deliberately set out to dupe us," he interrupted. "There is no excuse for it! We will not have it!"

"Be quiet, Robert."

The blunt command came from Allan, who up to this point had contented himself with watching things unfold in contemplative silence.

"Father, she—"

"Quiet, I say!" Allan Pinkerton focused his gaze on Lilly. It was clear to her that while the stroke might have debilitated him physically, it had done little to dull his intellect. "Please continue, Mrs. Partridge—excuse me—Mrs. Warner. I believe you were explaining your actions before my son's rude interruption."

Lilly looked into the detective's piercing eyes. "Though I am much younger than you might like, sir, and realize that I may lack the experience gained with years, it was never my intent to deceive, only to prove that I possess the necessary skill for this position, which I believe I did, since no one suspected that the three ladies who interviewed were one and the same."

"I'd say you proved that quite admirably, young lady," Allan said. "And I must say I admire your attention to detail as well as your tenacity."

"Tenacity!" Robert sputtered. "More like trickery!"

"Oh, hush, Robert!" A rare twinkle lit Allan's eyes.

"I apologize if my methods seem extreme and unorthodox," Lilly said, "but I understand that you're a proponent of various techniques as long as the ends justify the means."

"Indeed I am."

"It was that very reasoning that led me to go so far in order to be hired by your agency," she explained. "I ask that you give me this position, Mr. Pinkerton, if only on a trial basis. I will, of course, gladly accept any assignment, but because of my own background, my greatest desire is to help women who've been taken advantage of by deceitful men."

"A praiseworthy ambition."

"Thank you, sir."

Pinkerton sat there for long moments, lost in thought. "Will you step out into the anteroom, Mrs. Warner," Allan said at last. "I would like to discuss this with my sons."

Lilly sat in the outer office with the clerk, listening to the *clackety-clack* of the Remington typewriter Harris was using, while they both tried to ignore the yelling and cursing as the Pinkerton men argued over her like dogs over a meaty bone.

At the end of ten minutes, she was called back in. The tension in the room was palpable. Allan wore an unruffled expression, but his color was high. Thank God he had not suffered another shock on her account! William looked relieved. Robert was livid.

"Congratulations, Mrs. Warner," William said when she was

seated across from him once more. "You are the newest employee of the Pinkerton National Detective Agency, on that trial basis you mentioned."

The knot in Lilly's stomach unfurled, and her first true smile encompassed them all. "Thank you. I appreciate your confidence more than I can say and promise to do my best."

"I'm certain you will," William said. "We do have an assignment for you, a missing person—a missing family, actually. There will be no need for you to take on another persona. You will just be Lilly Warner, trying to locate a certain individual. It's up to you whether or not you'll be better served by letting people know you're with the agency. It may not be very exciting, but I'm sure you understand that as a new recruit, we can't throw you into the lion's den, so to speak."

She glanced at Allan, whose face was impassive. There was no mistaking the gloating expression on Robert's face at knowing her first assignment was one of little consequence.

"Thank you, sir. It's sound thinking on your part to give me something uncomplicated for my first assignment as a detective."

"For the record, my father has always preferred the use of operative instead of detective, since that word has come to mean someone with a less-than-savory reputation. You should also know that we have a code of ethics written by my father entitled *General Principles*. You will be given a copy. We expect all of our operatives to honor them."

"I will do my best."

Allan spoke up. "This is a high calling, Mrs. Warner. I'll be the first to admit that you are quite the expert at role-playing, which will stand you in good stead, but you must also become a close observer of people. To analyze those around you, judge their feelings, their actions, and the reasons behind those actions."

Lilly nodded, doing her best to store away every word he spoke.

"It's been my experience that people like to talk, even when they've done something wrong," the eldest Pinkerton offered. "It is up to the operative to judge just when to force the issue, as well as what means to employ to obtain the information. As you pointed out earlier, as long as justice wins out, the ends justify the means."

"I understand." Her head spun with all the information she was receiving. Perhaps it was better after all that this first job was somewhat trivial.

William handed her a small booklet. "This is an overview of the case," he explained. "We make a journal for each client. In it, you will find the client's name and problem, what he would like us to do for him, and a detailed plan of how to proceed. Look it over thoroughly tonight."

Lilly took the proffered book. "Thank you, sir. I will."

"We want you to come in each day for the remainder of this week and part of next for further instruction. At the end of that time, you will be sent to the southern part of the state, a town called Vandalia. Our clients are a wealthy man and his wife who wish to purchase some land and a house near there that they desire to turn into a home for unwed mothers."

"A noble undertaking," Lilly commented, thinking of her own mother.

"Yes," Robert interjected. "It's amazing how many young women have no moral standards these days."

Wisely, Lilly did not rise to the bait.

A red-faced William continued. "The house once belonged to a Reverend Harold Purcell and his family. He moved to the area approximately twenty-three years ago in the capacity of minister and bought a house some few miles outside of town, which he called Heaven's Gate. I understand it was quite a showplace in its day. This is the house our clients wish to purchase. The problem is that they have been unable to locate the Purcells to see if they will sell and, if so, at what price."

"No one knows where they went?" Lilly asked.

"Not that our clients have been able to find out. Thus, they came to us."

"You would think that one of the church members would know something," Lilly said with a frown. "That's a bit strange, isn't it?"

"Not so strange when you know that the preacher and his family left town in the dark of night in possession of all the church's money," William offered.

"Oh!" Lilly was silent a moment, then said, "I don't imagine it was the first time he had done such a thing."

"I'm afraid I don't follow you, Mrs. Warner."

"To the best of my knowledge, ministers do not make great amounts of money. If this Reverend Purcell came to town and bought a huge fancy house, where and how did he obtain the funds to do so?" She shrugged. "I suppose he could have been independently wealthy, but that seems somewhat improbable."

"Bravo, Mrs. Warner," Allan Pinkerton said. Approval gleamed in his eyes. "Excellent reasoning."

"Yes," William concurred. "Excellent."

Robert remained silent.

"Your job is to find the Purcells, see if they will sell, and report back to us. If they cannot be found, or they are opposed to letting go of the property, our clients will be forced to look elsewhere."

"I understand, and please, for the record I would like to be called by my maiden name, Long. I've taken steps to have it changed legally, when my divorce is finalized."

"Of course," William said with a nod.

After discussing a few more details about the position, Lilly thanked them once again and left. She stepped into the cold March air, her mind whirling, a wide, somewhat silly smile on her face. She felt like doing a jig down the street, but of course, she couldn't. She was a professional, a bona-fide agent of the Pinkerton National Detective Agency. Part of the "Eye That Never Sleeps."

Lilly Long. Female operative.

CHAPTER 11

Lilly awoke to daylight. Belching smoke and spewing sparks, the St. Louis, Vandalia, and Terre Haute locomotive rumbled through the early-morning sunshine toward its destination of Vandalia. They were due to arrive just after eleven o'clock, and she was past ready to do so. Her daily allowance from the Pinkertons did not permit a sleeping berth, which in any event she'd heard was comparable to sleeping on the floor. She'd spent the night in a seat, fleeing to the far corner of the passenger car when the heat from the woodstove in the center of the car threatened to broil her alive.

The makeshift accommodation had not been conducive to rest. Not only was there the snoring of various passengers, the whining of unhappy children, and the revelry of a group of rowdy young men the conductor said were traveling boxers, there was also the noise of the engine and the monotonous clacking of the metal wheels against the iron rails. All she'd managed was to doze off and on until pure exhaustion claimed her somewhere near dawn.

It had been a whirlwind week. Besides preparing for her

journey, she'd spent each day being schooled by William Pinkerton. She'd been taught how to "shadow" people, and various scenarios of former "stings" were outlined, with Lilly being asked how she would have proceeded. It was not necessary that she be correct; often there was no right way, only different methods. They'd brought in two other operatives with whom she carried on lengthy conversations in both French and Italian.

Allan, whose office was much like the backstage area of a theater with all its costumes and disguises, showed up twice to gauge her progress. She knew that despite any reservations he might have about her youth, he was impressed with her skill with the sword and pistol, as well as her education.

She'd learned there were criteria for both employees and clients. Before the heads of any office agreed to meet with a potential client, that person must present identification and letters of reference and also be able to afford the daily fee, which ranged from three to ten dollars a day. Only then was a meeting arranged. For a variety of reasons, no client ever met the operatives working on their case face-to-face.

All too soon it was time to leave. Pierce and Rose had given her a going-away party the previous evening. The thought of leaving for a strange city all alone was almost more than Lilly could bear, but she knew she couldn't let on, or Pierce would renew his efforts to persuade her to abandon her silly notion to become a Pinkerton.

Instead of giving over to her melancholy, she'd laughed and drunk too much champagne. She'd been hugged by her fellow actors until her ribs hurt, and her cheek bussed by so many women and mustached men that it still felt raw. With her head spinning from the unaccustomed alcohol, she found herself in Rose's embrace.

"I'm going to miss you, Lil." She heard the tell-tale huskiness in the older woman's voice as she whispered into Lilly's ear. "You're the only daughter I've ever had, and Pierce and I love you like you are our own."

"I know that," Lilly said, her giddiness giving way to the solemnity of the moment. "I feel the same."

"If ever you need anything—money or help of any kind— telegraph us and let us know. We'll be there."

In response, Lilly hugged Rose tighter. She knew that, too.

With a whisper for Lilly to take care of herself, Rose had taken her by the shoulders and stared at her for long moments, as if she were trying to commit Lilly's features to memory. Then, as a single tear slid down her cheek, she'd let go and fled from the room.

"Ten minutes to Vandalia!"

The sound of the conductor's voice curtailed her thoughts of the past. The closer she got to her new life, the harder it became to ignore the niggling suspicion that perhaps Pierce was right and she'd bitten off more than she could chew. It was one thing to let the pain of Timothy's deception and her own stubbornness ride on the coattails of her anger while she fought for her position with the Pinkertons. It was quite something else to go unaccompanied into a world about which she knew so little. She'd never been, or felt, more alone in her life.

She shivered. The blaze in the stove had died out during the night, leaving a definite coolness in the swaying passenger car. Determined to push her fears and loneliness aside, she checked the watch pinned to the lapel of her charcoal gray traveling jacket. The train was right on schedule. She gazed out the frosty window. Though there were small signs of spring here and there, a heavy cloud cover hid the sun, and a light veneer of frost covered the barren fields. She'd expected the farmland around Vandalia to be flat and treeless, but there was the occasional rolling hill, and groves of trees edged the fields.

Vandalia, a farming community of just under two thousand

people, was situated at the end of the old Cumberland Trail on the west side of the Kaskaskia River at a place once known as Reeve's Bluff. Vandalia had served as the state capital until 1839, when that title was bestowed on Springfield.

She shivered again in the chill of the railcar. Springfield. The place her mother had met the man who'd taken her life. The place Kate had been murdered and buried. Lilly had long ago concluded that she would never know who killed her mother. The problem was not necessarily the length of time that had lapsed, but the fact that her mind refused to relinquish the smallest memory of the day beyond her hiding beneath her mother's bed when Kate announced her lover had arrived.

Lilly sighed. Perhaps it was just as well. Like finding Tim, finding her mother's killer was not her purpose in life. Her most pressing need was proving to the agency that she was capable of completing her assignment to their satisfaction.

By the time the train slowed at the station, her emotions were once more in control. Squaring her shoulders and donning the persona of a woman well versed in the ways of the world, she began to gather her things. She was picking up the canvas bag that held a few necessities when she backed into something—or someone—and gave a little gasp. Whirling around, she whacked the person with the bag and stumbled a bit to regain her footing.

"Careful there!"

Lilly looked up into the face of an attractive man who'd reached out to steady her. Defying convention, his bowler was cocked back on his head and a lock of unruly hair—so dark it was almost black—fell over his forehead. His lean jaw was covered with a day's growth of beard that gave him a somewhat dangerous look. A well-tended mustache draped the upper lip of a mouth that was curved in an impertinent smile that was echoed in his sapphire-blue eyes. A nose that had been broken more than once and a thin white scar that trailed the crest of his left cheekbone saved him from conventional handsomeness and added to the impression of danger.

"Careful there, colleen," he said. "We don't want you falling, now do we?"

She didn't hear the teasing concern in his voice. All she heard was "colleen." It made no difference that the word was a common endearment for a young girl. To Lilly it conjured a mental image of Colleen McKenna, a painful reminder of Tim's betrayal. Also realizing that their encounter was almost identical to her first meeting with Timothy, she stiffened beneath the man's grasp and stepped out of his reach, breaking both his hold on her and their locked gaze. Gathering her dignity, she murmured a polite "Excuse me."

Without lingering to hear his reply, she stepped around him and headed for the exit. Waiting for the train to come to a full stop gave her time to regain her composure.

The conductor set a small stool on the ground, and Lilly stepped to the platform, her run-in with the stranger forgotten. Somehow she'd expected that Vandalia, which was more than 250 miles south of Chicago, would be warmer than the city she'd just left. It wasn't.

Lilly looked around, taking in the area. The train tracks ran more or less east to west, and the Vandalia House Hotel stood parallel to them. The tracks of the Illinois Central ran roughly northwest to southeast, with the town sitting in a pie-shaped area formed by the two rail lines.

She considered staying at the nearby hotel, but she'd learned from Pierce that one of the troupe's former actresses was playing at the Fehren Opera House, and since she hoped to enjoy a play and spend time with her old friend, it seemed smarter to find lodging closer to the theater.

The Dieckmann House, considered the finest hotel south of Chicago, was located kitty-corner from the Fehren, but it was a bit too much for her daily stipend, and William had cautioned her to keep close track of her expenditures. It seemed there had been a fair amount of expense sheet falsification and cash-flow problems in the past, and the agency's miserly accountant, Mr. J. G. Horne, now demanded scrupulous accounting of the agency's funds.

Though the Dieckmann was out, she was not the least concerned about finding agreeable lodging. She just hoped it was soon. After a long, uncomfortable night, she felt grumpy and rumpled and tired. She longed for a hot meal and to freshen up.

That bespectacled ticket agent, whose hair was whiter and wispier than the angel hair used to adorn Christmas trees, directed her to the Holbrook Hotel, which was located on the corner of Third and Johnson Streets, one block south of Gallatin, the main thoroughfare. He explained that the large home, which had been converted into a hotel, was reasonably priced and clean. It also had a dining room, and the food was good and plentiful.

Lilly thanked him and found a hack to take her to the hotel. The driver loaded her chest with help of a sturdy young man who assisted Lilly into the buggy and they started out, taking a left onto Sixth Street. The chill wind whipped color into her cheeks and made her brown eyes water. She took in her new surroundings with an eager eye. Vandalia seemed to be thriving, but it was far different from Chicago. She saw no fancy-dressed businessmen with hats and canes, no women out for a morning stroll in chic walking dresses. Most of the men wore clothing designed for hard work, and though many of the women wore hats of some sort and most wore gloves, their attire was, in most cases, a simple shirtwaist and skirt.

She spotted the Fehren on the corner of Fifth and Gallatin. The famous Dieckmann House sat on the opposite corner. The imposing three-story brick building did not disappoint. It was magnificent. As was customary, a hardware store, a restaurant, and dry goods establishment were located on the lower floor.

The buggy rolled down another block, passing the most

recent of three capital buildings to be built on the site. The Federal-style building had been built in 1836 and served as the courthouse since the capital had been moved to Springfield.

The driver took a right on Third, and the horse pranced past Ireland's, the livery stable where her driver and rig originated. The remainder of the block behind the stable was taken up with a shed and a somewhat muddy, tree-studded paddock. The Holbrook Hotel was located across the street from the horses, which were feeding on piles of hay.

The hotel exterior was painted a pristine white with forest green shutters framing the windows. A wide porch wrapped around three sides of the well-maintained structure. A hitching post complete with two horses was located in front of a flower bed, barren except for a few brave crocuses. A wooden watering trough stood on the opposite side of the porch.

All was protected by the enveloping arms of two huge maple trees whose branches blushed with the red of new buds. The stately trees would provide much-welcomed shade during the heat of summer. Willow rocking chairs lined the porch, and Lilly envisioned a warm spring evening with guests chatting while sipping lemonade and munching on tea cakes rich with plump raisins. She relished the idea of being able to enjoy that kind of leisure.

Tethering the rig, the driver helped her alight. Inside, she found the moderately sized lobby quite pleasant. The room smelled faintly of wood smoke and the scent of lemon balm, which, as she'd learned from Rose, was mixed with beeswax and used to polish furniture. The walls were painted navy blue. Lace curtains hung at the windows. Tan camelback sofas and wing chairs upholstered in navy, tan, green, and Indian-red tartan formed seating areas around hand-braided rugs.

Beyond the parlor, through opened pocket doors, was a large dining room. The mouthwatering smells reminded her once again just how hungry she was. The registration desk stood tucked beneath the staircase leading to the second floor, where there were six rooms, if the keys hanging on wall pegs were any indication. The third floor also had six rooms for visitors. No doubt Vandalia was a popular stopping-off place for settlers headed west, since it marked the end of the Old National Road, which ran east all the way to Cumberland, Maryland.

Hearing the jangling of the bell on the door, an attractive woman glanced up from a ledger and gave Lilly a welcoming smile.

"Welcome to the Holbrook Hotel," she said. "I'm Virginia Holbrook."

"Lilly Long," Lilly said, extending her hand. "I was wondering if you have a spare room for a week or so."

"As a matter of fact, two guests just checked out. Would you prefer the second or third floor?"

"Second, please." Lilly signed the register and paid for her week's stay in advance.

"Are you here for a visit, or just passing through?" the owner asked, after summoning her sons to carry Lilly's trunk upstairs.

"Business. I represent a client who is looking to purchase a place to put in a new business." At this point she saw no reason to let the woman know she was affiliated with the Pinkerton Agency.

"Really?" Virginia Holbrook looked a bit surprised by the fact that Lilly was a working woman, traveling alone. "I wasn't aware anything in town was for sale."

"Actually, it isn't in town," Lilly said. "It's a mile or so off the road that goes to Houston."

Virginia nodded. "You mean the Old Alton Road that goes to Mulberry Grove, or Shake Rag as it was called back in the days it was a stagecoach stop." Seeing the question in Lilly's eyes, she said, "When there was someone for the stage to pick up, the owners would send out a servant to wave a rag to stop the stage."

Lilly laughed. "Well, the property I'm talking about is out that way. The owner moved away several years ago, and I've been sent to look into the matter."

"Really?"

"Yes," Lilly told her. "The place is called Heaven's Gate. It belonged to a Reverend Harold Purcell. Perhaps you remember him?"

The suddenly closed expression that replaced Virginia Holbrook's interest and good humor made Lilly feel as if a door had been slammed in her face. She might be as unworldly as Pierce claimed, but even she realized that she had crossed some barrier she shouldn't have.

"I'm afraid I don't," Mrs. Holbrook said in a voice that had lost all vestige of friendliness. Without another word, she turned away and took a key from the wall peg. "Here's your key, Miss Long. We began serving lunch at eleven, if you care to eat with us, though there are several other places in town to get a bite if you prefer. I hope you enjoy your stay in Vandalia."

Chapter 12

A few minutes later, Lilly shut the door to her room and tossed her gloves, hat, and bag to the bed. She was stunned by Virginia Holbrook's brush-off. What was it about the mention of Heaven's Gate that turned Mrs. Holbrook from a pleasant, smiling woman to a cold, uncommunicative one?

Lilly stripped off her traveling dress and searched for fresh clothes. As she pulled things from her trunk, her stomach gave a sudden loud rumble.

She was too hungry to try to figure out anything at the moment. Breakfast had been an apple she'd purchased from the young news butch who'd been peddling not only yesterday's newspapers, but everything from cigars to sandwiches and dime novels. Whether or not there were other places to eat, she would definitely take advantage of the dining room downstairs.

Like the women of Vandalia, Lilly chose to dress sensibly, choosing a warm red wool dress. Like Mrs. Partridge, Lilly made the scandalous decision to forgo her corset. After all, she was a working woman, not a fashion plate.

Mrs. Holbrook was nowhere to be seen when Lilly passed through the lobby to the dining room. A young man, one of the sons who'd taken her luggage upstairs, was now behind the desk. Lilly entered a large eating area. A hall tree, adorned with several hats ranging from bowlers to the style favored by the western cowboys, stood just inside the door.

A family with two small boys occupied one table, and a lone man reading a newspaper sat at another. A long counter held six seats, and a large, framed piece of slate hung on the wall behind it. The day's menu was written with chalk in plain uppercase print. Other signage proclaimed that the hotel proudly served Chase & Sanborn coffee and Heinz ketchup.

The lunch choices made her mouth water. Steak or ham with gravy, potatoes, and a choice of several vegetables. Dessert was apple or rhubarb pie.

One of the counter seats was occupied by a rugged-looking individual wearing dungarees, boots, and spurs. No doubt the Stetson belonged to him. Two farmer types sat nearby. All were attacking plates of ham, potatoes, beans, and thick slabs of buttered bread along with mugs of steaming coffee. Lilly's stomach gave another growl.

A pretty golden-haired girl who looked like a younger version of Virginia Holbrook was taking payment from a well-dressed man. It seemed the entire family worked in the hotel. The paying customer was wearing a gray sack coat and matching vest. His collar was pressed into sharp wings, and a newly fashionable ascot tie of burgundy silk pierced with a pearl stickpin was a perfect match to the square handkerchief peeking from his breast pocket. His Alberts were polished to a high sheen. A banker, Lilly thought.

"Wonderful as usual, sweet pea," the man said to the young girl.

"Thank you, Grandfather," she replied, ringing up his purchase on the cash register. "I'll be sure and tell Sadie."

Seeing Lilly in the doorway, she said, "I'll be with you in just a moment, ma'am. Please have a seat."

Lilly chose a table near the window. From her vantage point she could see the horses across the street and the livery stable on the corner. A newborn foal gamboled next to his mother, who munched contentedly on a pile of hay.

"I'm sorry to make you wait, ma'am." The young girl, who looked to be in her late teens, filled the glass with water from a crockery pitcher. The apron covering the front of her simple blue shirtwaist was the same pristine white as the table-cloth and napkins.

"That's not a problem," Lilly assured her with a smile. "I've been watching the horses."

"That young one likes to raise a ruckus," the waitress told her with a smile. She pulled a small, lined tablet and stubby pencil from her apron pocket. "What can I get for you today?"

"I'll have what they're having," Lilly said, indicating the two men at the counter.

"Certainly. Would you like coffee or a glass of milk with that?"

"Coffee, please, and some Borden's condensed milk if you have it." Since trying the thick, sweet, canned milk some months back, Lilly had grown extremely fond of putting it in her coffee.

"I'm sorry, ma'am, but all we have is fresh cream."

"That will do nicely," Lilly assured her.

"I'll have it out in a few minutes," the young woman assured her. "By the way, my name is Helen, if you need me."

"Thank you, Helen. I'm Lilly. Lilly Long. Do your parents own the hotel?"

"Yes."

"I thought so. Your mother checked me in earlier. You look just like her."

"Really? I think she's beautiful."

"She is," Lilly said. "And so are you."

Helen blushed and disappeared through the door to the kitchen with Lilly's order.

While Lilly waited, she watched the two small boys with their parents. They were adorable. One was the spitting image of his father, the other a miniature portrait of his mother. She watched the woman wipe a milk mustache from the younger child's lips and saw her mouth curve into an indulgent smile as she raised her contented gaze to her husband. He returned the smile and reached out to touch her hand.

The happiness and love they shared left Lilly strangely sorrowful. As she had often of late, she considered love and its various incarnations: puppy love, familial love, and the rare, deep and abiding love a man and wife might share. She'd pondered the ways those kinds of love affected a person's attitudes and actions. Then she considered how the word was misused and distorted to cover baser feelings, like lust and covetousness and selfishness, just so that a person could have his way . . . like her mother's killer and Timothy.

How could a person be certain that the other was telling the truth about his emotions? She hadn't been able to discern Timothy's true feelings. Instead, she'd allowed herself to be caught up in his charming personality and pretty, lying words, mistaking her infatuation for the real thing. Could she ever trust herself to recognize truth in the future?

Without warning, a memory of the man she'd bumped into on the train slipped into her mind. Still smarting from Tim's betrayal and cranky from lack of proper rest, she'd responded to the stranger's simple act of kindness with anger. That wasn't at all like her.

Before she could give the matter any more thought, Helen approached with Lilly's lunch. It tasted as good as it smelled and looked, and even though she had a healthy appetite, she'd known when she placed the order that it would be far too much. Still, she did her best by it. She was finishing her third cup of coffee when Helen returned to check on her. The din-ing room had cleared of other occupants while Lilly enjoyed her meal.

"Was everything satisfactory?"

"It was delicious," she said. "Just more than I could manage."

"No dessert, then?"

Lilly gave a soft groan. "Not right now."

"Then I'll take your money at the register when you're finished," Helen said, whisking up the plate.

Lilly finished her coffee and went to pay. "Would it be a lot of trouble for you to make me a copy of my bill? I need it for my employer." She didn't intend to do anything to jeopardize her new job—not intentionally, anyway.

"Not at all. So you're here on business?" Helen asked as she began to write out a duplicate ticket. Like her mother, she seemed a bit surprised that Lilly was a working woman.

"Yes, I'm trying to locate someone who once lived here. Perhaps you could help."

"Of course, if I can."

"I need directions to the Harold Purcell property. Reverend Purcell. I have a client interested in purchasing the place." Seeing the girl's frown of confusion, Lilly added, "It was called Heaven's Gate."

"Oh, yes," Helen said with a nod. "I know who you mean. I never knew the family. They left town before I was born. My brother says one of his friends told him the preacher stole some money or something and fled in the middle of the night. No one in town talks about them much."

So William had been right about the reverend. She would have to talk to the local law and see if she could find out more about the theft, but not until she'd had a look at the property.

"Do you know where the house is located?"

"I know that it's a few miles west of town, going toward

Mulberry Grove, but I've never been there. My mother has forbidden it."

Not an unusual parental demand for a place deserted for some twenty years, Lilly thought. "Thank you, Helen. Do they rent buggies at the livery stable across the street?"

Helen's eyes grew wide. "Of course, but you aren't going out there, are you?"

"That was the plan, yes."

"Alone?" Helen asked. Her face wore an expression of disbelief and alarm.

Lilly was touched by the girl's concern. "I need to have a look at it for my client. Is there some reason I shouldn't go?"

"Well . . ." Helen's face flushed red. "I know it's a silly notion, but everyone in town claims Heaven's Gate is haunted."

The statement was as much of a shock as hearing that the reverend had stolen from his flock. Lilly suppressed a smile. At least a ghost added a bit of spark to an otherwise tedious assignment. Neither William nor his journal had mentioned a ghost. That tidbit—however ridiculous—plus the fact that the reverend had stolen from his congregation certainly explained why the townspeople were so reticent about discussing him.

"Haunted," she mused, tucking the expense receipt into her reticule. "And why would anyone believe that?"

Wide-eyed, Helen placed her elbows on the counter and leaned toward Lilly, eager to spin her tale. "Two boys who lived nearby were playing in the woods behind the house just after the reverend and his family came up missing and heard this eerie sound coming from inside the house . . . like a wounded animal . . . or a haint."

Helen gave a slight shudder. "I really wish you'd think twice before going out there alone."

"I appreciate your concern," Lilly told her, "but I must do my job, and besides, I am a pretty fair shot."

Helen's eyes widened. Lilly wondered if the girl was shocked by the fact that Lilly carried a gun or that she was handy with it.

Helen shook her head. "That won't do you much good against a ghost, Miss Long."

"I suppose you're right," Lilly said with a smile. "In that case, I promise to be very careful."

Grudgingly, Helen told Lilly that someone at the livery stable could tell her how to get to the abandoned property. Lilly left with another thank you. Seeing the apprehension lurking in the younger woman's eyes, she added, "If I'm not back by suppertime, you might send someone to come looking for me."

Helen nodded. "I just remembered that Billy Bishop is working at Ireland's these days. He was one of the boys who heard the ghost's howling. He can certainly give you directions as well as tell you more about the ghost."

Wonderful! Lilly thought with a little thrill of excitement. Detecting wasn't hard at all. It was just a matter of asking the right people the right questions. Talking up Helen had been a boon. The young girl had given her one eye witness so to speak, as well as a bit of interesting information. Perhaps this assignment wouldn't take long to wrap up, and she could go on to more challenging assignments.

CHAPTER 13

Back in her room again, Lilly took off her narrow-toed shoes and pulled on a pair of men's socks and some scuffed boots she wore when she and Pierce went horseback riding or shooting in the country.

Common sense told her that she should present her case to the sheriff before going off on her own, but Helen's story had kindled her curiosity and a burning need to visit the house that had been home to the notorious Purcell family. She also wanted to do as much snooping around as possible on her own before informing anyone about her employer. News that she was with the Pinkertons might scare people even more, so she would visit Heaven's Gate this afternoon and pay the sheriff a visit first thing in the morning.

Since the March day felt as cold as wintertime, she wore gloves and her heavy red cloak with its warm lining in case the day grew cooler later. Pierce always said one should try to be prepared for the unexpected, so she stuffed some money for the horse and buggy into a pocket along with matches and a flint wrapped in oilcloth, tied with a length of twine. The other pocket held her Remington over and under derringer and a handful of .41 caliber bullets. With her purse hidden in a compartment of her trunk, she was ready to start her assignment.

Billy Bishop was a husky man, somewhere on the shy side of thirty. As he was finishing hitching up a pleasing-looking chestnut to an open buggy, Lilly asked for directions to the Purcell property.

Bishop didn't answer for long seconds. When he finished rigging up the horse, he stepped around the front of the animal and stood looking down at her, his arms crossed over his brawny chest. "I don't mean to be poking my nose into your business, ma'am, but why would you be asking for directions to that evil place?"

Lilly extended her hand. Bishop's massive paw swallowed hers. "My name is Lilly Long. I'm trying to locate the former owners."

"Billy Bishop." The stable hand pumped her arm up and down. "Well, you won't find hide nor hair of them around here. They lit out after the preacher stole the church's money and ain't been heard from since."

"That's what I was told at the hotel. I was also told that you and a friend were playing near the house and heard something you thought was a . . . ghost." Lilly clamped her teeth down on her lower lip to keep from smiling. "I was wondering if you could tell me more about that."

"Not much to tell," Bishop said with a shake of his shaggy head. "Hank Gruber and I were playing out in the woods behind that big ole house, and we heard just what you said."

Despite the warmth of the sunshine, Bishop shuddered. Clearly what he'd heard or thought he'd heard had made an impression, if recalling it twenty years later could evoke such a response.

"It was a terrible wailing sound that come from inside," he said, his troubled gaze meeting Lilly's. "But it was faint and weak sounding. Like some animal was in terrible pain and dying, or"—he blushed blood red—"maybe mating. Beggin' your pardon, Miss Long."

"That's quite all right," Lilly assured him. "Are you certain the sound came from inside the house? Is there a possibility that it *was* an injured or mating animal somewhere in the woods?"

Bishop gave a hard negative shake of his head. "No, ma'am. It come from the house. I'm sure of it."

"What did you and your friend do?"

He looked away and gave a shrug of embarrassment. "Me and Hank was scared to death. We hightailed it to my house as fast as we could and told my mama. When Daddy come in from the fields, she told him, and he got his shotgun and went to fetch Hank's dad. They went over there to check on things. When they couldn't rouse anyone to the door, they went out to the barn and saw the horses and buggy were gone. They figured the reverend and his family had just gone off somewhere.

"Daddy said he knew he shouldn'ta done it since he was brought up better, but they went inside the house to see if they could find anything amiss."

Bishop swallowed hard. "There were bloody sheets on the bed in one of the downstairs bedrooms and a basin of bloody water in the kitchen. It scared them so bad they lit out like scalded cats. They figured someone had been killed in that bed, and they didn't want to stay and see if whoever done it was still hanging around. As they were leavin', they heard the same sound me and Hank heard . . . real faint-like . . . like it was comin' outta the walls or something.

"Figurin' it was the ghost of whoever had been killed, they skedaddled outta there and went to tell the sheriff. That's when they found out that the reverend had left town with all the church's money. The sheriff allowed that Purcell and his family had flown the coop, gone somewhere far away so they wouldn't get caught."

That part certainly made sense, Lilly thought. But what about the bloody bed, and the ghost . . . ?

"Did the sheriff go out and look around?"

"Oh, sure," Billy said with a nod. "Sheriff Mayhew's a good lawman. He was pretty new to the job back then, but him and a coupla deputies went out the next day and looked things over real good. They said it looked like the Purcells had left in some kind of all-fired hurry. Saw the bed and the bloody water and figured, like Daddy said, that somebody was slaughtered there and the killer tried to clean himself up."

Slaughtered. Bishop's choice of words brought a sickening picture to mind. "Did he try to find Reverend Purcell to question him?"

"Sure did," the livery hand said, running a gentle palm over the gelding's rump. "All we know is that Mrs. Purcell and her daughter didn't leave here by train, and the sheriff didn't have any luck picking up the trail of the missing rig, since a gully washer the night before wiped out any tracks it might have made. He had no idea where Purcell and his family went, so he sent telegrams to all the towns from Saint Louie to Chicago, but nothing ever turned up." He scratched his head. "It's a puzzle, that's what it is."

"Does Hank Gruber still live around here?"

Bishop shook his head. "Died a couple of years ago with the fever, but he'd just tell you the same thing I did."

Lilly hid her disappointment. "What about the sheriff? Mayhew, wasn't it?"

"He's still here. Still sheriff. His office is over in the old courthouse."

"Thank you, Mr. Bishop," Lilly said with a slight smile. "You've been a great help. Now, if you could just tell me how to get to Heaven's Gate, I'd greatly appreciate it."

His eyes widened in astonishment. "You still want to go out there? Alone?"

As touched as she was by his concern, Lilly was thankful that she was neither a fanciful nor superstitious person. "I do."

"Don't seem right for a woman to be doin' what you are."

"I'm very qualified, Mr. Bishop," Lilly told him, knowing she was far from it. "I'll be fine."

"All right, then," he said grudgingly. "You want to take the Alton Road toward Mulberry about five miles or so. There'll be some houses along the way, and you'll cross a wooden bridge over a creek. A ways past there you'll see a big dead tree near the turnoff road. Used to be a sign there, but I ain't been out that way in ages, so it may have rotted down."

"Are there any other houses once I turn off the main road?"

He shook his head. "No, ma'am. Once you turn off, it's a dead end."

The man in the dark suit frowned as the woman guided her rented rig down the street. He glanced up at the snow clouds above him and cursed beneath his breath. There was little doubt where she was headed. Why in the world she'd take off with the weather worsening by the minute was beyond him. Still, he had no choice but to follow.

CHAPTER 14

Lilly squinted against the cold wind blowing in her face as the horse and buggy traveled down the rutted road. The sky had grown even more overcast and snow had begun to fall, even though tentative sprigs of green pushed valiantly through the soil here and there. Though the days were growing subtly longer, and spring was just around the corner, snow wasn't uncommon this time of year. As a child, she'd once seen it snow on the first day of spring.

A hawk circled silently overhead, riding the air currents, searching for some unsuspecting mouse or inattentive rabbit to snatch for its dinner, a subtle reminder that bad things could happen unexpectedly.

The thought reminded her of Tim, and she felt a rush of regret for having given him even a portion of her life. Already, the brief interval spent with him seemed dreamlike, a few months plucked from another time. She'd been happy with him and equally miserable. She recalled Rose once telling her that without the low points in life, the high points would not be nearly so breathtaking and memorable.

She supposed it was true, but when she ever fell in love again—no, *if* she allowed herself to fall in love again—she would make certain that it was with a man who was not crooked, moody, and difficult like Tim, but steady and dependable and even tempered. A gentle man who made her feel safe and loved every moment of the day. Someone like . . . like Simon Linedecker, perhaps. Certainly not like the stranger she had run into on the train. Everything about that man cried out trouble with a capital "T."

The snowfall grew heavier. She thought of turning back and postponing her trip on a more suitable day; she didn't want to get stuck in an abandoned house in the midst of a snow-storm, but she was anxious to investigate the place for herself. Actually, she thought with a wry smile, with the dark, overcast skies, it was perfect weather to explore a house that was ru-mored to be haunted.

Her thoughts turned to her upcoming task, mulling over her conversations with Helen Holbrook and Billy Bishop. In spite of the tiny voice that told her ghost tales were nonsense, the story definitely piqued her interest. No matter how it turned out, her first assignment was shaping up to be more than a bor-ing missing-person mission. Ghost story aside, it was beginning to look as if something had happened at Heaven's Gate. Per-haps something heinous.

What was it about the preacher and his family that upset Virginia Holbrook so much she'd gone from warm and welcom-ing to cold and distant? Lilly had no answers to any of her ques-tions, and she had a lot of them. Like, why hadn't the agency's clients, the Stephenses, found out about the possible murder in the house when they searched for the Purcells? Was there any way they couldn't have heard about it? Perhaps the answer was simple. Maybe they had heard of the vacant house and learned nothing except that the preacher had taken the money, left town in the dead of night, and no one had any idea where he'd gone.

It didn't take a seasoned operative to see that few people were willing to discuss the incident, and it made sense that the Stephenses would have given up when met with such resistance. Most would. Should she send a telegram and ask William if their clients knew of the belief that someone had been killed at the property they wanted to purchase? It might make a difference in their desire to buy the place.

No. She wouldn't say anything until she knew more.

Tomorrow, she would make it a point to talk to the sheriff and see if he could shed more light on the story. Though Billy Bishop assured her that Mayhew had done his job, she wondered just how hard he'd tried to trace Purcell. Had the sheriff checked to see if there were signs other than the bloody bed that indicated a murder had been committed? Did he suspect, as she was beginning to, that the reverend could possibly be a murderer as well as a thief?

She gave a little shudder. What a horrible, disturbing thing to think about a preacher! Nonetheless, it was not an impossibility. She wondered if anyone else in town had come up missing at the time. A new thought occurred to her. What if the Purcells hadn't done anything wrong but take the money? What if someone had come in unannounced, killed one of *them*, and taken the others somewhere else to do them in? It was a possibility worth considering.

Seeing the fork in the road and the dead tree Billy Bishop had mentioned, she peered through the falling snow to make certain she was at the right place. What was left of the sign canted to the right. Snow was already starting to obscure the peeling paint, but there was enough print visible that she could make out the name of the estate.

She tugged on the reins and turned the buggy down the

lane. The wet snowflakes had begun to accumulate on the limbs of the trees that grew on either side of the road, creating a snowy archway that might have been plucked straight from a fairy tale or fantasy story of some kind. She half expected a wood nymph dressed in crystal flakes to step out of the silent woodland.

There was no sound except for that of the horse's hooves striking the ground. It was almost as if the forest creatures were afraid to break the profound silence of the moment with their chatter. Soon the canopy of branches would be covered with tender green leaves that would dapple the road with a pattern of sunshine and shade. It would be just as magical then as it was now.

Lilly guided the horse around a curve in the road shielded by trees. The buggy rounded the bend, and the house came into view. The front was encircled with black wrought-iron fencing. A wide archway with attached gates stood at the entrance of the brick pathway leading to the wide front door. Spelled out in ornate lettering were the two words: HEAVEN'S GATE.

Drawing in a deep breath, she got down from the buggy, tied the reins to the rickety hitching post, and pushed through the opening. The unused gate grated on rust-encrusted hinges, screeching a protest, almost as if the house loathed giving anyone entrance.

She stopped just inside, taking stock of the once-elegant dwelling. Perhaps it was the brooding cloud cover, but something about the place felt . . . wrong. She was not a fanciful person by nature, yet her first impression was that the house was not heavenly at all, but rather a place somehow sinister and foreboding.

Or as Billy Bishop claimed, *evil.*

A shiver ran through her, and she reminded herself that the

very nature of old, neglected houses lent them a spooky air. Add the tale of the ghost to the equation and there was no wonder the hair on the back of her neck stood on end.

Forcing herself to be analytical, she stared at the former beauty through the veil of snowflakes. The framework of the three-story house was simple. The left side was a gable front with a wing to the right, from which jutted two smaller gables. The front porch, which was deeper on the wing side, spanned both house sections and boasted an elaborate turned spindle railing. Even with her limited knowledge of architecture, Lilly recognized the style as Victorian. That influence was further revealed in the fancy eave brackets.

Once-immaculate white paint had peeled away like scabs from a wound, leaving the bare wood beneath exposed to the elements. In time, weather would cause it to decay and crumble. Thus far, only the corners of the house where wind had blown off the cedar shingles had succumbed to the rain and rot. Slate-blue shutters framed dirty windows whose emptiness reminded her of the vacuous expression in Colleen McKenna's eyes.

Lilly's critical gaze moved to the side garden to her right: a tangle of snow-dusted, winter-dead weeds, English ivy, and climbing roses run amuck. The wrought-iron fence gave way to stone walls circling the backyard, and the occasional absent rock reminded her of missing teeth.

The house was surrounded by huge maple trees as well as elms and cedars and oaks whose fallen leaves had been decomposing for two decades. Still, for all its spooky dereliction, there was something imposing about the place, like a proud woman who knows her beauty has faded yet refuses to acknowledge the fact.

Ready for further investigation, Lilly made her way to the front porch, where two wicker fern stands with long-dead plants stood sentinel on either side of the wide, leaded-glass door. More dead plants resided in the fernery on the right-hand side. The porch was rotten at the edges but sturdy enough further in. As she expected, the front door was locked.

Undeterred, she went down the broad front steps and picked her way through the side lawn and around the house, tugging her skirt free of the thorny rose brambles and hoisting it high to step over fallen limbs, some as thick as her thighs. At the center of the garden stood a bronze fountain, a life-size figure of a woman holding an urn that once trickled water into the pool below. The statuary was dusted with a film of snow, scaly with lichens, and come summer it would be slick with moss. The urn held the remnants of a bird's nest.

The Grecian-style statue was nude but for an intricate rose vine that swirled strategically over her breasts and across her most private places. While Lilly was impressed with the beauty of the piece, she felt it a strange choice for a minister's home and found herself wondering if it had come with the house or if the sculpture had been an addition of the Purcells.

Near the edge of the clearing at the back of the house, a low iron fence surrounded what must have been the family burial plot. She would have a look at it before she left. Passing through what was once no doubt an herb garden, she saw that the kitchen door stood ajar. Her pulse skittered and she paused, feeling for the gun in her pocket. Then she noticed that the aperture was filled with undisturbed leaves. The door had probably stood open for years. Testing the rotting floorboards nearest the door, she leaped over them into the Purcells' kitchen.

Inside, she pulled off her gloves, shook the snow from her clothing, and threw back the hood of her cape. A copper kettle stood on the wood-burning cook stove. Open shelving held sturdy crockery and an assortment of cooking pots, all covered with twenty years of dust. A pair of corroded scissors lay near a porcelain washbasin edged in gold and adorned with a pretty floral pattern. There was little doubt it was the very one Billy Bishop had seen as a boy. A flakey residue caked the bottom.

Next to the basin lay the yellowed remnants of a muslin towel with strips torn from one edge. A delicate china cup with ancient dregs of coffee or tea scaling the bottom sat next to a matching dessert plate. Any crumbs left there had long ago become a meal for the mice that had left behind their own contribution to the neglect of the house, testimony to the belief that the Purcells had left in a hurry—one step ahead of the law.

She shivered, unable to rid herself of the feeling that she was trespassing into the Purcell home and not a house they had abandoned with so little care. She made her way to the hallway and began her inspection of the lower floor. Even in a state of decline, the former glory of the parlor was easy to see. Magnificent. Yet it all seemed . . . too much.

Sun-faded drapes of crimson brocade hung in dry-rotted tatters. A tea cart held a crystal vase with a droopy bouquet of dried and dusty roses that sat next to a silver coffee service that was black with tarnish. Charred wood and ashes of a long-dead fire littered the fireplace, scattered about by tiny mouse feet. An exquisitely carved clock stood on the marble mantel, flanked by a pair of porcelain pheasants. Behind it hung a large landscape in the style of Landseer. The paint and gilt of the ornate gold leaf of the frame had begun to flake in the extremes of heat and cold that were slowly destroying the house and its contents. Dusty lace-edged silk antimacassars with delicate floral embroidery protected the backs and arms of the davenport that was upholstered in faded striped brocade.

An open Bible lay on a dainty table next to a gold damask wingback chair placed near the fireplace. Curious about what the reverend or his wife had been reading before they'd left in such a hurry, Lilly bent to blow away the dust and went into a paroxysm of sneezing. She wiped at her watering eyes with her fingertips and then swiped them down the side of her skirt.

One of the Purcells had been reading Psalms. There were five selections on the facing pages, and she scanned their beginnings.

"By the rivers of Babylon . . ."

"I will praise thee with my whole heart . . ."

"Lord, thou hast searched me . . ."

Nothing the psalmist had written struck a chord until she reached Psalms 140. *"Deliver me, O Lord, from the evil man: preserve me from the violent man; Which imagine mischiefs in their heart . . ."*

The words resonated in the deep recesses of Lilly's heart. A memory of Tim flashed into her mind, followed by a thought of the man who had taken her mother's love and then her life. She swallowed, her throat dry with sudden distress. She understood the evil and violence of men very well.

Drawing a deep breath and wondering if the passage held a special meaning, she straightened and let her troubled gaze roam the room's faded elegance once more. With a bit of surprise, she realized that the house conveyed something else. Sorrow. Something about the place reminded her of the whores at MacGregor's—any beauty once possessed faded with the passage of time and abuse.

No, not abuse. For some reason, no one had abused the empty house. What she saw was neglect, not destruction. Was it possible that the townsfolk were too frightened of the haint rumored to occupy the house to rob it, or did they have more respect for the man of God's property than he had theirs? Whichever it might be, it was strange, since even she knew the furnishings were worth a small fortune.

Recalling what she'd told William about preachers being unable to afford such costly things, her lips twisted into a bitter smile. The grand lifestyle suggested by Heaven's Gate and its furnishings would have been easily attainable if the reverend routinely fleeced his flocks.

Leaving the room, she crossed the hall and found herself in

a bedroom. A mahogany chest with cabriole legs, claw and ball feet, and decorated with carved shells and scrollwork sat on the far wall. A tin bathtub peeked from behind a carved dressing screen. A cherrywood chair, its needlepoint seat washed out from the sunlight, sat in the opposite corner.

Animals had helped themselves to some of the feathers from the rotting feather tick, and the tangle of sheets was stained with rust.

Her breathing hitched. Not rust. Blood. Lots and lots of blood.

Her temples began to pound, and her stomach clenched. The contents of the room grew fuzzy, as though she were seeing it through murky water. She swayed and reached out to grasp the back of a nearby chair, staring at her image in a hazy mirror, but it wasn't her own reflection she saw, it was her mother's. The room receded and she was suddenly sucked into a vortex of long-suppressed memories that washed over her in wave after wave of remembrance. . . .

CHAPTER 15

Eleven Years Earlier . . .

"He's here!" Kate dropped the lace panel at the window and ran to the mirror, where she pursed her rouged lips and arranged a curl of her auburn bangs just so. Eleven-year-old Lilly didn't know who the man was, just that her mother had met him when they were in Springfield four months earlier and that Kate was "completely besotted" with him.

"Hide, Lilly," Kate said, smoothing her palms over the soft yellow princess dress she'd chosen to impress this special man. "And for heaven's sake, don't make a sound."

Lilly dropped to the floor, her dress billowing out as she slipped beneath the iron bedstead, where she'd tossed a quilt in anticipation of a long stay. There was a sharp rap at the door. At her mother's call to enter, it opened with a squeak.

"Kate!" the masculine voice said. "You look divine."

Kate's throaty laughter filled the room. "So do you."

The door clicked shut, and Lilly heard nothing for several seconds but the sounds of kissing and rustling fabric. It was a familiar ritual, one she'd experienced many times from various hiding places during her life. Sometimes she built her little nest behind her mother's dressing screen. If the weather permitted and their room was on the first floor, she might play with her dolls outside the window. Often there was nowhere to go but beneath the bed. Above all, she was to be quiet and not peek.

Of course she'd peeked through the years, but she was always quiet. Her mother's encounters with her men friends were much the same. Kisses. A drink or two. Laughter. Moans. The creaking of the bed springs.

When she was younger, she'd thought the men were hurting Kate, but after a while, she realized the act was something her mother liked, something she wanted, or she wouldn't do it so often or with so many men.

Tonight promised to be no different. Kate's yellow dress puddled onto the floor like a pool of melted butter. The man's shoes, socks, and pants followed. Lilly squeezed her eyes shut, which served only to create a clearer image of what was happening. When the bed stilled at last, there was no sound in the room for long moments but that of ragged breathing.

"There's something I need to tell you."

The soft sound of her mother's voice told Lilly that Kate was afraid to say what was on her mind.

"What is it?" The man seemed wary, almost as if he knew beforehand the announcement would not be good.

"I haven't . . ." Kate's voice trailed away. "My monthlies haven't come around since we were here the last time."

The man was silent for long moments.

"Well, say something," she prodded.

The bed rocked roughly. "What would you have me say?" he snapped, all tenderness gone from his voice. "Am I to be happy about your ill-begotten whelp? Surely you didn't expect me to offer my hand in marriage, since I already have a wife."

"*My* ill-begotten whelp?" Kate cried. "As I recall, you had as much a part in the conception of this baby as I. As for your wife, you told me you were divorcing her."

Lilly's eyes widened at the word *baby*, but before she could ponder the meaning, she saw the man's bare feet hit the floor.

"And you believed me? From your behavior, I assumed you were a woman of the world." His voice mocked. "As such, you should know that a man will say anything to get what he wants. Besides, how do I know the brat's mine?"

Lilly heard her mother's sharp gasp. "Of course it's yours. There's been no one else since we met. And you did tell me you were divorcing your wife."

The man's laughter was cold, unkind. "A lie to get you into bed." He laughed, a sound without mirth. "It is beyond belief that you seriously thought I would leave my wife, when it's her money that helps me live the life I have."

Lilly heard her mother curse, something she seldom did. "You rich people are all the same." Bitterness laced her voice. "You believe having money somehow absolves you of taking responsibility for your actions. Well, not this time. Since you've no intention of doing what's right, and I'll bear the bulk of responsibility, it's only fair that you supplement the child's needs."

"You're daft, woman. I'll not give you a cent."

Lilly heard the finality in his voice.

"No?" Kate countered. "Then perhaps I'll pay your wife a little visit."

Lilly heard the sound of flesh meeting flesh and her mother's cry of pain. He had struck her!

The bed sank and swayed as the man climbed back onto it. "You will do nothing. You will say nothing. To anyone." The words were as sharp and flinty as stone on stone.

"Oh, won't I?"

Lilly heard another sound and clamped a hand over her mouth to stifle her own cry. Her eyes filled with tears. The man had hit her mother again. The bed began to move once more. There was more moaning, but this was different. Intuitively, Lilly knew something was very wrong. More afraid than she'd ever been, she squeezed her eyes shut and put her fingers in her ears. *Please, God, make him stop. Make him go away.* When at last she took her hands away and opened her eyes a crack, the bed was still and there was no sound in the room except the man's harsh breathing.

Lilly saw bare feet hit the floor, and the stranger reached down to pick up his trousers. One foot went in, then the other. He was leaving. The sound of her pounding heart was so loud she was afraid he might hear. Why didn't her mother say something?

A masculine hand reached to grab dark socks and one shiny leather ankle boot. Grunting, he groped beneath the edge of the bed for the other. Lilly's breath stopped. Her horrified gaze fixed on the square gold ring on his right hand. Centered in a black stone was a fancy letter that looked like a "T." Three shiny stones were clustered at one corner. Fearing he would look beneath the bed and see her, she reached out a trembling hand and edged the boot a scant inch closer to his searching fingers. Thankfully, he snatched it up, and the moment that seemed to last forever passed.

Finally, Lilly saw his feet move across the room, saw the door open and close, heard his footsteps fade down the wooden sidewalk. A shuddering breath of relief trickled from her. The scent of a spicy masculine cologne mingled with the odor of Lilly's fear. From far away she heard the sound of a horse's whinny. A carriage rumbled past. Someone called a greeting. When she was certain he was gone for good she eased from her hiding place.

Unclothed, her mother lay sprawled atop the muslin sheets, her hair fanned out over the feather pillow, her eyes open, but unseeing. Bluish-purple smudges ringed her neck and nestled in the hollow of her throat. Lilly shook Kate's shoulder but got no response.

"Mama, wake up," she urged, shaking harder. Nothing. A sudden pain knifed through her, along with the grievous certainty that her mother was not waking. Ever. The last thing she remembered was hearing someone screaming. . . .

CHAPTER 16

The sound of screaming jolted Lilly from the long-banished memories that had dragged her back into her past. Realizing that the sound had come from her, her tortured gaze found the bed once more; she was half fearful that she might see her mother's body lying there, but the ugly, painful memories had vanished as quickly as they'd come.

Light-headed, needing to escape the bedroom whose own dark secrets had sparked her suppressed memories, she bolted through the doorway. The sound of her boots echoed on the wood floor. Through the kitchen and out the back door she flew, unmindful of the rotted flooring, wanting only to be away from the murder bed, away from the lingering sounds of voices and the scent of masculine cologne that was not there.

Away from her past.

Outside, she drew in deep drafts of the cold air and battled the waves of dizziness that still threatened to drag her down into darkness. She remembered it all. Every ugly thing that had happened the day her mother was murdered. She'd heard it all as she lay hidden beneath Kate's bed: the loving and the fighting and the struggle as her beautiful Titian-haired mother fought for breath while the man she loved choked the life from her.

With a sharp cry of pain, she clutched her throat, and tears of sorrow for the mother lost to her so long ago slipped down her cheeks.

"You should know that a man will say anything to get what he wants. . . ."

It had been the killer's voice that drifted through her mind as she'd stood in her boardinghouse room trying to grasp how Tim could portray the loving husband even as he planned to walk away and leave her with nothing.

The man hiding in the deep shadows of the forest heard the spine-chilling scream and saw his quarry come barreling through the kitchen door as if the hounds of hell were chasing her.

What the devil?

He watched as she looked around wildly, started to run one way, then stopped and stood amidst the tangle of weeds, a splash of red against the whiteness of the gathering snow. Her hands clutched her throat and she was as still and unmoving as the nymph in the fountain.

He pushed away from the tree he'd been leaning against and took a few furtive steps closer, careful to stay hidden behind a cluster of shrubs barely touched with green, waiting to see what the obviously crazed woman would do. . . .

CHAPTER 17

Wrapping her arms around her middle as if to prevent herself from shattering into little pieces, Lilly closed her eyes and forced herself to breathe slow and deep. Unmindful of her misery, a cardinal perching on the shoulder of the statue sang a cheery song.

Kate. Her beautiful mother had been flawed, but as people are wont to do, Lilly tended to recall only the happiest times. Kate teaching her to play dominoes. Taking her to the mercantile and letting her choose fabric for a new frock. Letting her play dress-up with her laciest shawl, fanciest hat, and softest kid slippers.

Gradually, the selective, pleasant memories soothed Lilly's jangled nerves. With the return of her composure, she became aware of the damp cold and a prickling at the nape of her neck, that unaccountable sensation that told her she was being watched. Afraid to make any sudden moves, she opened her eyes and scanned the wooded area. She heard a rustling near the fringe of trees. A gray fox burst from the scrubby cover and streaked across the overgrown backyard to disappear in a tangle of undergrowth.

The breath she'd been holding whooshed from her. Her shaky laugh of relief sounded loud in the midafternoon silence. Though her insides quaked and her head ached abominably, she squared her shoulders and turned toward the kitchen door. It was the last thing she wanted to do, but if she hoped to prove herself worthy of her new position, she knew she must finish her exploration and get back to town.

Taking a breath, she forced herself to reenter the house. She skirted the morbid bedroom and gave the study a cursory glance before starting up the curving staircase. The second floor echoed the lower: clothes left hanging in armoires. Silver-backed brushes and combs arranged on marble-topped dressers. A petticoat flung over a chair. All evidence of a hasty departure.

Lilly even checked the top story. Like so many attics, it held a mishmash of discarded objects, all wearing a fine layer of dust and festooned with ancient spider webs. An octagonal window at the back of the attic drew her, and she found that it overlooked the family graveyard.

There was a single headstone in the weed-choked cemetery. She was staring at the marker when she caught a movement from the corner of her eye. With her heart beating hard and fast, her gaze probed the woods beyond the burial ground. Nothing moved in the shadows. After several moments, she was forced to admit that the movement had been nothing but a bush blowing in the wind.

Her heart rate slowed to a more normal cadence, and she noted that while she'd been in the house, the day had grown darker still. It was past time to leave the Purcell home and head back to town.

It was never a home.

The realization came to her quietly, and she paused a second before heading down the stairs. As beautiful as it had once been, as filled as it was with every imaginable amenity, it was just a house, a place the reverend and his family had lived. Never a home. Somehow, she knew that as surely as she knew the sun would set in the west. She shivered again, touched once more by the air of melancholy and despair—and even something that felt like fear—that seemed to ooze from every corner of the place.

You're getting fanciful, Lilly, letting all the talk of murders and ghosts and bloody beds get to you. Even as she told herself her qualms were unfounded, she ran down the two flights of stairs as if Satan himself were after her, eager to be out of the house and on the road.

What on earth was wrong with her? she wondered as she raced through the parlor and unlatched the front door. She'd never been such a pantywaist before. Yet here she was on her first assignment, and she'd already been frightened witless twice in one day. She slammed the door behind her and rushed down the steps toward the buggy where the rented horse waited.

Perhaps Robert Pinkerton was right, she thought, untying the reins and clambering onto the seat. Perhaps women were not well suited for the detecting business. Maybe Pierce was right, too. Maybe she was too innocent and untried to know how to handle herself in the unsettling situations that came with being a detective.

She turned the buggy around and tore down the lane, not slowing the animal until she reached the main road, leaving all the pain and fear and sorrow behind her . . . at Heaven's Gate.

From the cover of the woods, the man watched, wondering at the reason behind the woman's frantic departure. His mouth slanted with wry satisfaction. If she was as crazy as she seemed, ridding himself of her shouldn't take long, and then perhaps his own life could get back to normal.

Chapter 18

With her head throbbing the slightest bit from a night of restless sleep and the last lingering effects of the injury Tim had inflicted, Lilly sat in the hotel dining room, enjoying a tasty breakfast of ham, eggs, and toast.

Warmer air had moved through the area during the night and almost all the snow that had fallen the day before had melted. The bright sunlight streaming through the windows was a promise that spring was just around the corner and hinted of brighter tomorrows.

It whispered that now she knew the truth, she should let go of the circumstances surrounding her mother's death and move on with her own life. The alienist Pierce had hired to treat her after Kate's murder had said there was a possibility that when and if Lilly remembered that day, it would be in bits and pieces through the years. Another possibility was that some small, seemingly insignificant incident would trigger her memory and everything could come back in a rush, which is exactly what happened.

In truth, finally remembering what had happened that day

after so many years of wondering *was* liberating in a strange way. The return of her memory reinforced the certainty that far too many women were victims of self-serving men, which strengthened her determination to help them. More importantly, she no longer had to worry that she was somehow mentally impaired because she couldn't remember.

Driven by new resolve, she'd spent the previous evening rereading the journal William had given her on the Stephenses; then she'd immersed herself in Allan Pinkerton's *General Principles*. He was a man of great integrity with perhaps just a hint of Machiavelli in his soul. He considered the work he and his detectives did "a high and honorable calling." His *Principles* stated that the agency would not investigate a woman's morals unless there was a connection to another crime, and they would not handle divorce cases or those of a scandalous nature.

This, along with his willingness to hire women for a job that most men would not, made Allan Pinkerton a champion for women in a time when few could be found. Her new position gave her a freedom that her contemporaries would either envy or be frightened to death to possess, and at last she would have opportunities to use the skills Pierce had insisted she learn through the years.

Pierce. At some point she should telegraph him and let him know she'd recalled every gruesome detail of her mother's murder, but it could wait for the moment. What she needed now was to get her thoughts and course of action organized and move forward with her investigation.

Taking a sip of her breakfast coffee, she began making a list of things to do and people to see. Virginia Holbrook's name topped the page. There was some reason the woman had turned frosty at the mention of the Purcells, and Lilly intended to find out what it was. Unfortunately, the hotel proprietor had not been at the front desk when Lilly ventured down to breakfast.

Next on her list was the sheriff. She would see if he had anything to add to what Helen and Billy had told her about Heaven's Gate. If not, perhaps he would point her to members of the reverend's congregation or others who might remember some tidbit that could cast a glimmer of light on the preacher's whereabouts.

She should also stop by the church where Purcell had preached and see if there were any old records that might disclose some useful snippet of information. And though she dreaded it, she knew she needed to return to Heaven's Gate to search every nook and cranny. Hidden in a drawer or the pocket of an article of clothing could be some piece of information— a letter, a diary—something to suggest the whereabouts of the preacher and his family. It was up to her to find it, and she would not let an old, dilapidated house frighten her.

When she finished her breakfast, there was still no sign of Mrs. Holbrook, but there was a tall, rather nondescript man behind the desk who Lilly concluded must be the lady's husband. He smiled at Lilly's approach. "Good morning."

"Good morning. Are you Mr. Holbrook?" she asked, hoping her tone and demeanor conveyed the professionalism she was far from feeling.

"I'm David Holbrook, yes."

Lilly extended her hand. "Lilly Long. I was wondering if you had time to answer a few questions about a family who once lived here."

"I'd be happy to, if I can," David Holbrook assured her.

"The agency I work for has been retained by a client who wishes to purchase the place called Heaven's Gate. He was unable to locate the owners, a Reverend Harold Purcell and his family, and hopes I will have better luck in locating them. He's interested in negotiating the purchase of the property."

David Holbrook narrowed his eyes and stared at a spot

across the lobby as if in thought. "I'm sorry," he said at last. "The name doesn't ring a bell. They must have lived here before I came."

"I believe they left town some twenty years ago," Lilly offered. Why did she feel that Mr. Holbrook wasn't being completely truthful?

"Well, that explains it then," he said with a smile. "I only moved here seventeen years ago, but my wife is from here. She may have known the Purcells. Regrettably, she's under the weather today."

"No matter," Lilly said, recognizing the man's smile did not reach his eyes. Curious. She decided to move on for the moment. Her smile was a perfect match to his. "I'll be here a few more days. Perhaps I'll have a chance to speak to her before I leave. Thank you for your time."

"You're welcome."

Leaving the hotel, Lilly walked the block to the Federalist-style structure that served as the courthouse, more convinced than ever that the Holbrooks were hiding something.

Sheriff Mayhew was in, sitting behind a large, scarred desk, his boots propped on the top as he leaned back in his chair and perused a page of newsprint. When he did not put down his newspaper and stand as common courtesy demanded, it was all Lilly could do to keep from grinding her teeth.

"Sheriff Mayhew?" She was pleased to hear that her voice held no hint of her irritation.

The man regarded her over the top of the paper. "I am. And you are?"

Lilly narrowed her eyes. How rude! Her indignation on the rise, she crossed to the desk and extended her hand. The sheriff had no recourse but to lower his feet, stand, and reciprocate.

Though she strongly suspected he knew exactly who she was, she said, "I'm Lilly Long."

"Ah yes. Miss Long. I've heard all about you. Why, you're the talk of the town. A lone woman on her own asking lots of questions and looking for a missing family."

There was no mistaking the amusement on the sheriff's rugged face. Other than Robert Pinkerton, it was her first run-in with the male mind-set that held the notion that women were incapable of doing a man's job. She did not delude herself for one moment that it would be her last.

Ignoring his narrow-minded attitude, she opted to play her trump card. With a smile sweet enough to give him a toothache, she reached into her reticule and drew out her badge, placing it carefully on the desk.

Mayhew's surprise was almost comical.

"Yes," she said with another smile. "I can only imagine that the arrival of someone from an agency as prestigious as the Pinkertons would be cause for speculation." Without waiting for him to answer, she added, "May I sit down?" and did just that.

"By all means," the sheriff said. He picked up the badge, looked at it for a second or two, and then handed it back to her.

Lilly sat primly on the edge of the chair, and the sheriff retook his seat. She knew she had to present her case in the right way if she expected his cooperation. The town might be abuzz with talk of her looking for the Purcells so that a new enterprise could be started, but she hadn't told anyone whom she worked for or what that venture might be. Perhaps if she explained the noble nature of the undertaking the Stephenses proposed he would be more cooperative. To her surprise, the sheriff struck first.

"Begging your pardon, Miss Long, but you're really stirring up a hornet's nest by coming back and asking so many questions around town."

The anger in his eyes and the knot in his jaw told her that Mayhew was struggling to keep a tight rein on his resentment.

"You have no idea of the misery Harold Purcell caused the good people in this town. If folks around here never heard his name again, it would be too soon."

Act professional, Lilly. Don't antagonize the man. "I know about the stolen money, Sheriff Mayhew, so their feelings are perfectly understandable. I've spoken with Billy Bishop about the ghost and the awful discoveries in the house. I even drove out there yesterday, and—"

"You need to stay away from there!"

Lilly's heart raced at his tone and the fury on his face, but she refused to allow him to intimidate her. She raised her chin a fraction of an inch and regarded him with a narrow-eyed gaze. "Is that a threat, Sheriff Mayhew?"

"I don't threaten women. It's just a word of advice. Anything could happen to a woman out there alone."

"Well, I appreciate your concern, but I intend to do my job, whatever it takes. It would help me if I knew exactly when it was that you became aware the reverend had stolen the congregation's funds."

She could almost see the cogs turning in his brain. As one professional to another, he was compelled to assist her, but she suspected he would offer no more information than absolutely necessary.

"Lady, it's been almost twenty years," he said, the expression in his eyes cool and assessing. "How can you expect me to remember something like that?"

"I don't have to know the date, but I'm assuming it could not have been before Billy Bishop and his friend heard those . . . noises coming from the house."

Sheriff Mayhew leaned back in his chair and once again propped his booted feet on the desk in a deliberate show of disrespect. "And why would you assume that?"

Momentarily forgetting her need to placate the man, Lilly met his insolent gaze with an artless one of her own. "Why, because any *reputable* lawman who'd known about the theft would have ridden out to confront Purcell, or if there was no idea who had taken the money, to at least let him know someone had stolen from his flock."

The sheriff scowled. She wondered if he was rethinking his opinion of the nosey Pinkerton lady. She figured that few would dare to challenge how well he did his job.

He heaved a sigh. "You're right. Not half an hour before Robert Bishop and Jeff Gruber rode to town to tell me what their boys had heard and what they'd seen in that bedroom, James Reihmann, the bank president, came over and told me the preacher hadn't deposited the Sunday contribution. As I recollect, me and a couple of other men were getting ready to go out there to ask Purcell about it when Robert and Jeff rode in."

"And what day was this? Do you remember?"

She could see the uncertainty in his eyes. He might resent her coming and nosing around, but he didn't want to look incompetent in front of a woman.

"As a matter of fact, I do. It would have been a Tuesday afternoon. I recall the day, because Pop Powell took up the collection, counted it, and gave it to the reverend after Sunday night services. Purcell usually deposited it first thing the next day. When he hadn't come in by late afternoon on Tuesday, Mr. Reihmann got concerned and thought we ought to go see if everything was okay with the reverend and his family."

"So, already fearing that something was wrong at Heaven's Gate, and hearing the story about the bloody bed and the"— she offered him a slight smile—"ghost, you and the others went to check. Is that correct?"

"Yes, ma'am, it is."

"And what did you think when you got there?"

She could see the memories cloud his eyes. Memories and horror and pain.

"It was everything Bishop and Gruber said it was. The

bed . . ." He scrubbed a hand down his face, as if to remove the memory. "Frankly, Miss Long, I've never seen so much blood outside a hog killing."

Recalling the scene from the previous day, Lilly swallowed back a wave of nausea at the thought of what it must have looked like when the blood was fresh.

"It appeared the Purcells, the whole lot of them, had taken off and left everything behind," the sheriff added. "We don't know if Missus Purcell left before or after her husband, but we do know that he left town on Monday morning."

"Really? How?"

"When we got back here, news of the robbery was the talk of the town. Delton Jester at the train station came forward and said that Purcell had bought a train ticket to Effingham."

"And did you notify the sheriff there?"

"Of course I did," Mayhew said, visibly offended. "They couldn't find a trace of him. The thing is, Miss Long, with no one knowing Purcell from Adam, he could have bought a ticket to anywhere once he got to Effingham, and no one would have been the wiser. He just . . . disappeared."

She frowned. "Do you believe he left his wife and family behind?"

Mayhew shrugged. "They might have left before him. I have no idea. I do know that neither the missus nor her daughter was on any of the trains leaving from here, so they must have taken the buggy, since it was nowhere to be found."

"Were there any other children?"

The sheriff rubbed at the stubble on his jaw. "They lost a son while they were here, so there was just the daughter, Sarah. Prettiest thing you ever did see. She had the whitest skin and the bluest eyes and this gorgeous blond hair, just like her mother. She'd have been about fifteen when this all happened."

A hint of sorrow shadowed his eyes.

"What is it, Sheriff?"

"Beggin' your pardon?"

"You seem . . . sad."

"Oh," he said with a slow exhalation of breath. "It's just that the poor little thing got tuberculosis and had to be quarantined at the house. No one in town had set eyes on her for several months before they all up and disappeared."

"That is a shame," Lilly agreed.

"When Purcell first vanished with the money, several of the congregation thought that maybe he'd taken it to get Sarah better medical care in some bigger city," he offered. "Folks could almost forgive him for that. On the other hand, the church would have probably given them the money if he'd asked, so that idea didn't hold water for long."

"I'd think not. Besides, why would they need money for medical assistance? From the looks of things, it seemed to me that Purcell and his family lived in a pretty high style on a preacher's salary. The house alone had to be expensive, and it's furnished with some very costly pieces. If they were desperate for money, they could have sold some of their things instead of stealing from the church."

"I thought the same thing," he admitted with a nod. "Something didn't seem right about them from the first, but then, rumor had it that Mrs. Purcell came from money, and I had no way of knowing any different."

"If that was true, why steal?" Lilly asked, trying to take advantage of the sheriff's sudden willingness to open up.

"Again, I agree. When we started checking into things, Pop Powell told us that the weekly offering had always been considerably more than what the reverend had been depositing on Mondays, and James Reihmann said it went way up after Purcell left. It looked like he'd been skimming all along."

His eyes held a glimmer of his earlier anger. "He may be just a man, Miss Long, but I, for one, hold those in his position to a higher standard. A thief is a thief, preacher or not."

"It appears he *was* just a thief, masquerading as a preacher," Lilly said. "A true hypocrite." She smiled at the sheriff. "Did you know that hypocrite is a theatrical term?"

"You don't say."

"In the past, a player might perform several roles, so they wore masks to differentiate one from the other."

Mayhew nodded thoughtfully. "That means hypocrites wear masks so to speak, pretending to be someone they aren't."

"Yes."

"I'd say Purcell fits the bill perfectly." He looked her square in the eye. "I may as well stop beatin' around the bush, Miss Long. No doubt you'll find out sooner or later. I despised the man. He was nothing but a liar and a cheat and—" He stopped, aware that he was saying too much. "Sorry, ma'am, there's just some things I feel real strong about."

"As I do, Sheriff. And you never found any trace of Mrs. Purcell or Sarah . . ."

"Not a thing. There was a big storm Monday night, and whatever tracks they might have left were beat out by the rain by the time we got there on Tuesday. I sent some telegrams to other cities, but I never heard anything. Mrs. Purcell and Sarah seemed to have disappeared the same way the reverend did."

"What was your opinion of Mrs. Purcell?" Lilly asked.

"Prudence was a right handsome woman," the sheriff offered. "All the Purcells were easy on the eye, but Prudence had this sort of . . . I don't know . . . anxious look about her all the time. The reverend claimed it was because they'd lost three of their children, all sons. It wasn't that she was unfriendly, just sorta . . . well, not as outgoing and helpful as you'd expect a preacher's wife to be. The daughter was the same."

Hmm. Interesting. "Did you ever hear any of the family mention a place they'd lived or wanted to go?"

"I never did. Could be some of the church members did."

Lilly jotted something in her notepad. "You've been a lawman many years, haven't you, Sheriff?"

"All my adult life," he told her with a hint of pride.

"In your opinion, do you think someone was killed in that bed?"

"I can't think of anything else that would have made that kind of mess."

From what Lilly had seen, she would have to agree. She tossed out an idea that had been nagging at her. "Have you considered the possibility that one—or both—of the Purcell women might have been the victims?"

"Like maybe someone killed Mrs. Purcell and Sarah and did away with their bodies?"

Lilly gave a little shrug. "It would explain why they never turned up."

"I've thought about it," Mayhew admitted, a gleam of speculation in his eyes. "So did Doc. It was one of the reasons I didn't press harder to find them. With things just abandoned as they were, we also had a pretty good idea who might have done it"—he shrugged—"if that's what happened."

Lilly offered a slight smile. "The Reverend Purcell himself?" she suggested.

"You know, Miss Long, you're right smart. For a woman."

CHAPTER 19

Leaving the sheriff's office, Lilly walked the three blocks to the doctor's house, marveling at the mildness of the weather after the unexpected snow flurries the day before. Halfway there, she again experienced the nagging feeling that someone was watching her, but when she turned to check she saw no one. She concluded it was nothing but the surreptitious staring of curious citizens who knew she was in town asking a lot of questions.

On her second knock, a small, rotund man in gray pinstripe trousers, charcoal-gray vest, and wine-hued cravat opened the door. His snowy hair was parted down the middle and combed back with the aid of some sweet-smelling pomade. A neatly trimmed mustache brushed his upper lip and bracketed the corners of his mouth.

"Dr. Ramsay?"

"Dr. Nathan Ramsay, retired, yes," the physician said, his eyes twinkling with merriment. "And who might you be?"

Lilly extended her hand. "Lilly Long," she told him. "I'm with the Pinkerton National Detective Agency, and I wondered if you could spare a few moments to answer some questions about former patients of yours." No sense keeping her line of work under wraps now that she'd confessed to the sheriff. Everyone in town would know who she was and why she was here by nightfall.

The doctor released her hand and smiled, an action that made his eyes nearly close and pushed his plump cheeks into rosy knots that resembled dried crabapples. "Since I was giving my wife a terrible trouncing at chess, I'm sure she'd be pleased to take a few minutes from the game and make us some coffee. Please, come in."

Lilly stepped through the door and followed him into the parlor. A woman whose build and demeanor were almost an exact match to the doctor's sat with her round chin in a plump hand, contemplating a chessboard, her forehead puckered into a frown.

"You've been granted a brief reprieve, Hattie!" the doctor said jovially, gesturing toward Lilly. "This is Miss Lilly Long with the Pinkertons. She'd like to ask me some questions, and I'd like for you to make us some fresh coffee and bring us a slice of that marvelous spice cake you made yesterday."

The older woman's face had taken on a concerned expression when she heard the word *Pinkertons*, but she gathered herself in an instant and took Lilly's hand in a brief gesture of greeting.

Hoping to set her mind at ease, Lilly explained, "We have a client trying to locate a family who once lived here. I've been asking around hoping someone would be able to point me in a direction they might have gone."

"Oh? Which family is that?" Hattie Ramsay asked.

"The Reverend Harold Purcell." Her gaze included them both. "I understand you were the family physician, Dr. Ramsay. I wondered if you perhaps knew the family from church as well."

The doctor's expression changed little, but he nodded in affirmation. "I was their doctor, but we didn't attend the same church."

"Nathan and I are Lutherans," Mrs. Ramsay said. "So I didn't know them personally. I did see them around town from time to time. They were a handsome family. It was quite the scandal when the reverend took off with all that money."

"So I hear," Lilly said.

"I really can't tell you anything else, Miss Long, so if you'll excuse me, I'll go make the coffee."

"Of course."

After her hostess left the room, Lilly took the chair the doctor offered and watched while he relit the pipe that lay in a small brass tray. Finally he seated himself across from her.

"I treated them, yes," he said at last. "They were a pretty healthy bunch, just the usual garden-variety illnesses—colds, sore throats, influenza, and such. And I did see Mrs. Purcell during a pregnancy. She had a baby boy who was born prematurely and died soon after."

"So Sheriff Mayhew said," Lilly told him.

"I haven't a clue as to why it came so early," he said, his thoughtful expression suggesting that it was a subject he'd given much thought to. "The pregnancy seemed normal in every way, and when the baby was born at least two months early, it was perfectly formed."

"Perhaps it was God's will," Lilly said, remembering Rose's stock answer when awful, unimaginable things happened.

"Oh, clearly," the doctor said. He took a long draw on his pipe. "Prudence changed after that," he said. "She was never much of a talker, but she grew even more withdrawn. Then, when Sarah got sick, she hardly spoke, just sort of went away, like a turtle pulling into its shell."

"Sarah had tuberculosis, I understand."

"So I heard."

Lilly frowned. "You didn't diagnose her?"

"No," the doctor said with a negative shake that sent the cherry-scented pipe smoke swirling about his head. "Nor did I treat her. I assume they took her to another doctor somewhere. Perhaps someone in St. Louis or to St. John's in Springfield. I do know she was in strict quarantine. I never saw her once in the months before they left."

Mrs. Ramsay arrived with the refreshments, effectively ending Lilly's questioning. Neither the doctor nor his wife could shed any light on the Purcells' stealthy departure, but agreed that perhaps the speculation that Harold had taken the money so that he could seek treatment for his daughter was correct, but unlikely.

After partaking of the excellent cake and coffee and thanking the Ramsays for their hospitality and help, Lilly took her leave, more perplexed than ever about the Purcells. What possible reason could they have had for not using their family doctor for Sarah's illness?

CHAPTER 20

Lilly went to the church next, a lovely redbrick building with a towering steeple surrounded by several budding trees that sheltered the adjacent cemetery. She found the current minister, a stooping, scrawny individual with more hair on his face than his head, working on his Sunday sermon.

After introducing herself and explaining her situation, she asked, "I was wondering if you have access to any records or correspondence from Reverend Purcell's tenure here that might tell me a bit more about him? Things about the congregation, his family, where they moved here from, or some other clue as to where they might have gone when they left? I'm eager to find out anything that might lead me to them now."

"It was a terrible thing, what he did to the people of this town," the preacher said. "It gives the church a bad name, but what's done is done, isn't it?" He offered her a wan smile. "All my predecessors' records are in the storage room. If you'll come with me, we'll have a look."

Lilly followed him to a stuffy little room whose only source of illumination was a single window overlooking an alley. The small space held an old podium, some pews that needed repair, and a wall of whitewashed shelving. The shelves held odds and ends, stacks of old songbooks, and ledgers with years and names of the previous ministers written on the spines. It didn't take long to find one with Harold Purcell's name, and a quick thumbing through told Lilly it was just what she needed. It held a list of members, and a registry of births, marriages, and deaths. Another ledger itemized the church's finances. They also found a small bundle of letters, tied with twine, bearing Harold Purcell's name.

"Would you mind if I take these with me, so I can look through them at my leisure?" Lilly asked. "I'll return them in a few days."

The preacher smiled. "Keep them as long as you like. It isn't as if I have a need for them."

"Thank you," she said, arranging the journals and letters into a neat stack.

By the time she left the church, it was almost noon, and she decided to have lunch at one of the restaurants on Gallatin Street and look over the contents of the books while she ate.

An hour later, she was fed and had a new goal in mind: to speak with as many of the church members as possible. She'd conferred with her waitress about the list and made notations in her notebook as to which of the church members were still alive and living in the area. Among those still living in town were the banker and one of the town's attorneys. One of the women, Lilly was told in a whispered aside, was the town's tart. Another was the elusive Mrs. Holbrook. If not fruitful, Lilly's afternoon promised to be at least interesting.

After talking to half a dozen men and women who'd worshiped at the reverend's church, she began to get a clearer picture of the man and his family. Though many were cautious with their comments, others seemed to have known the preacher only in a superficial way. Most of Purcell's former brethren described him as a "no-account scoundrel," a "rotten thief," or worse, which certainly didn't speak well of the reverend.

The women, too, were unable to tell Lilly anything meaningful. For all that he had preached a good sermon, not a one had commented on his having made a positive impact on her life, yet without fail, they all described him as handsome, or charming, or charismatic, and one even said that in her opinion, he'd been a bit of a flirt. More often than not, knowing their comments might be construed as uncomplimentary to the preacher, they were accompanied by a blush and a ducking of heads. Men and women alike claimed he knew his scriptures, delivered a good sermon, and had a way about him that drew people. He'd seemed so devout, but then, actions spoke louder than words, didn't they?

Prudence was described much as the sheriff had depicted her. Pretty, but aloof, with her daughter much the same. Like the sheriff, they all felt terrible about the young girl's awful disease, and a few of the ladies concurred with Sheriff Mayhew's theory that the preacher had taken the money for his daughter's treatments. Evidently, few, if any, knew of the abundance left behind at Heaven's Gate, or they might not have been so charitable about the reverend's trespasses.

She decided to do one more interview before returning to the hotel, but seeing the telegraph office across the street, she decided to send a message to Pierce, telling him of the return of her memory the previous day.

As she stepped inside the small office, she decided that the room's greatest asset was an abundance of sunshine. The varying shades of wood tones on the walls were as bland as the man behind the counter. Youngish and prematurely balding with spectacles and a bow tie, the softness around his middle spoke of his lack of physical activity.

He waited with patience while Lilly tried to think of how to word the message so that the whole town of Vandalia would not know her business. Operators were supposed to be discreet, but she was sure that this man would not hesitate to pass on any juicy tidbit that might cross the wire. She decided to settle on simplicity. She would see Pierce and Rose soon enough and explain everything then.

Finally know everything after so many years.
Two died instead of one. Will explain when next we meet.

Satisfied that Pierce would understand what she meant, she paid the operator and stepped back out onto the sidewalk. She was so intent on returning her change to her reticule while holding the church ledgers in her arms that she didn't notice the man passing the office until she'd careened into him, something that was becoming an annoying habit. Reaching out to steady herself by grabbing his arm, Lilly looked up and saw the sheriff looking down at her with a quizzical expression.

"I'm so sorry," she said, stepping back.

He tipped his hat and smiled at her. She imagined he'd been an attractive man in his youth; he was still fine looking with his craggy features, sardonic smile, and thick salt-and-pepper hair.

Looking at the books she carried, he said, "I see you've been busy. Do you have any ideas yet about where the Purcells might have gone?"

"I have a lot to process," she hedged. "So I believe I'll look things over and have a piece of pie at the restaurant across the street while I mull things over." Lilly forgave herself for the small fib. Actually, she was interested in the sheriff's actions.

Realizing that his questions would get him nowhere, he offered her a mocking smile. "I wish you luck, Miss Long," he said, stepping aside for her to pass.

"Thank you, Sheriff Mayhew. Good day."

Chapter 21

Asa Mayhew watched Lilly cross the street to the restaurant. Once she was inside, he turned and went into the telegraph office.

"Hello, Sheriff," the telegraph operator said. "How've you been?"

"Fine, Charles. You?"

"Very well. What can I do for you this afternoon?"

"The lady who was just in here. Did she send something?"

"Sure did. Message went to St. Louis. Who is she anyway?"

"She's a Pinkerton agent trying to locate a missing person."

Charles Presley's eyes grew wide behind his wire-rimmed spectacles. He gave a *tsking* sound. "A Pinkerton agent! What's the world coming to?"

"Going to hell in a handbasket, that's for sure," Mayhew said by way of agreement.

"Who's she looking for?"

"Reverend Harold Purcell and his family," Mayhew supplied. "I doubt you'd remember them. You'd have been just a kid when they lived here."

"I don't remember them, but I've heard the talk," Presley

said with a disbelieving shake of his head. "None of it good. I can't imagine any preacher stealing from his flock."

"Me either. Anyway, people around here just want to forget the past, and she's running all over town stirring up old memories."

Mayhew offered the younger man a conspiratorial, man-to-man smile. "I don't suppose you could tell me what was in the message she sent?" Seeing the reluctance on Presley's face, the sheriff softened the request. "I know you're not supposed to blab about that stuff, but it would sure put everyone's mind at ease if I knew she planned to be moving on soon. The quicker she finds what she's lookin' for, the sooner she'll leave town."

Charles Presley nodded. "I understand." He turned and reached for the piece of paper that held Lilly's message and handed it to the sheriff. "It went to someone called Pierce Wainwright. Sounds like she's on to something, doesn't it?"

Mayhew read the cryptic message aloud. *"Finally know everything after so many years. Two died instead of one. Will explain when next we meet."*

"Do you think this Wainwright person is the one who wants to buy Heaven's Gate?"

"I don't know," Mayhew said, jotting down the message and then handing the original back to Presley. What was going on? What had Miss Long stumbled across out at Heaven's Gate that led her to believe that Prudence and Sarah had both been killed there? No doubt about it, the Pinkerton lady was smarter than he'd given her credit for, and sure enough bore closer watching.

"Let me know if she gets a reply, will you?" he asked the telegraph operator.

Presley rubbed his palms down his pants legs. "Sure thing, Sheriff. Sure thing."

CHAPTER 22

Though she wasn't all that hungry so soon after her meal, Lilly crossed the street and returned to the café, choosing a seat where she could watch Sheriff Mayhew's actions. He'd been passing by when she'd barreled into him, so the only reason he would go inside would be to snoop around about the message she'd sent. She forked up a bite of raisin pie and smiled with a sort of perverse satisfaction. Well, he wouldn't get much information from the brief missive she'd sent to Pierce. Let him make of it what he would. She might have been more forthcoming about her progress into the investigation if he had been more helpful to her.

A few moments later, she watched him exit the office and don his western-style hat. Even from across the street, Lilly could see the dissatisfaction on his face. He glanced down at a small piece of paper in his hand and then stared at the restaurant. Lilly was glad she was seated at one side of the window where it was doubtful he could spot her. Then he stuffed the paper into his breast pocket and headed down the street. Lilly had little doubt that the message she'd sent to Pierce was on the scrap of paper, and wondered what he thought of her mysterious comment. Amused that he was checking up on her, she paid for her refreshment and went toward her final stop of the day, Eloise Mercer's place.

The small house where the town's shady lady lived and plied her trade was a shotgun affair, with a sagging roof, peeling paint, and a rotting porch with an ancient canine lying near the door. Lilly approached the porch warily, uncertain of her reception from the mongrel. But he only lifted his head to regard her with milky eyes and thumped his tail by way of a welcome.

Eloise Mercer answered Lilly's knock promptly. Though it was late afternoon, she was wearing a faded pink seersucker wrapper over little else if Lilly had to guess. Near Virginia Holbrook's age, the years had not been so gentle with Eloise Mercer. Her dull brown hair was tangled, and powder caked the lines fanning out from the corners of her eyes. Her face was puffy from too much sleep and too much liquor. Indeed, she held a glass of some golden liquid in one hand and a pungent-smelling cigarillo in the other.

Drunker than Cooter Brown, she seemed to float in a smoke and alcohol cloud. Like Colleen McKenna, there was a hard edge about her, yet the challenging lift of her chin seemed to dare Lilly to find fault. Instead, she found herself comparing the stranger to the house at Heaven's Gate. Even with years of misspent living having taken its toll, it was obvious that Eloise Mercer had once been quite beautiful.

"Miss Mercer?" Lilly said with a slight smile, holding out her badge. "My name is Lilly Long, with the Pinkerton National Detective Agency. I was wondering if I might ask you a few questions."

The woman's eyes narrowed in suspicion. "It's Mrs. Mercer," she corrected. "Why on earth would you need to talk to me?"

Lilly wasn't sure why the news that Eloise was married was

such a surprise. Tamping down her curiosity, she went into her spiel about the potential buyers and their inability to locate the Purcells. "I saw your name on the church membership roll and wondered if you could tell me anything about him or his family."

Without a word, Eloise Mercer stepped aside. Encouraged, Lilly entered the small, shadow-shrouded parlor. The obese yellow cat dozing in a nearby chair raised its head to peer at her through squinted eyes. Like the dog, it reached the conclusion that she was of no importance, lowered its head, and closed its eyes once more; the loud sound of its purring seeming to vibrate the chair itself.

Clothing, dirty glasses, and various other bits and pieces of clutter littered every surface. The furnishings, though once nice enough, had grown shabby with time and lack of care. A fire smoldered in a fireplace whose chimney needed cleaning, if the smoky interior was any indication. The closeness of the room emphasized the woman's discomforting odor. While all Lilly's senses rebelled, she couldn't deny a pang of sympathy, an emotion she knew instinctively would not endear her to Eloise Mercer.

"Have a seat," her hostess said, scooping up the cat.

Lilly regarded the fine covering of cat hair in the chair's sagging cushion and the questionable blob of something on the arm. "Thank you," she said, "but I'm a bit chilled. I'll just stand by the fire."

"Suit yourself." Eloise sat in the chair and settled the cat on her lap.

"So you want to know about the Reverend Purcell." Smiling a smile that could only be described as derisive, Eloise drew deeply on the slender cigarillo, but the cloak of bravado she wore didn't obscure the torment in her eyes, a look Lilly had seen too often in her own eyes after marrying Timothy Warner.

"Any information you may have about him or his family

would be greatly appreciated. For whatever reasons, those I've talked with so far have been a bit close-mouthed about him, including the sheriff."

Eloise laughed and took another deep draw that sent her into a fit of coughing. When the spell passed, she said, "Well, Pa never was too fond of the preacher."

A jolt of surprise widened Lilly's eyes. "Sheriff Mayhew is your father?"

"Oh, yes." Eloise gave a grandiose wave of the hand that held the glass of liquor. "Asa Mayhew, citizen of the year. Deacon in the church. Pillar of the community. Hypocrite." This time, instead of favoring the smoke, she lifted the glass to her lips.

Deciding that it was wiser to leave that insult alone, Lilly said only, "I admit your father didn't seem overly fond of Reverend Purcell, though he didn't say anything overt against him."

"Of course he didn't." Eloise didn't elaborate, just sat there looking at Lilly with that direct, challenging gaze.

At a bit of a loss as to how to continue, she said, "I suppose it's natural for people to be hesitant about discussing him after the way he took advantage of the congregation."

Eloise's mouth twisted into a bitter smile. "Oh, no, good Christians that they are, they wouldn't want to speak ill of anyone."

She stood, dumping the cat to the floor, where he landed squarely on his feet. Heading toward the fireplace, Lilly's hostess flung the small remainder of tobacco into the halfhearted blaze and turned to face her. Lilly resisted the urge to take a step back.

"Fortunately for you, I have no such problem, departed as I am from the narrow path," she said with a bit of bravado.

Lilly wasn't sure when she'd ever felt so uncomfortable in someone's presence. Not even Colleen had made her squirm so.

Eloise Mercer had a "devil take you" attitude that was as fascinating as it was disturbing.

Without warning, she proceeded to call Harold Purcell names Lilly had seldom heard, even among the theater troupe, whose language was often as colorful as a sailor's. "He was a taker," Eloise said finally, her hate-filled gaze daring Lilly to look away, daring her to say otherwise. "A taker, and a user and a leaver. He tore apart a lot of families in this town, and I pray to God he rots in hell."

"What do you mean, tore apart?"

"You seem like a smart woman, detective lady. Figure it out. Now get out of here. I have a friend stopping by after work."

Startled by the venom in the woman's voice and unable to make sense of what she'd said, Lilly did as she was told and headed for the door. Standing in the aperture, she turned. "Did he ever mention to you where he'd come from, or where he might have gone, or wanted to go?"

"Not to me."

"Can you tell me if there was anyone in town he was particularly close to whom he might have confided in?"

"I suspect he was *close* to a good many people, Miss Long, and he did them all wrong."

Struggling to make sense of the statement, Lilly murmured a soft "Thank you" and closed the door behind her. She stood on the small covered stoop, her mind whirling. Standing on Eloise's front porch, Lilly decided to call it a day and think through the things she'd learned. She wondered what could have happened to bring Eloise Mercer to this point in her life, and how Harold Purcell, charismatic, well-prepared, knowledgeable preacher . . .

. . . *and thief* . . .

. . . could have ignited such hate in her.

On her way to the hotel, Lilly stopped by the telegraph office again, this time sending a message to William, telling him she would soon exhaust her leads in Vandalia and that she planned to go to Springfield in two days. She didn't fail to notice that—thanks to the sheriff's visit—the telegraph operator regarded her with a speculative gleam in his eyes that had not been there earlier. Nor did she doubt that as soon as she was out of sight that the man would waste no time informing the sheriff of her plans. She smiled. She really didn't care if he knew where she was going or when.

It wasn't that she expected to find the Purcells in Springfield, but since more than one person had mentioned the city in connection to treatment of Sarah's illness, it was worth checking out. Besides, she had no idea where to go next, and she hated to admit defeat. She would explore every possible avenue before giving up and returning to Chicago.

Telegram sent, she started back to the hotel, mentally exhausted from trying to make sense of what she'd learned, physically weary from walking all over God's creation, and emotionally spent from the inexplicable sorrow she felt in the presence of Eloise Mercer.

What she needed was respite from the questions and speculation roiling around in her mind, but she wouldn't get any real relief until the following evening when she attended the play her friend Lenora Nash was performing at the Fehren. Nora, a competent actress a few years older than Lilly, had been with the troupe in the days when Arnold Feldman managed— or mismanaged—the company. She'd left several months before Arnold absconded with their funds and Pierce had taken over the ensemble. Lilly had always liked the spunky, freckle-faced Nora, who lived life with an enviable zest.

Unlike the once-beautiful Eloise. Blast it all! Why couldn't she forget Eloise Mercer? Poor thing. She'd had a husband at some time. Lilly wondered if he still lived in town. Had they parted because she possessed loose morals, or had his poor treatment of her caused her to turn her back on decency? As a young, impressionable girl, had her faith been crushed when she realized that the very man who was supposed to be helping her to heaven had lied and stolen from his flock? Is that why she'd given up on God?

She had no idea what lay behind the woman's hatred of Harold Purcell, but she understood well the anger and disappointment at realizing someone you cared for had feet of clay. Kate had been one of those people. When Lilly had grown up enough to understand the meaning of the parade of men who'd shared her mother's bed and understand the circumstances of her conception, Kate had become one of those people. Lilly's feelings for Kate had undergone a drastic change, and for a while, she'd detested her mother. Despised what she'd done, what she was. She'd even hated her mother for getting herself killed.

As a woman grown, Lilly realized that it had taken a lot of courage for Kate to accept the scorn of society by bearing a child out of wedlock rather than take vows she'd known she couldn't keep. At least her mother had possessed enough maternal instinct to not end Lilly's life by swilling a potion of pennyroyal or seeking out some quack to gouge her unplanned child from the womb. Neither had her mother left her on the doorstep of some orphanage in one of the cities the troupe passed through.

Fighting the wave of depression that always accompanied memories of Kate, Lilly forced her thoughts back to Eloise Mercer and her puzzling comments. What had happened between her and her father? Was her chosen occupation the wedge that had driven them apart the way she'd felt separated from Kate? What had Eloise meant when she said Harold Purcell tore families apart and that the reverend was *close* to a lot of people and wronged each and every one? The most obvious possibility was that he'd dallied with the women of his congregation, but thus far that was pure speculation on Lilly's part. Not a breath of such a suggestion had crossed anyone's lips.

All she really knew was that the more questions she asked, the more were raised, and so far, no one had given her any clue to where the Purcells might have gone. Which left only Springfield on the off chance they had gone there to seek treatment for Sarah.

Shoulders slumped, footsteps dragging, she stopped to peer in a window filled with spring dresses in pastel prints. As she stood there, she again felt the eerie sensation of being watched. Not wanting to alert the observer, she used the storefront glass as a mirror, trying to spot someone who was paying her undue attention. She saw no one.

She ground her teeth in frustration. She was exhausted, and her mind was a muddle of unanswered questions and old memories. She didn't need some phantom following her. Squaring her shoulders, she turned and started toward the hotel. Passing by the Presbyterian Church at the corner of Main and Third Streets, she walked south along the courthouse block. A wagon loaded with grain-filled gunnysacks headed east on Gallatin, and a man crossed Third. Something about him seemed familiar. At the corner, he unrolled a paper and began nailing it to a tree.

Drawing closer, Lilly saw that the broadside touted a boxing match on Friday afternoon on the courthouse square. She realized that the man doing the nailing was none other than the one she'd bumped into on the train. Somehow she wasn't surprised to learn that he was one of the rowdy boxers who'd kept her from getting any sleep.

Hoping to pass without him noticing her, she started around him, giving him a wide berth. At that precise moment, he stepped back a couple of paces to check his handiwork and almost knocked her over. She staggered backward, the books she was carrying tumbling to the ground. Once again, he turned and grasped her shoulders to steady her.

A trifle shaken and more than a little embarrassed, Lilly looked up at him. When she'd stumbled against him on the train, she was so taken aback at the realization that their meeting was so similar to hers with Timothy that she hadn't realized just how attractive the stranger was. He was. Very. She squelched the thought and cursed the maddening trait she'd inherited from her mother. She would not be swayed again by a charming man.

Recognition lit his eyes, and he favored her with a cocky smile. "Well, hullo, there. I was hopin' I'd run into you again. But mayhap not quite so literally." He regarded her with a narrowed, considering expression. "You're not followin' me, are you, lass?"

Following him? The utter gall of the man! "I beg your pardon?" she said in a frosty tone.

"No need to get huffy, now. It's just that we've bumped into each other twice now, and I thought maybe you were flirtin' with me just a wee bit." The observation was accompanied by an audacious wink.

Lilly's mouth dropped open in surprise, but before she could think of a suitable set down, she caught the familiar scent of bay rum. Timothy's scent. The aroma enveloped her, leaving her awash in memories . . . Tim laughing, teasing, holding her, kissing her, telling her she was the most important thing in the world to him. . . .

With a little sound of annoyance, Lilly pushed both the man and the hateful memories away. "I'm fine, thank you," she snapped. In an act of self-preservation, she took a backward step to put some distance between them and stooped to pick up her books. He squatted to help her and their hands touched. Their gazes met and locked. Fighting the pull of his personality, she glared at him. Without a word, he stacked a book on top of the others in her arms. They stood almost simultaneously and she started to step around him, but his voice stopped her.

"If I've offended you, I beg your pardon. It's just that I don't think there's anything wrong with a bit o' flirtin' now and again."

Lilly lifted her gaze to his and favored him with a withering look. "I do not flirt with strange men, sir," she said. "And if I did, I would never flirt with the likes of you." Pulling her skirts aside, as if brushing against him might give her the plague, she swept past him.

She'd taken no more than two steps when his voice halted her again. "Never say never, colleen. It's a very long time."

Muttering beneath her breath, Lilly walked away, her heart racing. Whether it was from her reaction to the man or from her anger, she could not have said.

CHAPTER 23

After another delicious dinner, Lilly headed to her room. Mrs. Holbrook still hadn't made an appearance. As Lilly climbed the stairs she wondered if she dared confront the woman at home. She decided to do just that if her hostess didn't make an appearance at the hotel the next morning.

Dressed in her gown and wrapper, she propped up in bed, intent on studying the ledgers and letters she'd borrowed from the church. Though she scoured the pages for hours, she found nothing of interest about the Purcells except a page listing deceased church members, where she found the name of the reverend's infant son, Joel David Purcell.

One of the letters to Harold had been sent from a fellow in New Orleans, but the contents revealed nothing but the fact that the writer, a Nelson Hargity, was thinking of leaving his preaching position and going into the mercantile business. If there were any other clues about where the Purcells might have gone when they'd fled Vandalia, or any bits of information that might have given her insight to the preacher's motives, she was unable to recognize them.

She fell asleep with a letter in her hand, but her sleep was shallow and dream filled. Now and then, just to make things more exasperating, random scenes featuring Timothy crept in. In one muddled dream sequence, the boxer from the train met Tim in the ring and knocked him flat on his posterior.

That dream awakened her. What on earth was that all about? She punched her pillow and scrunched up her eyes, willing her mind to stillness and praying that she could gain a few hours of restful sleep.

While Lilly courted sleep in her hotel room, the sheriff was busy pulling down the blinds on his office windows. The two men he'd summoned settled into chairs across from his desk. They were there to discuss the long-term ramifications of the Pinkerton agent's unexpected arrival and her ongoing inquiries into things they thought they'd left far in the past.

The first man was tall and elegantly dressed, clean shaven and clearly unhappy about the unanticipated meeting. The second, though shorter, was just as properly attired. There was nothing in his calm demeanor to suggest that he was in any way distressed over the latest happenings.

"What's all this about, Asa?" the taller of the two asked, accepting the squat glass of whiskey the sheriff offered.

"I thought you should know that Miss Long went out to Heaven's Gate yesterday to have a look around. Today she sent a telegram to someone named Pierce Wainwright and another to William Pinkerton," the sheriff told them.

"William Pinkerton?" the tall one asked. "Why would she do that?"

"The lady is a certified Pinkerton agent."

"I hadn't heard that. Are you certain?"

"She showed me her badge."

"Well, isn't that just dandy? A Pinkerton snooping around."

"There's not much we can do about it," Mayhew said.

"Obviously she said something that worries you," said the shorter of the two, tapping the ash from the sweet-smelling cigar he was smoking.

The sheriff nodded. "The one to Wainwright said something about finally knowing everything after so long a time and two dying that night. She said she'd explain more later." To verify his statement, he pulled the piece of paper with the words written on it and handed it to the taller man.

When he finished reading it, he passed it to his cohort. "What do you think it means? You don't think she suspects—"

"I don't know what to think," the sheriff interrupted. "But I thought you two ought to know about it. It just seemed strange to me. She says she's here to locate Purcell and see if he'll sell his property, but I'm beginning to wonder if that's really why she's come."

"Why else would she be poking into the past?"

"I don't care a fig why she's here. I want her gone. We have to think of ourselves and our families," the taller one said.

"We are," Mayhew told him. "I think we've done a pretty good job of burying things."

"I thought so, too, until now," the man said. "Is it possible that some young woman still wet behind the ears has discovered something at Heaven's Gate that was overlooked all those years ago?"

"Something that I overlooked, you mean?" the sheriff snapped, tossing back the shot of whiskey and grimacing as it burned down his throat.

"Now don't get your hackles up, Asa," the short man said in a conciliatory tone. "You were new to the job back then. It's possible you overlooked something, but there's no shame in it if you did. Miss Long may be a woman, but the Pinkertons aren't known for surrounding themselves with imbeciles."

The sheriff gave a disgruntled nod. He'd already come to that realization.

"So what should we do? Find a way to suggest that she mind her own business?"

"I don't think that's necessary just now," Mayhew told them. "Her message to William Pinkerton said she was leaving for Springfield the day after tomorrow."

"Springfield!" the tall man exclaimed. "I wonder why she's going there."

"I have no idea."

"It doesn't matter," the shorter man muttered. "It sounds as if she's about to give up on finding out anything about Purcell. If our luck holds and no one cooperates with her, she'll leave here with nothing, and our lives will settle down to normal. Or as close to normal as they will ever be."

CHAPTER 24

Lilly woke the following day to sunshine and birdsong and a much clearer mind. Her natural hardheadedness was back in full force. She might not be able to locate Purcell, but she would not let anyone frighten her away from trying—man *or* ghost! She'd promised William Pinkerton she would do the job he'd sent her to do, and she intended to fulfill that promise, especially since her assignment was turning out to be far more interesting than she'd first expected.

She was heading out the door for her breakfast when she saw the envelope that had been slipped beneath the crack. Had she received a telegram from Pierce, or even William after she'd gone to bed? She reached down to pick it up and with a bit of trepidation, pulled the heavy vellum from its envelope. Unfolding it, she found herself staring at a beautiful Spencerian script.

Your presence is unwanted. Leave us alone, and leave town at once.

Her heart seemed to stumble. A threat? She hadn't counted on that when she'd thought to become a detective. Hands shaking, she carried the note to the window, where she examined it again. Each time she read the missive, her alarm lessened and her anger grew. How dare someone threaten her! She worked for the most respected law enforcement agency in the country. Still, common sense told her that even though it might be nothing of true importance, she should not ignore it. She was not stupid. She decided to show it to the sheriff and get his opinion.

After fortifying herself with several cups of coffee and a bowl of molasses-topped oatmeal, Lilly crossed to the square and entered the courthouse. Since criminals made no distinction for the weekend, she found the lawman in his office in what seemed to be his favorite position: booted feet on his desk. Again, he was reading a newspaper, but this time when he saw who'd entered his domain he lowered his feet to the floor.

Lilly tossed the letter to the top of his desk.

"What's that?" he asked, shaking the newsprint closed.

"Perhaps you could tell me," she said as he reached for the letter. She stood with her arms folded over her chest, one foot tapping out an impatient rhythm.

Sheriff Mayhew unfolded the note, rubbing his salt-and-pepper mustache with his forefinger as he read its content. When he finished, he muttered a mild curse. "Where did you find this?"

"Someone slid it beneath my door while I was sleeping. I must say, Sheriff, it doesn't make me feel very welcome. I was wondering if you have any idea who might have left it for me. If you don't, perhaps I can narrow it down for you."

She ticked off her ideas on her fingers. "One, I don't think it was you, though I know you don't like me poking around and asking questions. Two, I don't think it's your daughter, whom I met, by the way, and who tells me you're a hypocrite. Perhaps before I leave town, you would tell me why. You do remember what a hypocrite is, don't you?"

The sheriff's eyes narrowed in irritation.

"Three, I don't think Billy Bishop or his ilk would do such a thing, since I doubt they have a source for vellum, not to mention it's doubtful they could write so well, which brings us to the conclusion that it was someone highly educated. I'm thinking a merchant. Teacher. Lawyer. One of the preachers in town. Mr. Reihmann at the bank—"

"I know who wrote it," the sheriff interrupted. "I'll take care of it, and it's not a threat. It's a warning."

Lilly's eyes flashed with indignation. "Perhaps you would be so kind as to explain the difference."

"Actually, I think it's just a request for you to stop disrupting so many lives."

Lilly rested her palms on the desktop and pinned him with a furious gaze. "Do you stop trying to find out who committed a crime when it ruffles a few feathers, Sheriff Mayhew?"

"Of course not."

Lilly's unflinching gaze met his. "Well, neither do I," she told him in a deceptively soft voice. "Finding Harold Purcell's whereabouts is my job and I intend to do it, so if you'd be so kind as to pass that on to the person who wrote me the . . . *request,* I would greatly appreciate it. Since you seem to know who it is, you would save me considerable time and trouble." She straightened. "Now, I have people to question. Good day."

She was at the door when his voice stopped her. She didn't turn around.

"I don't normally talk about personal things with strangers, Miss Long, but since Ellie brought it up, I may as well try to set the record straight. She thinks I'm a hypocrite because there was a time in our lives that I rushed to judgment. By the time I learned the truth, it was too late for forgiveness."

Lilly thought of herself and the hurt she still dealt with daily because of Tim's behavior. She thought of the hate she felt for the man who'd killed Kate. She had not forgiven either of them and wasn't sure she ever could.

She turned to face the sheriff, who at that moment looked much older than he had when she'd first come in. "I won't be judging you, Sheriff Mayhew," she told him with a stiff, sorrow-filled smile. "I have my own demons to wrestle down."

CHAPTER 25

After leaving the sheriff to take care of the anonymous message, Lilly was trying to decide whom she should talk to next. When she passed by the bank, she saw James Reihmann sitting in his office. Deciding he would do as well as the next, she tapped on the window.

When he looked up and saw her he frowned and went back to his work. Lilly reached into her bag, took out her badge, and tapped the metal against the glass. His eyes narrowed in irritation, but he got up reluctantly and disappeared toward the front of the bank. In a few seconds she heard the key scraping in the lock. The door swung open and he stepped aside for her to enter. He made no effort to hide his displeasure.

"Mr. Reihmann," she said, extending a hand that he took reluctantly. "I'm Lilly Long with the Pinkertons. I'm sure you've heard why I'm in town. I'm sorry to bother you on a Saturday morning, but when I saw you through the window, I thought that perhaps today might be better for you than a regular workday."

"I know who you are and what you're doing," he told her, "and I'm very busy."

"I just have a few questions. It won't take long."

"Very well. I can give you a few moments."

How very kind of him, Lilly thought, pressing her lips together to keep from saying something she shouldn't. Without another word, he ushered her into a spacious office, rounded the gleaming desk, and resumed his seat. It looked as though he'd been making entries into a ledger.

"I'll just be a moment," he said, resuming his work.

As she took the chair across from him and waited for him to finish, she remembered Helen calling him grandfather the morning of her arrival. With nothing else to do, she took stock of him. Clean shaven, nary a hair of his graying dark blond head was out of place. He was dressed in a brown three-piece tweed suit, typical bankers' attire. He was attractive enough for his age if one liked the cool, pompous look.

Her gaze moved from his bent head to his well-shaped, soft-looking hands. His nails were clean and pared close, and the only ring he wore was a wide gold wedding band. Her gaze meandered over the desk, and her pulse quickened. His handwriting was exactly like that of the warning note she'd received, and there was a short stack of vellum on his desk. Her patience vanished. Apparently, he intended to try to intimidate her as he no doubt did those who fell behind on their notes. She cleared her throat.

He condescended to look up, and she saw that he at least had the grace to blush. "I'm sorry," he said, a bit shamefaced. "I really need to finish those accounts within the hour. I have an appointment."

Lilly pegged him for a rich coward who bluffed his way through life because his money gave him a false sense of superiority. Just like Kate's killer. She had no use for his kind.

She reached down and picked up a piece of vellum, turning it this way and that. "Lovely paper."

"Thank you," he muttered in a low voice.

She gestured toward the open ledger. "And you have beautiful handwriting."

"Thank you," he said again.

She let the full force of her untroubled gaze rest on his. "I received a note on this exact paper in this handwriting just this morning. Someone slipped it beneath my door."

James Reihmann's face drained of color. He couldn't meet her gaze. "Indeed."

"Yes, indeed." She smiled at him. "I wouldn't imagine there are too many folks in town who have mastered Spencerian script since it is relatively new. Or who can afford vellum to write on. You know, Mr. Reihmann, you really ought to think twice about repercussions before threatening people."

"I . . . I don't know what you're talking about," he blustered.

"Oh, I believe you do," Lilly countered, looking him squarely in the eye.

He dropped his gaze. "Does . . . anyone else know about the . . . note?"

"No one but me," she told him. "Oh, and Sheriff Mayhew. I turned it over to him this morning."

Reihmann's gaze dropped to the desktop. He began to rearrange papers.

"Mr. Reihmann," she began, clasping her hands together in her lap, "I'm here on a very simple mission, and that is to see if anyone knows where the Purcells might have gone when they left. The sooner I have somewhere to look, the sooner I will leave this town and its citizens in peace."

Reihmann nodded, looking much like a child who'd been put in his place.

"However, everyone seems intent on making my job harder by being less than forthcoming. I've learned some things about the preacher and his family, and I understand that when he left here, he was not much liked. Under the circumstances, those feelings are understandable.

"I know he did his banking here. I know that he didn't make his weekly contribution deposit before he vanished. I know in general the things that happened afterward. All I need to ask you is if he ever, during the time he did business with you, mention where he might have lived before coming to Vandalia, or where he might have . . . say, wanted to go if he left."

"Not that I can remember."

She favored him with a benign smile. "See? That wasn't so hard, was it?"

"No."

Deciding to see if another tack might render some useful bit of information, Lilly stood and picked up her handbag from the desktop. "Well, I'll be going then. I need to speak with your wife, and perhaps I can finally catch your daughter at the hotel."

James Reihmann leaped to his feet. "Leave them both alone!" he demanded, finding a bit of backbone at last. "Mirabelle can't tell you any more than I have, and Virginia was just a girl when the Purcells were here. No one in town knows where the scoundrel went when he took off."

Well, well. It looks as if we have someone else who isn't overly fond of the reverend. Was theft enough to provoke such hatred? Finding out Purcell's whereabouts was rapidly becoming secondary to Lilly's need to satisfy her own curiosity about the preacher's actions. But she'd upset the banker enough for one day. She rose, said her good-byes, and left the banker stewing in the bitter juices of his own concoction.

Chapter 26

Lilly spent the remainder of that day asking more questions of Purcell's former congregation. Many of the older members had passed away; a few had moved. Phillip Townsend, one of the two lawyers in town, met her at the door of his house, which was situated near the edge of town. He shook her hand and agreed to give her a few moments, though, like the banker, he was "a busy man."

He led Lilly through the foyer of his impressive two-story house into a book-lined office where he rounded the desk and indicated that she should take a chair opposite his. They both sat and he reached out to straighten a stack of papers. Her gaze went unerringly to the ring on his right hand, and for an instant she couldn't draw her next breath. Then she realized that though the stone was onyx with a "T" in the center, it was not the style worn by her mother's killer as she remembered it.

She took a handkerchief from her reticule and dabbed at the dew of perspiration that had appeared on her upper lip. Now that she'd remembered that day, was she doomed to suffer those pangs of panic every time she saw a man with a signet ring?

After a few moments of conversation, she learned that Phillip Townsend and his wife had been members of the reverend's flock, but he did not know anything of consequence to add to her slim dossier on the preacher.

She gave a sigh of disappointment. "What about your wife? Perhaps she recalls something Mrs. Purcell might have mentioned—woman-to-woman."

"I don't mean to be rude, Miss Long," the attorney said, "but under no circumstances are you to speak to my wife. Her mental state has been precarious for some time."

A bit shocked by the vehemence in his voice, she nonetheless acquiesced. "I understand, Mr. Townsend, and I'm sorry. It truly is not my wish to cause anyone any undue pain. What about your daughter, Rachel? Does she still live here?"

"Unfortunately, no. Rachel moved away about the time the Purcells vanished," he said.

Sensing that she'd received as much information from the lawyer as he was willing to give, she thanked him, took up her purse, and started to leave. At the door, she turned. "One more thing. I just learned that Eloise Mercer is married. Do you know where I can find her husband?"

"Buddy's dead," the attorney said. "Has been for many years."

Lilly thanked him and left.

Many of the people she tried to question either refused to talk or gave her answers along the same lines she'd received the day before. By that afternoon, there was no one left who might be able to offer viable information but Virginia Holbrook.

Pushing James Reihmann's warning from her mind, Lilly walked the four blocks to the Holbrook home, hoping to find Virginia there. She was surprised when the banker's daughter answered the door. From the expression on her face, it was clear that if she'd had any inkling of her caller's identity, she would not have been so eager to answer the knock.

"Good afternoon, Mrs. Holbrook," Lilly said before the woman could slam the door in her face. "I hate to bother you at home, but I received a list of Harold Purcell's church members from Reverend Lawrence a couple of days ago, and saw your family's name on the roll. If you have the time, I'd like to ask you a few questions."

There was a distraught expression in the woman's eyes. "If I agree to talk to you, will you go away and leave us alone?"

"Us?"

"The town," Virginia said with some asperity. "You have no idea the misery you've caused by opening old wounds."

Shades of the warning letter, Lilly thought, wondering once more what was behind the town's paranoia. "I'm truly sorry. Upsetting the town was not my intent. I'm just trying to do my job, and you're the last person I need to talk with."

"I honestly don't want to talk about the man—ever," Virginia said. "But if you promise to leave here without troubling us anymore, I'll let you come in."

"I hope to wrap up things here by this evening, and leave on the morning train," Lilly assured her.

The announcement had the desired effect. Without a word, Virginia stepped aside. The contrast between this home and Eloise Mercer's was dramatic. Nothing was out of place. Windows glittered in the sunlight. Dust would not have dared to collect on the gleaming furniture.

Virginia Holbrook gestured toward the parlor, where a small fire banished the chill of the spring day. Lilly settled into a chair near the fire; Virginia took the rocking chair across from her. Lilly would have loved a cup of tea or coffee, but it seemed unlikely that Virginia's hospitality would stretch beyond a grudging discussion.

Ignoring the anger blazing in her hostess's eyes, Lilly tugged off her gloves. It seemed there was no way to approach the subject except head-on, so she did just that.

"I'll try to be as brief as possible, Mrs. Holbrook."

"Please do."

"Though there are many people who won't talk to me at all about Harold Purcell, I've found out that he stole from the church, that his daughter was ill, that they have not been heard from since they slipped out of town in the dead of the night, and that no one seems to have any idea where they might have gone. Over the past few days I've gained somewhat of a feel for what kind of person he was, and I've heard all the strange tales of ghosts and murders that are believed to have happened at Heaven's Gate, yet even with all that information I don't feel as if I'm being told the whole truth."

"There are often many versions of the truth, Miss Long. You say you have a feel for what kind of man Harold Purcell was, but I doubt that very much," she said in a cold voice.

"He came to this town with his engaging ways and hellfire and brimstone sermons, and made us believe the things he told us about heaven and hell. Then, he fleeced his congregation, took our"—she swallowed—"our innocence and trampled us under his greed and self-importance. He's an evil man, Miss Long, and I hope he rots in hell!"

She lurched to her feet and clasped her shaking hands together. "I'm sorry," she said in a trembling voice. "I can't do this. I'm afraid you'll have to leave."

There was no denying the woman's agitation. It would be churlish to stay. Lilly stood. "I'm sorry for upsetting you, Mrs. Holbrook. I'll see myself out."

She thanked Virginia and left, more bewildered than before. She understood that by asking questions about the past, she'd brought back unpleasant memories to many people, but for the life of her, she didn't see how it could be as upsetting as the reactions she'd stirred up. It didn't take a seasoned opera-tive to know there was more going on here than Purcell taking money, but how was she to find out what it was when no one would talk to her?

She was left with no recourse but to speculate. By all ac-counts Purcell was handsome and charming. Charismatic. A flirt. The sheriff mentioned something that had happened that he couldn't forgive. Virginia Holbrook spoke of engaging ways and stripping the congregation of their innocence.

The possibility that the reverend *had* behaved indiscreetly with some of the ladies of the church was gaining credibility. Had Eloise or Virginia's mother been among his conquests? Was Mrs. Townsend's precarious mental state caused by her being found out by her husband and the town folks? That would certainly explain the sheriff's and Mr. Reihmann's ani-mosity.

If Harold Purcell had been unfaithful to his wife and had seduced the women of his congregation, it was no real surprise to Lilly. He was a man, after all, and in her opinion, men were in general rakes and reprobates, concerned only with them-selves, their desires, their needs. Her theory made sense, but she doubted she would ever know the truth, and as eager as she was to know what had happened, it really didn't matter. None of it had any bearing on her assignment. All she needed to be concerned with was finding the Purcells and asking them if they wanted to sell Heaven's Gate.

With her leads exhausted, she went back to the hotel, longing for a hot bath and something to take her mind off the case. One of the Holbrook boys stopped her as she started up the stairs, handing her a telegram. It was from William, who in-structed Lilly to return to Heaven's Gate once more before she left for Springfield. She was to look for anything that might shed some light on the past.

Though she hated revisiting the place, William left her no

choice. Maybe with her wits more about her, she would find something that would point her in a new direction.

But that chore was for tomorrow. She'd had enough of the town's hostility for one day. Just now there was nothing more pressing on her agenda than to have a leisurely bath and go watch Nora Nash at the Fehren. The familiarity of the theater and seeing a new play would go a long way toward getting her mind off her work. Just the kind of evening she needed.

CHAPTER 27

The three-story Fehren Opera House stood on the corner of Fifth Street, kitty-corner from the Dieckmann House. The brick façade, with its arched windows, faced Gallatin. The opera house itself was located on the third floor of the building, while doctors dispensed medicine and lawyers, including Mr. Townsend, dispensed legal advice on the second. The first floor was comprised of various shops.

Lilly couldn't help the excitement coursing through her as she watched Nora play the lead in *Esmeralda*. Though her friend was perhaps not as polished as Hallie Elliott, who had made the lead role of the popular comedy her own, and even though the other performers in the troupe were not on the same par as Jacob Bunn, Will Tracy, et al, Lilly deemed the overall performance still quite respectable.

When the final curtain closed, she made her way through the throng to the dressing rooms located on the northeast corner of the theater. As in many venues, heating was too little or none at all, and once away from the relative warmth of the lights, it was easy to become chilled.

After telling one of the stagehands who she was, she was let in. Giving little heed to the bawdy laughter and crude comments flying between the actresses as they scrubbed away the heavy stage makeup and shucked their costumes for their own clothes, Lilly scanned the group of women for her friend. It was impossible not to spot Nora's frizzy, silver-blond hair among the group of chattering, laughing women.

"Hey, Blondie!" Lilly called into the melee. "Come and say hello to an old friend."

Hands wiping makeup stilled, half-clad bodies became motionless, and every head turned at the sound of her voice. She knew the exact moment Nora recognized her. The question disappeared from her brown eyes and her mouth widened into a comical O of surprise.

With a little squeal of delight, Nora launched herself across the room, enveloping Lilly in a familiar embrace. "Sweet heaven, Lilly girl," she said, holding her at arm's length, "you've grown into a proper woman the last two years. What on earth are you doing here?"

"You won't believe me when I tell you," Lilly said. "But we can talk over a late dinner, if you don't have any previous commitments."

Nora grinned. "Now what would I have going on in a strange town?" She laughed gaily. "Just give me a few minutes, sweetie, and we'll be on our way."

Fifteen minutes later, Lilly and her friend were sitting in a restaurant down the street. A few places had grown smart enough to take advantage of the theater's presence the nights they were in town by staying open to indulge theatergoers in a late meal or a hot beverage and dessert. Over rich black coffee and perfectly decadent slices of chocolate pie with mile-high meringue, the two friends caught up on the happenings in their lives over the past two years.

Lilly told Nora about the turnaround in the troupe's success since Pierce had taken over its management, about her recently being given some lead roles, and the whole sordid tale of Timothy. It would do no good to hide it, since all their common friends knew the truth.

"He hit you?" Nora asked in horror. "And Rose?"

"Yes." Lilly went on to tell her about her trip to MacGregor's and what she'd discovered about her husband there.

"Well, all I can say is that it was meant for you to find out the truth. Better sooner than later, I say."

"I know."

Lilly went on to tell her friend how the incident with Tim had played a part in her decision to try to help other women who had been taken advantage of. She even told her about applying for the Pinkerton position as three different women. Nora sat listening with wide eyes. When Lilly got to the part about Mrs. Partridge taking off her wig and revealing her identity, Nora laughed until tears ran down her freckled cheeks.

"Oh, Lilly, that's rich!" she said, wiping at her eyes. "So did they hire you?"

"Indeed they did," she said, "which is why I'm in Vandalia. I'm tracing a missing person."

"You're joshing me!"

"I said you wouldn't believe me," Lilly reminded with a smile. "It's true." She gave Nora a sketchy version of her assignment, and confessed, "I haven't been able to find out much, so I'm off to Springfield day after tomorrow. Because of their daughter's illness, that's the only lead I have, and if nothing pans out there, it's back to Chicago for me. And besides," she added with a guilty grin, "the Pierced Rose Troupe is filling in a cancellation at a small theater in Springfield for two weeks, so I'll have a chance to see Rose and Pierce. I haven't been gone but a few days, yet I miss everyone already."

"That's normal," Nora said. Looking thoughtful, she rested her pointed chin on her palm. "So, Lil, with the divorce from

Timothy in the works, you'll soon be footloose and fancy free."

"I don't feel footloose and fancy free. I feel like an imbecile for being taken in so easily."

Nora covered Lilly's hand with hers. "Don't be so hard on yourself. Men like Timothy are professionals. Taking in women is an art form to them. Someone will come along someday who will be everything you want and need, and then you'll live happily ever after."

There was no denying the soft glow of happiness in her friend's eyes. "Nora . . ." Lilly said with a smile. "What's going on? Have you found someone?"

Nora's eyes glittered with tears and she nodded. "I have. His name is Elijah Wilkins, and he lives in Ft. Worth."

"Texas?"

"Yes, he's a cattle rancher and he's looking for a wife."

"A wife!"

Nora nodded. "I signed up to be a mail-order bride."

"Oh, Nora, you didn't!" Lilly said, scandalized.

"I did, Lil," she said with a defiant lift of her chin. "Lots of women are doing it." She stared down at the dregs of coffee in her cup for long seconds and then lifted her weary gaze to Lilly's. "I'm tired of sleeping in a different room every week or so. Sick of not having a place to call my own. I want a regular life with a husband and kids. I want a porch with a rocking chair."

Lilly couldn't argue with the sentiment. It was the same reason she'd decided to spend her savings on a house some-where and settle down to a non-nomadic life. But that was im-possible now, thanks to Timothy.

"How do you know you're getting a decent man, since you've never seen him?" Lilly asked.

"You met Timothy face-to-face and were fooled, so how

can anyone know what they're getting without spending time together?"

"True," Lilly said with a sigh.

"Elijah and I have been corresponding for several months," Nora said. "He asked me to marry him, and I accepted, and I'll be leaving for Texas in a couple of weeks."

"You'll keep in touch, won't you?" Lilly asked.

"Of course I will. Who knows? The troupe might play in Ft. Worth or Dallas sometime."

"And you don't mind moving to Texas?"

"Not at all," Nora assured her. "It will be a wonderful new experience."

Lilly still had her doubts, but her friend was so excited it would have been rude to belabor the issue. After more than two hours, they hugged and parted company, both promising to keep in touch.

As Nora released Lilly, her friend met her gaze, and said, "It's a good thing you're doing, Lil," she said, giving Lilly's hand a pat. "A really good thing."

CHAPTER 28

On Sunday morning, Lilly's mind felt fresher for having put her assignment aside for a few hours. Since she'd exhausted her list of people to question, there was no reason to delay the dreaded trip back to Heaven's Gate. She left as early as possible, packing a canteen of water and having Helen tie up a fried-egg sandwich in brown paper and twine.

Since the mornings could still be quite chilly and the empty house was bound to be cold, Lilly left her cape in the room and took out a warm gray wool coat and matching tartan scarf. Once again, she armed herself with her derringer on the off chance that the sheriff had not been able to convince the writer of the "appeal" to leave her alone. Assuming James Reihmann was the culprit, she doubted he would have enough gumption to come after her in person, especially since she'd confronted him. He didn't seem the type who'd want to get his hands dirty.

Knowing it was useless to protest, Billy Bishop rigged up a buggy. The morning was pleasant, and by the time she reached Heaven's Gate, the sun had already begun to warm the air. Squirrels played tag up and down trees. Soon the animals and birds would mate, babies would be born, and life would begin a new cycle. Despite her loss of faith in men and her fear of being like her mother, she couldn't stifle a twinge of longing for a love as strong and true as the one Pierce and Rose shared. At some time, she also wanted a child. She wondered if the day would ever come when she felt able to trust a man again.

At Heaven's Gate, she tied the horse to the sagging hitching post and, leaving her lunch and coat in the buggy, headed for the front door, which she'd left unlocked when she fled the house a few days earlier.

Determined to take William's advice and search carefully, Lilly started in the kitchen. She didn't expect to find anything helpful there, but looked nonetheless. Next, she checked the library. The walls were lined with copies of the classics, their leather covers splotched with grayish mold. Pictures of men on horseback fox hunting and hounds giving chase hung behind the desk and over the fireplace, which was flanked by two brown leather chairs also covered in mold.

She stood in the doorway, vacillating. There was no way she could check all the books, but she could check the contents of Purcell's desk. Inside a drawer, Lilly found a journal containing Prudence Purcell's household expenses. She thumbed through it and saw a bit of the minister's wife's life unfolding before her. Listed in a prim and proper hand were itemized expenditures and the dates the items were purchased.

Sarah: five yards yellow muslin, seven yards Irish lace and makings, $3.87; trimming, 33 cents, 14 abalone buttons, 35 cents, April 11, 1861.

Ten yards sheeting, five bottles iodine, two bottles quinine, May 27, 1862 (for Union Army).

It came of something of a start to realize the War had been raging when the Purcells lived here. She added the book to those she planned to take with her and riffled through the other papers in the desk. Another ledger with different handwriting noted receipt of Harold's salary and the itemizing of the purchases he'd made. She frowned. There was no way he could afford this opulence on his minister's wages. There were pages with notes and Biblical passages—most likely in preparation of his sermons—and books with excerpts underlined. A dust-coated copy of Dante's *Divine Comedy* lay on the desk. She added the lot to her growing stack.

Throughout the house, she collected letters and tintypes and other records. As she stood surveying the parlor, she spied the family Bible she'd seen before. On impulse, she added it to her cache.

The morning was almost spent. She felt she'd gathered everything of importance from inside the house and decided to have her sandwich before visiting the cemetery. Looking at the graveyard shouldn't take long, and it would help sate her curiosity about the Purcells. Then she would get back to town in time to have a leisurely dinner and pack for her trip to Springfield.

She was carrying her cache to the buggy when one of the books slipped from her grasp and fell to the floor. Bending to pick it up, she noticed a large discoloration at the bottom of the stairs. It looked as if someone had broken a decanter of wine. No doubt an excellent vintage, she thought, recalling the preacher's expensive taste. She must have been too preoccupied with her fears to notice it during her last visit.

Back in the warmth of the sunshine, she deposited her plunder in the floorboard of the buggy, unwrapped her lunch, and ate her meal sitting on a fallen tree and listening to the earth waking from its winter slumber. As Rose would no doubt say, God was in His heaven, and all was right with the world. Recalling her terror when she'd been here just days ago, Lilly laughed. She'd never been so fanciful before.

After finishing her lunch, she once again made her way through the overgrowth clogging the garden path to the small family burial plot. A large tree limb had fallen at some time, blocking the mildewed, lichen-encrusted headstone and knocking one side of the fence askew.

She pushed through the gate and picked her way across the small plot toward the stone. A chubby cherub sat on the memorial, a serene expression on its granite face. Carved into the speckled gray rock were these words: JOEL DAVID PUR-CELL. PRECIOUS SON, GONE TOO SOON.

The son whose death had been recorded in the church records. Recalling the sibling whose life had been sacrificed when her mother was killed, Lilly felt a prickling beneath her eyelids and swallowed back the threat of tears. The monument was a reminder of the fragility of life and how swiftly it could be snatched away.

As she turned to leave, her gaze was drawn to the house. A covered porch spanned the entire back side. On the second floor, a pair of dormer windows looked out over the yard. On the attic floor, she spied the octagonal attic window she'd looked out of the day she'd gone through the house. Another, smaller window with square panes was located some eight or ten feet to the right of that one. She didn't recall seeing another window, but then, she hadn't really been looking.

She was about to leave when she spotted the remains of a wooden cross. The whitewash once covering it was all but gone, and a severe case of rot caused it to lean left. She worked her way through the weeds and briars to get a better look, but if there had been a name on the cross, the elements had long since obliterated it. The Purcells had lost three sons. Was this the grave of another? If so, why was there no stone marker? And why wasn't this child listed in the ledger noting the congregation's deaths?

It's probably the grave of a family pet. Don't you remember when Boots died you made Pierce bury her?

Her cat had gone to kitty heaven complete with a wooden casket and wrapped in a satin blanket Rose had edged with lace. Lilly and Pierce had sneaked into a cemetery in Terre Haute and dug Boots a grave beneath the low boughs of a cedar tree, hoping no one would notice it.

Lilly was so lost in her memories that she was halfway through the side garden before she recognized that niggling feeling that someone was watching her. Anger instead of fear rose inside her. She'd had about enough! Who the devil was it? She certainly didn't think it was a ghost. Had the telegraph operator given the sheriff the message William had sent and had he followed her? Had she misjudged James Reihmann, or had he sent someone else to do his dirty business?

Resisting the urge to whirl around and see if she could spot anyone, she slipped her hand into the pocket of her skirt, reaching for the comfort of her derringer, only to find that it wasn't there. With a thrill of alarm, she remembered that she'd left it in her coat pocket, and her coat was in the buggy. Heart racing, she kept walking at a normal pace, determined not to panic, or at least determined not to let whoever was watching her *know* she was panicked.

She managed to keep her steps slow and steady until she reached the rig, untied the horse, climbed up, and let the gelding trot down the lane and around the sharp curve in the road. Then she gave the animal his head and raced to the main road as fast as he could take her, her rear bouncing up and down on the wooden seat as the wagon wheels skimmed over the rough road. Ireland's Livery was going to start charging her double if she kept bringing back their horses all lathered up.

★ ★ ★

The man who'd followed Lilly to Heaven's Gate returned to town at a leisurely pace. While she was busy inspecting the cemetery, he'd been inspecting the ledgers she'd taken from the house as well as the contents of her coat pockets. When his fingers closed around the four-inch over-and-under Remington derringer in her coat, he'd been a bit surprised. He pulled it out and gave it a cursory once-over. A sardonic smile lifted the corners of his mouth. It was almost identical to the one he carried in an ankle holster above his right boot. The woman might be a bit batty, but she wasn't stupid.

By the time Lilly got to town, the horse had cooled out and once again her fears seemed ridiculous. Berating herself for her foolishness, she sent a telegram to William to let him know she was leaving for Springfield the following morning. She requested he check out Nelson Hargity in New Orleans and said she would be in touch soon. She sent another telegram to Rose and Pierce in Springfield telling them she was coming the following morning. Then she left the buggy at the livery stable and tied up the things she'd gathered at Heaven's Gate with a piece of twine she begged off Billy Bishop.

She was leaving the barn when her attention was caught by movement across the street. On her way to the livery, she'd seen that the boxing ring, mostly hidden from nonpaying customers by a makeshift fence, had been erected on the south side of the courthouse lawn. Now a crowd had gathered, and from where she stood, she was able to see two bare-fisted, shirtless men in high-topped shoes who waited to enter. Neither man was the audacious Irishman.

A memory of the arrogant boxer surfaced. He was strong, she thought, recalling the feel of his hands on her shoulders. And polite and concerned. Truth to tell, just because he'd flirted with her a little was no reason for her to have been so short with him. Perhaps if she saw him again, she would apologize. She squelched the thought as soon as it entered her mind. He meant nothing to her. There was no sense trying to make things right, just because she found him attractive. She'd learned her lesson. The hard way.

CHAPTER 29

Early Monday morning, a well-dressed man watched the Pinkerton agent board the train bound for Springfield. Thank God. He stood staring after the slow-moving train; then he turned and walked away, filled with satisfaction. The status quo might have been shaken, but it was still intact, and she was gone.

Springfield was the juncture for no less than five rail lines. Six thousand miles of track crisscrossed the state and more was under construction. Lilly settled into her seat. All she knew was that despite its many drawbacks, train travel was much easier than stagecoach.

She hoped she was not wasting her time and the agency's money on this trip to the capital, but she truly felt it was necessary to be thorough in her search for the Purcells if she hoped to impress the Pinkerton men.

While the clacking wheels ate up the distance between Vandalia and Springfield, she had ample time to read the ledgers, letters, and journals she'd confiscated at Heaven's Gate. As she thumbed through *Divine Comedy* she saw an underlined passage: *Halfway through life's journey I came to myself in a dark wood, where the straight way was lost.* Had the reverend attached any special significance to the section, or perhaps planned to use it in a sermon?

She set the book aside and continued her search, gleaning a name or two that might bear checking out if this trip bore no fruit. She studied the daguerreotypes of the Purcell family with an intensity that, were it possible, would force the inanimate people to whisper all their secrets.

Sarah was a beautiful young girl, having received the most perfect features of both comely parents. Lilly imagined the portrait in color. Sarah's oval face was the perfect setting for the blue eyes the sheriff had mentioned. She had a straight patrician nose. The blond hair she'd inherited from her mother was pulled back at the sides and hung to her shoulders in barley-sugar curls, revealing small ears that hugged the sides of her head. Her lips were full and softly curved with a slightly pouty look.

The handsome preacher's dark hair was parted just off center and brushed back, shiny with brilliantine. Straight, heavy eyebrows rested on the bony ledge above wide-set eyes, which, if Lilly had to speculate, were the same blue that his daughter's eyes were said to be. His jawline was lean and angular with a deep cleft in his left cheek, and the mustache draping his upper lip drew attention to his finely molded lips. He stood straight and tall and somber in his black frock coat and white vest. His left hand rested on his wife's shoulder.

Though the pose was formal, stiff even, Lilly fancied that the slight lift of his chin and the gleam in his eyes hinted that he believed himself to be just a cut above his fellow man. She wasn't sure if the comments of the Vandalia citizens had skewed her thinking about Purcell, or if her own less-than-perfect experiences with the opposite sex were to blame.

Prudence was a lovely, older version of her daughter, but Lilly imagined she saw tenseness in Mrs. Purcell's shoulders, tightness around her pretty lips, and an expression of melancholy in the eyes that stared straight into the camera. Lilly touched the woman's face with her fingertip.

What did he do to you to make you so unhappy? Did he flaunt his affairs with his female church members? Did he shame you by making you feel you were less than what you thought yourself to be? Did you know he was a thief when you married him, or did learning the truth take the smile from your eyes?

Lilly couldn't fault the preacher's wife. Centuries of submissiveness and dependence had fostered a fragility of both spirit and will in women. Few of her contemporaries would have the courage to speak up if they found themselves wed to a man whose deeds were less than honorable. Fewer still possessed the courage or the wherewithal to walk away. Once again, she thanked God for the assertiveness Pierce and Rose had instilled in her.

Sighing over the unfairness of a world that relegated women to such a fate, she put the picture away and took out the journal William had compiled for the assignment. She hoped a fresh look at it would give her renewed vigor for this last leg of her investigation. She did not want to be the reason her clients were forced to abandon their dream.

The couple who wanted to purchase Heaven's Gate resided in St. Louis. Noah Stephens was an attorney, and his wife, Rachel, was a schoolteacher. Appalled by the number of young women giving birth to babies outside the sanctity of marriage, the couple's goal was to provide a haven where those unfortunates might find sanctuary and comfort instead of censure.

Lilly wondered if Kate might have taken advantage of such a place had it been available when she'd learned she was expecting a child, but knowing her mother's penchant for thumbing her nose at the world and its rules, she doubted it.

Weary with the questions roiling about in her mind, she

put everything back in the carpetbag and leaned her head against the window, hoping to catch a few winks of sleep. It was hopeless. All she could think of was what she would do when she arrived in Springfield.

She would visit churches and see if Harold Purcell was still preaching. Pierce had always been adamant about the notion that people did not change their habits, but she felt that in this case it was a gamble. She believed Harold had been stealing from his church members even before the incident at Vandalia, and that the odds of him abstaining from that practice for twenty years was unlikely. It was also unlikely that he was still in the area. How could he continue pilfering for so many years in one spot without being found out? Still, even if he *had* run true to form, someone might be willing to talk, providing another thread to unravel.

She would go to doctors' offices, since Prudence would have been of childbearing age when they left Vandalia. There were legal records of every kind regarding births, deaths, and property sales, not to mention newspaper morgues. And, as weary as she knew she would be at day's end, she would visit with Pierce and Rose whenever she could, and of course she would go to Chatterton's Opera House.

When Pierce had received her telegram saying she was heading to Springfield, he'd informed her that she must not miss Mary Anderson at Chatterton's. The popular performer would be playing the lead in *Romeo and Juliet*. Though the actress was often criticized by reviewers, most audiences, including Pierce Wainwright, adored Miss Anderson.

Seeing the play at the Fehren and visiting with Nora had made Lilly realize that it wasn't as easy to walk away from one's past as she'd imagined. It would be wonderful to see someone of Mary's acclaim perform.

Somehow, she drifted into a restless sleep until the train halted at its destination. By the time she got checked into the hotel, the day was half gone. Though she longed to go straight to the theater to see Pierce and Rose, she knew she must prioritize her time. The sooner she searched for the missing family through every avenue available, the sooner she could devote time to visiting with her loved ones.

The afternoon was warm. Looking at all the evidence of spring around her, it was hard to believe she'd driven in a snowstorm just days before. The streets of Springfield were broad and generously decorated with shade trees. Knowing she had to be careful with her money, she decided to start out walking and rent a phaeton only when she tired.

Her first stop was one of the two daily newspaper offices, where she spent two hours examining back issues, looking for any mention of Harold or Prudence Purcell, or any reference of thefts of local congregations' coffers. Finding nothing, she walked the few blocks to the second daily, with no better results.

After a late lunch, she decided there was no reason to question the nuns at St. John's Hospital about the possibility of Sarah having been a patient there, since Lilly had learned that the hospital had not been in existence twenty years earlier.

Instead, she decided to finish the day's search at city hall, where she checked land sales, deeds, census reports, and birth and death records. There were three different families of Purcells living in Springfield.

Armed with the facts she needed, she started to leave, but without actually meaning to do so, she found herself thumbing through the death records until she found the date of her mother's murder. And there it was: Katherine Viola Long, age twenty-eight, death by strangulation. Lilly was a bit surprised to learn that her mother was buried in a cemetery just a few blocks away. Feeling that familiar tightness in her chest, she slammed the book closed and headed out into the bright sunlight.

Deciding she had done quite enough sleuthing for one day, she instructed the driver to take her to the theater where Pierce and the ensemble would be performing. There might be time to enjoy an early dinner with him and Rose before the evening performance.

On the way to the theater, the horse and carriage trotted past a park, where she saw a boxing ring set up beneath the canopy of new green leaves. The broadside nailed to a tree was an exact replica of the one put up by the Irishman in Vandalia.

She was struck by the sudden, irrational notion that the boxer was following her. She dismissed the idea with a laugh. It seemed she was growing paranoid since becoming an agent! There was no logical reason a group of pugilists with broken noses and cauliflower ears would follow her from town to town. The truth was simpler and much less forbidding: Like theater troupes, boxers went from place to place in search of new audiences and new revenues. It was inevitable that she would run into some of the same groups. Unfortunately, the life of entertainers was neither simple nor easy.

To Lilly's delight, Pierce and Rose were only too glad to treat her to a meal before the evening performance. They went to a place on Fifth Street called the Café de Paris. The food was excellent, but she was more interested in catching up with what had happened since she'd left the ensemble than with enjoying the culinary fare.

"So, luv, tell us how you like the detecting business."

"Yes, Lil," Rose said. "How is your investigation going?"

Happy to comply, Lilly recounted everything from the time she'd gotten off the train in Vandalia. She told them about the missing family, the town's attitude, the abandoned house, the bloody sheets, and the ghost. She related her discussions with Eloise Mercer, Helen and Virginia Holbrook, the sheriff, the banker, and the attorney. And she told them about her growing feeling that something more than thievery had sent the Purcells running.

She did not mention the warning note that had been slipped beneath her door, or her feeling of being watched at Heaven's Gate, or her chance encounters with the pugilist. Neither did she mention what a failure she felt she was for not uncovering a single valid lead, and definitely not how she was beginning to fear that Pierce and Robert Pinkerton might have been right that she was not suited to the work. She did not want to worry Pierce and Rose unduly, or to admit defeat just yet.

"Of course I think the ghost story is nonsense," she said at the end. "But it is spooky to go inside and see such a fine house abandoned with everything just as it was when they walked away. From all appearances, the entire family left with nothing but the clothes on their backs. And that bloody bed . . ." She gave a little shiver.

"Bed?" Pierce asked, his keen gaze finding hers. "Is seeing the bed what made you remember the day Kate was killed? That's what you meant in the telegram, isn't it?"

Picturing the room in her mind, Lilly's heart began to beat faster, and she tried to hide the trembling in her voice. "Yes. If it is blood, and the sheriff assured me it is, it must have been a grisly slaying. When I saw it, everything about Kate's murder came back with a rush."

Neither spoke, but Lilly knew the time had come to tell them the things her mind had kept locked away from her for eleven long years. Looking from Rose's concerned expression to Pierce's, she related in vivid detail all the remembered horrors of her mother's murder.

"I still wake up nights reliving it," she told them. "And I've become obsessed with men's signet rings. Whenever I see a man wearing one, I find myself checking to see if it looks like the one I remember the killer wearing." She offered a quavering smile. "Still and all, I'm glad I finally remembered what happened. It helps to put the past to rest."

"It will put it to rest for all of us," Rose said, casting a glance at her husband.

"Remembering about the . . . baby was . . . disturbing," Lilly said. She cast a questioning look at Pierce.

"I'm sure it was."

Her mention of the baby Kate had been expecting ushered in an awkward silence. It was impossible to miss the sorrow in Pierce's eyes.

Sensing that the two of them needed a moment, Rose said, "If you'll excuse me, I need to find the necessary."

When she was out of earshot, Pierce said, "She's missed you."

"I've missed her, too. She's the only mother I've known since Mama died." *And you're the only father I've ever known.*

Pierce had always been there between the men who flitted in and out of Kate's life, the one constant in an existence spent traveling the country with a fey, flighty mother whose very nature was as changeable and tumultuous as the sea.

Long before Rose had come into the picture, Lilly recalled herself and Kate, accompanied by Pierce, eating at some of the fanciest hotels in the towns they passed through. He'd always let Lilly order whatever she wanted from the menu. Lilly realized now that he'd been wooing Kate. Aching to know the truth of her paternity and figuring this might be the best opportunity she'd have to ask, she took a steadying breath.

"Pierce?"

"Hmm?"

"I've often wondered if . . ." She hesitated, uncertain how to phrase the question. "I wondered if you knew if I . . ."

He smiled, a wry lift of his lips. "You want to know if I'm your father."

"Yes." It was almost a whisper.

It was his turn to draw a deep breath. The gaze that met hers was steady, unflinching. He reached out and tucked a stray tendril of her dark red hair behind her ear. "I truly don't know, Lilly. I always trusted that Kate was faithful to me the time we were together, but when I gathered enough courage to ask her, she just laughed and asked me if I really wanted to know. At twenty-six, I decided that perhaps I didn't. I had faults and trouble enough of my own, and even then, I knew she wouldn't be happy if I insisted she marry me."

"You loved her." It was as much a question as a statement.

He didn't reply at once. He reached out and covered her hand with his. Its strength and warmth was steadying as always. "A part of me will always love her," he confessed.

"Didn't she love you back?"

"For a while." She saw the need to make her understand in his eyes. "Your mother was like the wind, Lilly. Gentle sometimes, sometimes strong and wild, but always restless, searching for the next good time. You're like her in many ways."

"I certainly hope not!" she cried, and Pierce laughed. "I don't want a parade of men traipsing through my life."

He smiled. "You're nothing like her in that way," he assured her. "But you can be as impulsive and headstrong as she was, something that's more apparent the older you get."

"How?"

"Well, the way you change up dialogue to suit your mood when you're performing, or the way you take impossible jumps when we're riding horses, or—"

"I see," she interrupted, understanding exactly what he meant. "So you don't really know the answer to my question."

He offered her a self-deprecating smile. "There's no way I can ever be sure. I will tell you this. In my heart you're my daughter, and I love you completely."

Lilly felt her eyes fill with tears and saw the sheen in his. Though far from a certainty, it was enough.

"We traveled the same circuit for about five years," he said, continuing the story, "and every day was hell for me, seeing her with other men. I only stayed as long as I did because of you. Finally, out of self-preservation, I took a position with another troupe."

"And met Rose?"

"And met Rose," he said with a smile. "I adore Rose, Lilly. Kate was the love of a young man, but by the time Rose came along, I'd grown up enough to realize what qualities were really important in a woman. Finding her was like finding home again, something I hadn't had since I left England."

There it was again, the infrequent mention of his homeland. All she'd been able to piece together was that as a young man he'd been studying to become a physician, and for some unknown reason, he had abandoned that dream to come to America. He'd never been back to the land of his birth.

"When I met up with Kate again, you were nine. I saw soon enough that nothing had changed. Kate was still Kate, and though I cared for her in many ways, Rose had taught me about the kind of love that lasts a lifetime."

"What did she think about your being in such close contact with Kate again?"

"She knew me well enough to know that I would never betray her. After a year or so, I talked with Rose about confronting Kate again about your paternity. We both felt we could handle things if she said yes, but before I could ask her, she was murdered and I was robbed of the opportunity."

"What did Rose think about you taking me in?"

"She thought it was a wonderful idea. She knew you would need someone. Who better than a childless woman and the man who believed he was your father?"

"Do you have any idea who the baby's father might have been?"

"None," he said with a shake of his head. "Kate was pretty secretive about her liaisons."

They saw Rose coming back, and the conversation came to an abrupt halt. After Pierce helped her into her seat, he cleared his throat, and said, "About your investigation. I agree that something more than Purcell taking the money is at the root of the folks in town refusing to talk about him. And you could be on the right track about him indulging himself with the women of the congregation. That would be an embarrassment to everyone, something they'd not want some stranger resurrecting. It's easy to see how your questions might put them on edge."

His intelligent gaze found Lilly's once more. "Did anyone in the area come up missing about that time? If so, it might suggest who the victim was."

"No one I interviewed mentioned anyone."

"Would you feel better knowing for certain the stains are indeed blood?"

Lilly's expression brightened. Since Pierce had been studying medicine before the incident that had forced him to leave his native country and come to America, he was still interested in the subject and he made it a point to keep up with all the newest happenings in the medical world. "Are you telling me there's something I can do to prove it?"

"Indeed there is," he told her. "Guaiac. It's a compound made from parts of a West Indian tree called Guaiacum. It's been used for centuries to treat syphilis, arthritis, and coughs, but they've found out that if you use it in conjunction with hydrogen peroxide on stool samples it reacts to blood."

"Pierce!" Rose admonished with a frown. "This is hardly polite dinner conversation."

"Sorry, luv," Pierce told her with a smile. "Just trying to help. Peroxide alone might be a better choice for this, though.

And then of course, there's benzidine, which is used in dye making. It would work, too."

"Dye making?"

He nodded. "When it comes into contact with blood, it turns blue. The problem is that the stains are so old, I'm not sure any of these compounds would work."

"Well, I thank you for the suggestion, and it is all very fascinating, of course," Lilly said, "but the thing of it is that while my curiosity is aroused about what went on in that house, it has no bearing whatsoever on my assignment. My job is to find Purcell and see if he'll sell, which is how I wound up here. This was the only place mentioned they might have come, because of their daughter's tuberculosis."

"And did you find out anything today?" Rose asked.

"Not much of use. Located three Purcell families living here, and I plan to visit them tomorrow. If none of them is the preacher, I have no choice but to go back to Chicago and admit to William I've failed—but not before going to Chatterton's to see Mary Anderson," she added with a smile, hoping to turn the conversation to a more pleasant topic.

"Speaking of seeing people, did you get in touch with Nora before you left Vandalia?" Rose asked.

"I did," Lilly said with another smile. "We shared a late dessert after the play."

"How is she?" Pierce asked. "Still the same fun-loving Nora?"

"Very much so," Lilly said. "But she's leaving the theater in a couple of weeks to go to Texas and become a mail-order bride."

"A mail-order bride! I can't believe it!" Rose said, placing her palms on her cheeks in incredulity.

"Neither can I," Lilly said. "But she says she's tired of living a nomadic life, and she wants a family."

"Well, she's a fine woman," Pierce said. "Whoever this rancher is, he's lucky to get her."

Lilly said good-bye to them thirty minutes later and returned to her hotel with depression weighing heavily on her. Tomorrow it would be back to the job and asking questions to which she would receive few satisfactory answers. Back to being alone.

This is what you wanted, Lilly.

As Rose always said, "Be careful what you wish for; you might get it."

CHAPTER 30

Two of the Purcells Lilly located the next day had no connection to the reverend. The first was a little prune-like man whose gnarled, arthritic hands were covered with liver spots and shook with the palsy. He clearly suffered from dementia. After speaking with him for less than a minute, Lilly wondered how he'd found his way to the door. She thanked him and went to her second stop, a young wife with a baby on her hip and a toddler clinging to her skirts.

It was late morning when the driver pulled the rented hack to a stop in front of the third house, her last hope of finding Harold Purcell in the capital. She approached the Greek Revival–style home, torn between thankfulness that her search was nearly at an end and a deep-seated hope that this final stop would prove to be the right one. Either way, she should be finished with her inquiries by noon. Somewhat disheartened, she banged the brass knocker against the Federal blue door that was flanked by narrow sidelights and topped with a transom of rectangular lights.

However this meeting turned out, she would go back to

the hotel knowing she had done all she could to find the preacher and his family. In fact, she would celebrate the end of her inquiries by luxuriating in a hot bath with a generous handful of the rose and chamomile bath salts Rose had given her for Christmas. She would treat herself to a nice dinner at Delaney's French Café and Saloon, which was just down the street from her hotel, and then she would hire herself a cab to transport her to Chatterton's. Tomorrow she would go back to Chicago and see what new assignment William had for her, if he decided to keep her on. She was so caught up in her plans for the evening that when the door opened, she gave a little start.

The years had not been kind to Prudence Purcell, but there was little doubt in Lilly's mind that she was indeed staring at the minister's wife. Though probably in her early fifties, the woman looked much older. Even the red merino Garibaldi blouse worn over a black skirt and belted around her still-slender waist was old, a style more likely to be seen during the sixties. Her blond hair was threaded with skeins of gray. Her delicate features were now drawn and haggard, and the firm lines of her face had given way to sags, wrinkles, and dark pouches that not even a dusting of powder and a touch of rouge could hide. Lilly felt a glimmer of admiration for Prudence's valiant attempt to hold her own against the encroaching years.

"May I help you?"

There was nothing soft about the voice. The older woman's tone was all business, almost sharp. "Mrs. Harold Purcell?" Lilly asked.

"Who's asking?"

Smiling, she extended her gloved hand, where her badge rested. "Lilly Long. With the Pinkerton Detective Agency."

Prudence's eyes widened and then narrowed. She withdrew her partially extended hand.

"There's no need for alarm, Mrs. Purcell," Lilly said, tucking the badge into her reticule. "I'm only here representing some clients who are trying to contact your husband regarding a business matter."

The wariness on Prudence's face vanished. "I see. I'm sorry to say that my husband was"—she paused, as if searching for the right words—"cruelly snatched from the life he so loved several years ago, Miss . . ."

"Long," Lilly supplied again, taken aback by the news of the preacher's death. "I'm so sorry for your loss, Mrs. Purcell. Please forgive me for bringing up such a difficult topic."

"That isn't a problem, Miss Long. There is no way you could have known."

"Do you perhaps handle your husband's affairs now?" Lilly asked.

"With the assistance of my attorney," she said with a nod.

"I hate to impose, but would it be possible for me to come inside and discuss the matter with you? It won't take long, and I've traveled some distance to locate you."

"Certainly, my dear. I was just brewing a pot of tea, and you can join me. Do you mind waiting here for just a moment, while I put the dog in another room? Strangers upset him."

"Not at all."

Prudence was back in no time, stepping aside and leading the way to the parlor. "Please make yourself at home. The tea will be ready in a few minutes."

It was getting on toward noon, and Lilly was glad for the offer of refreshment. From the kitchen, Prudence's low, soothing voice could be heard as she spoke to the dog.

While her hostess was preparing the tea, Lilly pulled off her gloves and strolled about the room, examining the décor and hoping to find some clue to the personalities of the occupants. The walls were papered with a panoramic landscape, something only the very wealthy could afford. The oak floors gleamed with beeswax and lemon balm. Delicate lace and crisscrossed draperies in heavy bronze-green brocade graced the leaded glass windows, and two crystal chandeliers hung suspended from the ceiling.

The preacher had spared no expense, either in purchasing the house or in its décor, using his ill-gotten money on ornate furnishings reminiscent of those at Heaven's Gate. This house, too, was stilted and formal, far too elaborate for Lilly's taste, not to mention it was somewhat depressing. It was as stripped of personality as the Purcell family photograph in her carpetbag.

There were no photographs sitting around the parlor, no portraits on the wall, no knitting bag with a half-finished muffler trailing over the side, and no books that might suggest an outside interest. Only a cabinet of bird's-eye maple displaying a collection of pistols gave any clue to the homeowners' personalities.

From her shooting days with Pierce, who felt it necessary to study various aspects of anything that snared his interest, Lilly recognized a .67 caliber weapon, reported to be the choice of George Washington; a flintlock, which was considered the first accepted military pistol; a breechloader; a percussion pistol; and a fancy little derringer with a scrimshaw grip. The others were unfamiliar and fancier, no doubt crafted as much for their beauty as their usefulness.

She was contemplating the inadequacy of her own little derringer when Prudence returned bearing a gleaming silver tea service and a plate of coconut cookies.

"Harold collected those." Prudence set the tray on an intricate inlaid table that sat in front of a medallion-back sofa upholstered in Indian-red velvet.

Lilly imagined she heard disapproval in her hostess's voice. "It's quite a nice collection." *But a strange one for a preacher.*

"Oh, yes," Prudence said, settling onto the couch and concentrating on pouring the steaming tea into a delicate Spode cup. "Harold was quite the collector . . . of many things. Sugar?" she asked, the silver tongs poised over a plate of sugar cubes.

"Two, please," Lilly said, taking a seat in a paisley wing chair. "No cream or lemon."

She took the bone china cup and added a couple of the proffered cookies to her plate. While they shared the tea, the two women chatted about the beautiful spring weather, books they had read, and Mary Anderson's upcoming performance, which Lilly confessed she planned to attend that evening.

She finished the cookies and declined a second cup of tea. "That was delicious, thank you. It was kind of you to offer it."

"I enjoy a good cup of tea," Prudence said with a slight smile. "But there is seldom anyone around with whom to share a cup." Refilling her own teacup, she leaned against the sofa's back. "Now what was it you wanted to discuss?"

"As I said earlier, the agency I work for was approached by a couple who would like to buy Heaven's Gate. They hoped to turn it into a home for unwed mothers, but they were unable to locate your husband to see if he might sell. They contacted the agency, and Mr. Pinkerton asked that I try to locate the reverend."

From the room next door, a loud crash sounded. Prudence stood, her eyes narrowed once more, and her thin lips turned upward at the corners into a semblance of a smile. She gave a despairing shake of her head. "That scoundrel dog! I know better than to bring him inside. Forever into something. He'll be sorry when I get in there to him. Please excuse me, Miss Long."

Lilly offered an understanding smile.

Prudence was back in a couple of minutes, a smile of satisfaction curving her lips. She did not speak until she'd taken another sip of her tea. "Where were we? Oh, yes, the home for unwed mothers. I must say it is quite noble of your clients to want to help young girls who find themselves in such dire straits." Her tone and expression suggested thoughtfulness.

"It is," Lilly agreed. "It seems it is always the females who are doomed to suffer the consequences of an unfortunate liaison, or . . . worse." As soon as she said the words, she wished she could call them back. The last thing she wanted to do was remind Prudence of her husband's indiscretions, if indeed he *had* sullied his marriage vows.

Prudence's smile never reached her eyes. "I agree wholeheartedly. Men are much more callous—even indifferent to a woman's lot, yet we love them anyway, don't we?" Her steady gaze met Lilly's. "Have you ever been in love, Miss Long?"

What a strange question coming from someone she'd just met. Nevertheless, she considered how Tim had made her feel, at least for a short time. Again she wondered if her feelings were love, or if she'd been in love with the notion of loving him. "I'm not sure," she said at last. "At the time, I believed I was."

"Then you know full well that when you love someone you'll do anything for them, don't you?"

Lilly thought of how she'd given Timothy money, knowing he would use it to fuel his gambling habit, knowing he had no intention of replacing it, no plans to change his life.

"Unfortunately, I do." Uncomfortable with the turn of the conversation and the reminder of her misplaced feelings, she sought a more neutral topic.

"I went out to Heaven's Gate before coming here. The house needs a lot of work after sitting empty for so many years. Many of the furnishings are in bad condition, but others need only a cleaning up, and the bric-a-brac and dishes and such are all intact. I would think they would fetch you a good price, if you decide to sell. Or perhaps you'd like to keep some of the nicer pieces for yourself."

"I have all I need right here," Prudence said. "And I want nothing from there to remind me of that time in my life."

Lilly immediately thought of the baby boy who'd died. She recalled the name on the headstone: Joel David Purcell. Then there was a daughter's sickness and a husband's thievery and possible unfaithfulness. She didn't blame Prudence for wanting to leave it all behind.

Her hostess dabbed at her mouth with a damask napkin and set down her cup. "I do wish these nice people success with their venture, Miss Long, but Heaven's Gate is not for sale."

Expecting Prudence to jump at the chance to rid herself of the reminder of her unfortunate past, Lilly was stunned by the firmness of the decision. She struggled to form a suitable reply besides the obvious *why*. "Perhaps you're saving it for Sarah, then," she said, trying and failing to make sense of the refusal.

"Sarah?" Prudence repeated with a puzzled frown. "Oh, dear, no." Her eyes clouded with memory. "Sarah died before we left Heaven's Gate."

It was all Lilly could do to hide her shock. Why had no one in Vandalia told her? Poor, poor Prudence! A scoundrel for a husband, and all her children dead. "I . . . I must apologize again, Mrs. Purcell," she stammered. "Had I known, I would never have brought up the subject. Her passing must have been quite grievous for you."

"Her loss was . . . very difficult for both of us," Prudence replied, "but I believe her father took it the hardest."

There was something in the older woman's tone that Lilly couldn't put her finger on, so jumbled were her thoughts. "Was that Sarah's grave out back, then?" Lilly asked. "The one with the wooden cross?"

For a moment, Prudence looked confused, then a bit agitated. Then she smiled a bright, artificial smile. "If there is a grave there, then I suppose it must be, mustn't it?"

What a strange answer. But then, Prudence Purcell was a strange woman. Why could she not recall the grave of her daughter? Was it possible she suffered from hardening of the arteries?

Clearly disturbed, the older woman rose and went to stare out the window. "I did what I could, Miss Long . . . what I had to do. Harold was in a hurry to leave, and there just wasn't time . . ."

Guilt, then. She feels guilty because there had been no time to have a proper headstone made before she'd left Heaven's Gate and was forced to use a wooden cross. "Was your time cut short because of the money Harold took from the church?" Lilly asked, finding the nerve to pose the prying question.

Prudence turned toward Lilly, her face pale, her eyes wide with shock. "Harold took money from the church?"

Either Prudence knew nothing of the theft, or she was a consummate actress, Lilly thought. "You didn't know." It was a statement, not a question.

"I had no idea." Prudence gave a shake of her head.

"Do you think he'd done it before, in other places you lived?" Lilly asked, daring to put forth one of her theories.

Clasping her hands together against her chest, Prudence shook her head and turned back to the window. "I have no idea. He handled all our finances, of course. He told me his family sent him money. His part of a trust fund or some such thing."

Lilly's already low regard for the preacher sank to new depths. Harold had left the impression that it was Prudence who received money from someone. She longed to probe deeper, to ask about the bloody bed, but she'd already ruined the woman's day by dredging up painful memories and breaking the news that her husband had been a thief. She sighed. Besides, as she'd told Pierce and Rose, her own curiosity had nothing to do with her assignment, which she had now completed.

Heaven's Gate was not for sale.

"Well, since you won't sell, I have no choice but to let my employer know so that he can contact our client." She pulled on her gloves and picked up her reticule. "Thank you for your hospitality, Mrs. Purcell. And again, I apologize for any grief I may have caused you."

"There are many kinds of grief, Miss Long," Prudence said. "As Christians, we must accept it with as much grace as possible and deal with it as best we can."

Lilly thought of all Prudence had suffered. Strange or not, she was a remarkable woman to have come through her difficulties and still maintain such a wonderful attitude.

"Yes," she replied, standing. "You're right. I'll see myself out. Thank you again for the tea and hospitality."

She was almost across the room when she heard her hostess mutter something beneath her breath. She wasn't certain, but it sounded like, "What else, Harry? What else?"

Lilly stepped out onto the porch, filled with conflicting emotions. Her first assignment as a Pinkerton was completed, but her sense of accomplishment was tempered with a bit of dismay for having disrupted Prudence's life and informing her of her husband's misdeed.

She headed down the brick walkway to the street where her buggy and driver waited. As she approached the thoroughfare, she saw an ancient, rail-thin woman with a straw hat tied beneath her chin. Hoe in hand, she was attacking a flower bed near her front fence with more vigor than Lilly would have dreamed possible. As she neared the rig, the woman glanced up. Dropping the hoe, she gave a wild wave of her skinny arms.

"Yoo-hoo!" she called in a quavering voice, hurrying toward the fence as quickly as her legs would take her. "You there! Oh, miss!"

Lilly paused and then walked toward the elderly woman. "Yes?" she asked with a patient smile.

"I'm Victoria Langley. I see you've been visiting with my neighbor."

"Yes," Lilly acknowledged with a slow nod, wondering where the conversation was leading.

"I just moved here last fall, and I've barely set eyes on her all winter," Victoria Langley said, blotting her pink cheek with the back of her hand. "How is the poor thing? I worry about her, her having so much to do and all."

Lilly felt bad. She had mistaken Mrs. Langley's concern for prying. She wondered what it was that Prudence had to do besides clean the huge house. And, if Lilly were a betting person—which she certainly wasn't—she'd wager Prudence hired that done for her.

"We had tea, and she seemed well." Lilly smiled. "I'm sure she would love to have you visit. She said she hardly ever had anyone over to share tea with."

"Oh, I hate to bother her. He takes up so much of her time."

Lilly's smile faded. "He?"

"Yes, her brother. He's wheelchair bound. Some sort of riding accident years ago, I think she said."

Prudence locked the door behind her departed guest. Picking up the tea service, she carried it through the dining room and used her hip to push open the swinging door to the kitchen. Setting the tray onto a long wooden table, she turned a bright smile to the man sitting in a wheelchair, a napkin tied around his mouth and his wrists bound to the chair's arms with strips of leather. A wooden tray sat on the table next to him and a shattered cup lay next to the chair in a puddle of tea.

Lilly would not have recognized the once-handsome preacher. His dark hair was mostly gray and hung to his shoulders. His lean body was nothing but an awkward frame for the covering of papery-white skin. Grooved cheeks had become hollow, and the beautiful mouth was now twisted into a grotesque half smile—when it was not gagged. His good looks were gone, stolen by time and the ravages of a series of strokes. Only the fire in his eyes and the twitch of the fingers of his right hand suggested that there was life inside the cadaverous body.

Ignoring his blistering gaze, Prudence unfastened the napkin from his mouth. She paid no more heed to the hatred that burned in his eyes than she did the drool of saliva that trailed down his chin. Wiping his mouth, she untied the leather restraints. His face contorted with the effort of trying to speak. Nothing emerged from his mouth but garbled grunts and moans.

She gave his mouth another swipe, and said, "There, that's better, isn't it? I'm sorry I had to restrain you, my love. I know you don't like it, but I've told you to be very quiet when we have guests, and now see what happens when you aren't. We both know you knocked over that cup deliberately, to get Miss Long's attention."

She gave him a loving smile and brushed back an errant lock of his hair. "You're such a naughty boy, and you must be punished. I know you get lonely with just me for company, but we couldn't have Miss Long seeing you, now could we? Not when I led her to believe you were dead, and we've managed to keep your whereabouts a secret for so many years. Just think of what a scandal it would be if people found out you're still alive," she crooned.

The man in the chair heard and understood every word she said, but he could not respond in any way, imprisoned as he was in his bodily hell. His answer was a guttural grunt.

"No! Don't blame me," she said in a stern voice. "You brought it all on yourself." She wagged an admonishing finger at him. "Miss Long said you took from the congregation in Vandalia. Good heavens, Harry! What were you thinking? The good book says 'your sins will find you out.'"

Stepping behind him, she gripped the chair's back and pushed him out the hall door toward the rear of the house. Sunshine filled the room, which boasted windows on three sides and a plethora of plants. The cheerfulness of the room matched her voice and mocked the man in the chair.

"Are you ready for your lunch?" she asked. "I made some

lovely asparagus soup. When I get it warmed up, we'll have lunch and then we'll have our nap. Law! I'm just worn out. I'm not used to company anymore."

Bending over, she closed her eyes and rested her cheek against the top of his head, circling his neck from behind. "Oh, Harry, the last years have been wonderful, haven't they? Just the two of us. You know how much I love you, don't you? For better, for worse, in sickness and in health. Till death do us part."

A single tear rolled down his cheek. Filled with a rage he was helpless to exhibit, Harold Purcell closed his eyes and prayed. If the past seventeen years had done anything, it had improved his prayer life. Death was something he prayed for every day. Death for them both.

CHAPTER 31

Back in her room, Lilly stripped down to her chemise and pantaloons, donned her wrapper, and tried to rest, but after more than an hour of flouncing around on the bed, she gave up, dressed in a simple skirt and blouse, and went down to the hotel restaurant for a cup of coffee.

She sipped at the murky brew and wondered why she was in such a strange mood. Certainly the time spent with Prudence Purcell had not been what one might call an enlightening hour, though she had accomplished what William Pinkerton had asked of her: located the Purcells—or what was left of them—and found out that Heaven's Gate was not for sale. William would have to advise the Stephenses to locate another property for their venture. End of case.

It was not, however, the end of Lilly's questions, questions that had no relevance to the assignment, but refused to give her peace. Prudence wouldn't sell at any price. Why? She'd lost a son and daughter while living at Heaven's Gate. Her husband had stolen from his church, so she would never again be welcome in the area, nor had she any plans to go back and claim any of the many treasures still housed within the crumbling walls. Clearly she wanted no reminders of the place or the time, which was understandable. So why not sell and be rid of it once and for all?

And what of this brother the neighbor spoke of? Where did he fit into this strange tale? According to Victoria Langley, Prudence's brother had been injured when they were in their teens. She had cared for him for years—since their parents passed. Lilly wondered why no one in Vandalia had seen fit to mention a brother. Had it been too much of a chore to take him to town? Had there been so few visitors to the house? Had he only come into her care since she'd left Heaven's Gate? Did the people of Vandalia even know of his existence?

"She's a saint, Prudence is! A wonderful Christian woman."

Lilly didn't know if Prudence was the saint Victoria believed her to be, but suffering the indignities and sorrows of life and still maintaining her positive nature made her a good Christian woman in Lilly's book.

A tinkling laugh from across the room banished her worrisome feelings and brought her thoughts back to the present. She glanced at the watch pinned to her jacket. It was high time she started her preparations for the evening.

An hour and a half later, Lilly regarded her reflection in the cheval mirror. She was bathed, powdered, rouged, and dressed in her best finery, a dress of champagne-hued gossamer satin overlaid with chiffon. She'd found a woman who worked for the hotel to lace her into her corset while she muttered about the misery the undergarment brought. It was amazing how quickly she had grown used to going without it. Now she could scarcely draw a satisfactory breath, but seeing how the fabric of the gown clung and how tiny her waist looked, she allowed herself a rare bit of vanity, deciding that perhaps she could stand the torturous contraption for a few hours.

A swathe of the delicate fabric draped the low-cut bodice of her gown, almost resembling cap sleeves over her shoulders. The narrow skirt was overlaid with sheer fabric in horizontal, swag-like draping down the front of the skirt, and was caught just below her waist in the back. It tumbled down over her bustle in a cascade of lush fabric that fell to the floor in a swooping train.

Her critical gaze moved up. She'd swept her dark red hair away from her oval face and rolled it into a classic chignon at the nape of her neck. Since she had no bangs, she had coaxed some shorter strands around her face into curls with the help of the curling rod Rose had insisted she bring.

"You cannot allow yourself to lose your femininity, Lilly, even though you will be doing the work of a man."

A light dusting of powder gave her skin translucence, and her cheekbones and lips had been pinked with so deft a hand that only the most critical scrutiny would detect it.

Since she had no fine jewelry, Rose had fashioned a wide brown velvet ribbon that fit perfectly around Lilly's slender throat and pinned a delicate cameo brooch to it. The brooch was one of the few good pieces she'd inherited from Kate, likely a gift from a lover.

As she stood before the mirror, checking her handiwork, her eyes widened. Rose would be pleased, Lilly thought. Gone was the skinny, plain, red-haired girl and the average-looking woman who'd returned her gaze from the mirror for twenty-two years.

Tonight a stranger stared back at her. She was not fixed up to look like a stage character. She hadn't been made up to look like the Southern belle, Mrs. Cartwright. She looked feminine. Stylish. She looked, she thought on a sharply indrawn breath . . . very much like her mother.

The realization should have been pleasing, and it was, yet the pleasure was tempered by the fear that had plagued her from the time she'd figured out the truth about Kate's lifestyle. She didn't want to be like Kate. Wouldn't.

She reached for her wrap and paused. Was that fear the reason she'd chosen to portray a picture of drabness to the world? Oh, she was always neat and tidy, but her choice of clothing had always been simple, unassuming, and unadorned. Her hairstyle, usually a no-nonsense knot atop her head, reflected that unpretentiousness. Had she downplayed her looks all these years because she was trying so hard to distance herself from her mother? Was she inviting some sort of disaster tonight?

Just because you see some of Kate's beauty in yourself for the first time doesn't mean that you will somehow take on her bad tendencies.

The reminder set her mind at ease. She was going to the theater, and she would enjoy the night, whatever it brought. Grabbing her bronze-toned velvet wrap, she went downstairs and hailed a cab to take her to dinner.

The drive to the restaurant was short and uneventful. As she entered the eating establishment, she decided that Delaney's French Café would be worth whatever it cost. The elegantly appointed restaurant was impressive with its white linens, silver flatware, and gleaming wood. Paintings in the style of the Pre-Raphaelites adorned the wine-colored walls, and strategically placed statuary and hothouse ferns added a touch of elegance.

As she followed the maître d' to the table, she could not deny that many masculine heads turned her way. Neither could she deny that the attention pleased her. She wondered fleetingly what her mother would think of her. Would she be as proud of her grownup daughter as Pierce and Rose were?

It doesn't matter a fig!

Except that somewhere deep inside, it did. Even in death, Kate had the ability to influence Lilly's thoughts and feelings. Still, as long as she was careful to not imitate her mother's behavior, perhaps all would be well.

After perusing the menu's offerings, she treated herself to a veal cutlet in a wine sauce, with tiny baked redskin potatoes dripping butter and sprinkled with parsley, as well as fresh asparagus that had been shipped on a refrigerated rail car. For dessert, she chose a cup of coffee and a slice of decadently rich chocolate cake topped with fresh-whipped cream. Then, feeling as if she needed a nap instead of an evening out, she gladly paid her exorbitant bill, then hired a cab to take her to the theater on Jefferson Street.

Her driver pulled up behind a rig with SALZENSTEIN'S emblazoned on the door and took his place in line so as to let her disembark near the chain-suspended overhang that offered protection to the arriving patrons in the event of inclement weather. Several other hired hacks were lined up, waiting to discharge their passengers in front of the unprepossessing building.

Formerly Rudolph's, the new Chatterton's Opera House was the result of a reconstruction effort by George W. Chatterton, Sr. He had purchased the building after it suffered a devastating fire five years earlier.

With its reputation of being "the finest theater in the middle west" and of showcasing the crème de la crème of the theatrical world, her first impression was disappointment, especially since it was well-known that Mr. Chatterton had used the talents of a New York architect. The building sat in an area amongst several saloons, with one called Sullivan's next door. Most likely, they did a brisk business before and after the performances.

Stifling her disillusionment, she dismounted, paid the driver, gathered her skirts in one hand, and stepped through the main door. Looking around, she saw the ticket booth inside to the left. Thankfully, she was able to bypass it. When she'd first arrived in town, she'd asked for information about purchasing a ticket at her hotel and was told that since she'd waited until the last moment, she should make haste to Chatterton's Jewelry store to purchase a ticket before the performance sold out.

Off to the jeweler's she had gone. Reserved seating was out

of the question, and she was thankful to snare one of the few remaining balcony tickets for one dollar, though even that was a bit rich for her blood. She would have been just as thrilled to watch the play from the lower-priced seating in the gallery, as long as she had the opportunity to see Miss Anderson's performance.

When Lilly told the austere female behind the display counter she would take the balcony seat, the odious woman had leaned over the glass encasement filled with expensive baubles and snatched the money from her hand. Then she'd pointed her nose toward the ceiling and told Lilly in a haughty tone that if she should ever hope to attend such a stellar performance in the future, she should buy her ticket well in advance.

At the last minute, on the off chance that the woman might remember, she showed the clerk a sketch she'd made of the signet ring and asked if she recalled anyone purchasing such an item. The answer had been a chilly, unequivocal "no," which was what Lilly expected.

Now, as she checked her wrap with a young woman who handed her the stub of a claim ticket, she asked if there was anyone who might have worked there eleven years earlier. Maybe someone would remember a man with a signet ring and the letter "T." The young lady pointed toward Chester Carpenter, the ticket taker.

Along with other theatergoers, Lilly made her way toward Mr. Carpenter. Now was not a good moment to conduct an interview, but she did ask him if they could speak at some other time. Giving her an inquisitive look, he assured her that if she came back after the performance, he would be happy to oblige her. She smiled and thanked him.

She then was pushed along by the crowd, which split into three lines as they made their way to their allotted seats: Lilly to the left and the gallery; the balcony viewers to the right.

The patrons bearing tickets for the coveted, reserved, dollar-and-a-half seats went straight ahead.

The sound of the orchestra warming up set her heart racing. Unseen fingertips danced over keys, offering pitch and running through finger-limbering scales. Violin strings twanged and whined, a backdrop for the clear sweet sound of horns of every kind. It was seldom she was on this side of the stage, and never before had she been permitted the opportunity to watch an actress with the accomplishment of Mary Anderson. It was a night she knew she would remember forever.

Lilly's first glimpse of the auditorium brought a gasp of surprise and pleasure. If she'd been disenchanted with the building's exterior, the inside more than made up for it. She lifted her gaze to the ceiling where a scattering of trumpet-blowing cherubs cavorted over the highly wrought expanse. The marvelous, new-fangled wonder of electricity sent dozens—if not hundreds—of bulbs aglow from the enormous chandelier that hung from the center, illuminating the rich and not-so-rich of Springfield society. They were all decked out in their finest, with jewels glittering from wrists and ears and necks while others nestled in the cleavage of plump bosoms.

Red and gilt abounded. Curtains draped the walls, many surrounded by framed advertisements of local businesses: Myers Great Bargain Emporium for men's clothing, hot and cold baths for the whole family at the St. Nicholas Hotel and Barber Shop, fine dining at J. Maldaner's European Restaurant on Fifth Street, and all sorts of grocery items—from plain to fancy—could be found at Connelly's and Wickersham's.

The lights had not yet gone down, and her rapt gaze moved from the figures in the orchestra pit to the double tiers of boxes on either side of the proscenium. She gave a sigh of purest plea-sure and sank into her seat. It wasn't long before the lights went down and the audience began to settle in, shifting and whispering, eagerly awaiting the first line. A man wearing just his shirt sleeves and a derby hat peeked around the curtain, and the footlights went up. The curtains swished open revealing the set director's vision of a public place in Verona, Italy. *Romeo and Juliet,* the tale of young star-crossed lovers, began.

Lilly was so caught up in the story that it was intermission time before she realized it. She joined the others making their way to the lobby, more in the hope that standing might ease her protesting ribcage than a desire to mix and mingle.

The area was packed. Soon cigar and pipe smoke floated on the currents of dozens of conversations and the occasional burst of laughter. Dark-clad bodies brushed against ivory skin and a shifting rainbow sea of satin, taffeta, and lace gowns. Feeling a bit out of place, she was admiring a framed broadside of Miss Anderson that touted the play, when a gravelly voice said, "Quite lovely, isn't she?"

Lilly turned to see a tightly coiffed, too-rouged woman of indeterminate age, who introduced herself as Matilda Hawthorne and immediately launched into an account of her recent trip to Philadelphia. She gushed over her meeting with Diamond Jim Brady and seeing the incomparable Lillian Russell's performance at The Walnut. Lilly was only half listening to the woman's garrulous praise when she looked up and saw a familiar figure.

The boxer! While her mind registered the phenomenon, he gave her his familiar audacious wink. For a moment, she was too stunned to do more than stare at him. When reason returned, she deliberately focused her attention back to the ancient dowager.

"My, my," the woman said, her fan swishing back and forth in front of her face. "What a forward young man. Do you know him?"

"No, I've just seen him . . . around." Was he following her as she'd first thought when she'd seen the notice?

"Well, he certainly seems smitten with you. Oh, dear! Here he comes." Clearly interested in whatever was about to transpire, Matilda Hawthorne moved closer to Lilly and watched curiously as the "forward young man" approached them.

He looked to be in his late twenties, Lilly thought. Other than the scar on his cheek, the bump on his oft-broken nose, and the breadth of his shoulders, which was somewhat rare in the aristocratic circles of the upper class, there was little about him to suggest he was anything but a well-heeled young man about town. His hair had been touched with brilliantine in an effort to subdue the unruly dark waves into a semblance of neatness. He was clean shaven but for his neatly trimmed mustache. A two-button black dinner jacket with a satin shawl collar covered a wing-collared, stiff-fronted white shirt. Black, narrow-toed dress shoes and a white bow tie completed his fashionable evening attire.

His smile included Lilly and her companion.

Her initial impression of the boxer in Vandalia had been that he was flirty and supremely confident. His easy charm, so reminiscent of Timothy's behavior, was apparent by the way he moved through the crowd, smiling and speaking to every man and woman along the way. As the Red Sea had for the Israelites, the sea of bodies parted for him.

As he drew closer, his discerning blue gaze found hers. His mouth, beneath the dark mustache, lifted in another of those lazy smiles. Her fingers tightened around her beaded reticule. He stopped in front of her and Matilda, and made a huge show of kissing the older woman's hand and complimenting her on her attire. Matilda blushed and fluttered about like a bird in spring.

Good grief! The man was an inveterate flirt. If his behavior as he crossed the room was anything to go by, he chatted up anything in skirts. As she stood watching him and Matilda bantering back and forth, she became aware of the manly scent that emanated from him. It wasn't the bay rum he'd favored before—thank goodness—but something that smelled of sandalwood and patchouli and whispered of the Orient. She pressed her lips together and stiffened her spine.

Another well-dressed matriarch approached and took Matilda's arm, tugging her toward a small group across the way with a murmured apology. They gave a little wave to Lilly and sailed into the crowd.

The stranger focused his attention on her, his considering gaze traveling from her feet to the top of her head. Missing nothing.

"Hullo, ma'am," he said with another smile. "It seems our paths were destined to cross again." His rich Irish brogue fell from his finely shaped lips with lilting ease.

"By no fault of mine, I assure you," Lilly responded in a chilly tone, her awareness making her forget her vow to be pleasant to him. "I begin to think you are following me."

"And why would you be thinking that?" he asked, suddenly solemn.

Why was it, she wondered, that most dark-haired, blue-eyed people were exceedingly attractive?

"Perhaps because you do not appear to be the type to enjoy the theater."

He placed his right hand over his heart, as if her words wounded him. "Ouch! Pretty to look at, but sharp of tongue." The expression in his eyes was serious as he said, "I assure you, madam, that I have connections to the theater that go back to my youth, and I am not following you. I'm merely goin' where I'm sent, tryin' to make an honest living. What type of person *do* you have me pegged for, if I may be so bold to ask?"

"Well, after assessing each of our meetings, I think you are a man who uses his looks and his charm to get your way with women. I believe you are as good an actor as Miss Anderson is an actress."

He laughed softly. Despite her determination, the husky sound sent a shiver of responsiveness through her.

Unmindful of her inner turmoil, the stranger gave a negligent shrug. "I told you I see no harm in a little flirting, and I cannot deny that I've had my share of success with the fair sex."

"Oh, I do not doubt it," she replied crossly.

Drat the man! He was too likeable for his own good or anyone else's for that matter. *Think of Timothy hurting you and Rose, of him stealing and spending your hard-earned money. Think of him doing that to all those other women.*

"And you think that the attention I'm payin' to you is an act, that I have no real interest beyond my . . . 'gettin' my way' with you?" he asked, that teasing glint back in his eyes.

"I dare say you do not want to know what I think, sir."

He stared down at her, and before she knew what he was about, he reached out and touched her mouth with his fingertip. " '. . . teach not thy lip such scorn, for it was made for kissing, lady, not for such contempt . . .' "

Lilly gasped, whether in surprise that he knew Shakespeare or shock at his boldness, she could not say. How dare he quote the bard to her! How dare he touch her! "Sir, you go too far!"

The teasing light in his eyes vanished, along with his smile. "Perhaps you're right, ma'am," he said. "My most humble apology." With a slight bow, he turned and left her to stew in her own ire.

CHAPTER 32

Lilly stood there for several seconds, willing calmness. Rude, obnoxious man! She fluttered her fan in front of her face, trying to cool her anger and the heat of her embarrassment, but both raged too hotly inside her. Blast Tim, and blast the boxer, whoever he was! She had a job to do, and she would do it right, and Robert Pinkerton, Timothy Warner, and this burly buffoon could just go to Hades!

Seeing that the intermission was almost over, she started to return to her seat, but all pleasure in the evening had fled. Enjoying the remainder of the play would be impossible, since she could not rid her mind of a bold smile, husky laughter, and the lilt of an Irish accent. No, it was best that she return to the hotel and try to forget her encounter with the annoying stranger.

Furious at having her evening ruined, she took the claim ticket from her bag and retrieved her cape. As she pushed through Chatterton's entrance, she noticed that many of the patrons were drifting back to their seats for the second part of the play.

She made her way down to the street and looked around, hoping to catch a ride, but the cabs had yet to return to collect the theater's patrons. Few people were about: a couple climbed into a lone hack that rolled smartly down the street; across the way, a man strolled toward a woman standing beneath a streetlight. A prostitute, she thought. An enclosed buggy sat, horse waiting patiently for its owner to exit the theater.

Frustrated over her lack of conveyance, she stood, tapping the toe of her satin slipper. There was nothing to do but wait for the hired rigs to come back for their return fares. She spied a millinery shop across the street and decided to check out their spring offerings.

Though it was difficult to see clearly with only the streetlight for illumination, the straw and flower confections arranged in the window proved unsatisfactory in catching her interest, as did the dresses in the windows of the shop next door. Her run-in with the boxer had definitely soured her evening. What, if anything, should she make of him? *Was* he following her, or were their encounters random as he claimed?

Random or deliberate, he was taken with her, else he would not have instigated two conversations—or been such a flirt. She was equally pleased and distressed by the notion. Heredity warring with common sense. Interested in her or not, she realized that he was a hazard to anyone in a skirt.

Seeing nothing to interest her in the window displays of three more shops, she decided to go back to the theater and wait for a cab. Crossing the thoroughfare, she pulled a small watch from her reticule, but it was too dark to see the time. She was unaware that the buggy down the way had moved from its position and the horse had been whipped into action. Hearing the rumble of hooves, she stopped and turned to see the conveyance bearing down on her at the same moment she realized she was in the middle of the street.

For an instant, she could only watch as the rig thundered nearer. *Run, Lilly!* Before she could act on the thought, something iron-hard circled her waist from behind and snatched her out of harm's way.

A string of curses assailed her ear before she was set to the ground. Hard hands gripped her shoulders and spun her around. Once again, she found herself staring into the angry face of the pugilist. Was it her imagination, or had fear leached the color from his face and darkened his eyes?

He gave her a little shake. "What in the world were you doin' standin' in the middle of the street like that?" he demanded in a harsh voice. "You came within inches of bein' killed!"

Lilly stared up at him in disbelief. Her life had been in jeopardy, and he attacked her with anger? Her limited knowledge of men prevented her from knowing that rage was the typical masculine response to fear and situations over which they had no control.

Relief, the remnants of her own fear, and more than a bit of guilt for her own stupidity prompted her tart reply. "That, sir, is none of your business, and you are not my keeper."

In frustration, he rammed his fingers through his dark hair and muttered something indistinguishable beneath his breath.

"I beg your pardon?"

"I said it is obvious that you need one."

"How was I to know that the horse and buggy was being handled by a moron?" she asked, pulling free of his grasp and stepping away from him.

"Moron? That driver knew exactly what he was doing. He pulled away from across the street and headed straight toward you at a dead run. I saw the whole thing and aged ten years! You're lucky I got to you in time. Who've you angered lately?"

The biting comments came at her like bullets from a gun.

"No one." The notion that someone had tried to run over her deliberately might have been laughable if her knees were not still knocking together. Then, without warning, she remembered the feeling of being watched while she was at Heaven's Gate and again as she'd walked to the hotel in Vandalia. And there was the note warning her to stop upsetting people's lives. She'd taken none of it seriously, but was it possible there was a real threat to her out there somewhere?

This man was in the same town as you both times.

She blinked at the thought and how much sense it made, yet contrarily, she felt no fear of him. "Were you following me?" she demanded, narrowing her eyes in suspicion.

"Guilty as charged," he snapped with brutal frankness.

Lilly couldn't hide her surprise.

"I wanted to see if I could somehow make amends for my earlier behavior."

The explanation defused both her anger and her suspicions. She gathered her wrap around her and regarded him with a thoughtful expression. Whether or not he had followed her from Vandalia was known only to himself and God. At worst, the man standing before her had saved her from death; at the very least, from severe injury. To refuse him forgiveness and a thank you would be the height of rudeness.

"Apology accepted," she told him, though her tone held an undeniable chill. "And thank you."

"There now, that didn't hurt too much, did it?" he mocked. Before she could reply, he held out his arm, and said, "Would you accept an invitation to dinner tomorrow night?"

"I don't plan on being here tomorrow night," she said, "and

even if I were, you are the last person in Springfield I would agree to have dinner with."

He shook his head and made a *tsking* sound. "Coyness is not your forte, is it, colleen?"

Colleen! Memories of the woman Timothy had slept with swept into her mind. "Don't call me that!" she snapped. "And playing coy is for women who wish to land a man."

"And you have no desire to do that?" he queried with a lift of one heavy eyebrow. "Most women do."

"That is a folly I have already committed, much to my regret. And I am not most women."

"You certainly are not," he agreed. "And you must have made a poor choice."

His observation was too close to the truth. "My choices are none of your concern, sir, and I believe you pass the bounds of propriety with this line of conversation."

"Indeed I do," he told her. He offered her his arm once again. "Let's get you back to your hotel."

"That's where I was going," she told him. "And I'm quite capable of getting myself there if you will be so kind as to secure me a cab."

At some time during the harrowing escapade, a few carriages had begun to arrive in hopes of capturing prime spots in front of the theater. With nothing but a considering glance and a wry lift at the corners of his lips, the boxer gave a piercing whistle and waved at the driver of a shiny black calash, which promptly pulled up next to them.

"Will you permit me to act the gentleman and help you up, or can you manage that by yourself as well?" he demanded in a tone that straddled amusement and exasperation.

The heat of embarrassment suffused her face. Instead of answering, she held up her gloved hand for assistance. Ignoring it, he spanned her waist with his strong hands and swung her up into the four-wheeled buggy. As she settled into her seat beneath the folding half top, she saw him hand a bill to the driver. "The lady will tell you where to take her."

Before she could protest, he stepped aside and gave her an abbreviated bow. "G'night, Lilly," he said, his eyes glittering with something closely akin to exasperation. Without another word, he turned and headed back toward the theater.

CHAPTER 33

On her way back to the hotel, Lilly forced her thoughts away from the boxer. It was not an easy thing to do. As she was reliving the evening, she realized that she had left the theater without having her conversation with Chester Carpenter. She supposed she could be forgiven for having forgotten, since she'd almost been killed. She sighed. There would be other opportunities to delve into the circumstances behind her mother's death.

First thing in the morning, she would telegraph William that she had found what was left of the Purcell family, that Prudence had no intention of selling, and she was coming back to Chicago. She would not tell him of the carriage incident or mention the fighter.

Feet dragging as she entered the hotel lobby, she summoned the woman to help her get out of her corset, then got into her nightclothes and fell onto the feather tick, hoping her eventful day would bring an easy rest.

It was not to be. She could not forget her meeting with the man at the theater. She remembered the teasing good humor in his eyes, the fear, and the irritation she'd seen there when she'd challenged him about following her.

While it was true that she was unafraid of him—perhaps naïvely so—she was equally certain that something about him was less than genuine . . . or was she once more measuring an attractive man with the same yardstick she'd used when looking at the daguerreotype of the Reverend Purcell? Were the two men really flawed, or had her limited and disastrous experiences with smooth-talking men tainted her judgment?

She thought about the fighter's comment about the horse and carriage deliberately trying to run her down. That disturbing notion took her thoughts back to the events in Vandalia and her encounters with him there. All that aside, she still could not believe he meant her harm. If that were his intent, why come to her rescue?

It didn't make any sense. Who would want to harm her? She decided to concentrate on her conversation with Prudence Purcell. Considering the widow's circumstances, her refusal to sell Heaven's Gate held no more logic than it had when she'd last tried to make sense of it. It had something to do with the reverend, but what?

"He's an evil man . . . fleeced his congregation . . . took our innocence . . ."

". . . user . . . taker . . . hope he rots in hell."

"Sarah died . . . her father took it the hardest . . . my husband was cruelly snatched from the life he so loved . . . What else, Harry?"

There was much about this strange assignment Lilly didn't understand, but one thing was certain. Something had happened at Heaven's Gate, something no one knew about. But what? Was Prudence afraid that if she sold the place the new owners might stumble across that secret, whatever it might be? While it was possible that she'd been ignorant of her husband's thievery, Lilly suspected that the Widow Purcell was privy to whatever secrets lay behind the doors of the crumbling house.

What other explanation could there be for her reluctance to sell?

For all her growing certainty that she was on to something, Lilly felt she was missing a vital piece of information. Knowing she might be going on a fool's errand, she made a decision. She would not return to Chicago just yet. She would go back to Vandalia and the Purcell house just long enough to make one last search. Since the trip was to satisfy her own curiosity, she would pay for all her expenses. That would be fair, and the agency would have nothing to complain about.

"I hope he rots in hell."

Yes, she was missing something . . . unlike the keen-eyed boxer, who she suspected missed very little. Groaning at the memory of him that intruded yet again, Lilly flounced onto her side and yanked the covers over her head.

"G'night, Lilly."

Lilly bolted upright in bed. They had not exchanged names, yet the stranger had known hers. Her heart raced. Despite his seeming carelessness and cocky demeanor, there was an aura of danger surrounding him. Foolish perhaps, but somehow she did not believe that he meant to harm her. But like Heaven's Gate, she did suspect that there was more to him than met the eye.

CHAPTER 34

Without contacting William, Lilly took the early train back to Vandalia on Thursday morning. On the way to the depot, her carriage passed the park where the boxing ring still stood. She wondered if chance would bring her face-to-face with the pugilist again. Perhaps she had finally convinced him that she had no interest in him. Except, of course, she did. She wondered how he knew her name, and why he had troubled himself to learn it.

When she arrived back at the Holbrook Hotel the desk was being manned by one of the Holbrook boys. Lilly had her things taken up to her new room and went straight to the dining room for a cup of coffee. Helen was nowhere in sight when Lilly took her favorite table near the window, but the young waitress soon emerged from the kitchen. She spotted Lilly, but instead of her usual smile of welcome, her gaze darted away, and she concentrated on serving the middle-aged woman and child seated at a nearby table.

Helen looked sad and pale, and her eyes were red, as if

she'd been crying. Trouble with a beau, perhaps? The poor child might as well accustom herself to the fact that if a male were the source of her misery, it wouldn't be the last time she would suffer. Lilly turned her attention to the blackboard menu.

When Helen finally approached the table, the corners of her lips were quirked upward a tad, though the action seemed forced. Without asking about the Springfield trip, without any conversation at all, Helen took Lilly's order and disappeared into the kitchen once more. Concerned by this turn of events, Lilly wondered if she should question Helen about her change of manner, but when Helen returned with the food a few moments later, Lilly thanked her and kept silent.

By the time she finished her meal she'd decided to ask Helen what was bothering her, but before she could frame the question, the girl blurted, "Miss Long, may I have a word with you?"

"Of course, Helen. Sit down."

Helen glanced around the room, her nervousness apparent, even though everyone had left but Lilly. "Not here. I'll take your money and find an excuse to step out back a moment."

"All right," she agreed, wondering once more what was going on.

Carrying the dirty dishes, Helen started toward the kitchen, but spun around quickly. Her troubled gaze met Lilly's. "I didn't expect to see you again."

"I didn't expect to come back."

"I'm glad you did."

Lilly's curiosity was definitely piqued. After paying for her meal, she went through the front lobby and around the house to the back, where she found Helen pacing in a tight circle.

"You must not have found the reverend, since you came back here," she said, as Lilly neared.

"I found his widow. It seems the reverend passed away a few years ago." Lilly thought she saw surprise in Helen's eyes. Surprise and something else she couldn't define. Relief?

Instead of commenting, Helen burst into tears.

"What is it?" Lilly asked, all thoughts of the Purcells and Heaven's Gate vanishing in the face of the young woman's distress. "I knew the moment I saw you that something was wrong."

"Everything is in a muddle," Helen cried, sobbing into her apron.

"Is it because of me?" Lilly felt the need to comfort Helen in some way but was held back by a sense of inadequacy. What did she know about comforting a young girl? "Has my nosing around caused your grief?"

"More than you'll ever know."

Lilly's heart took a sickening plunge. All she'd wanted to do was complete the work assigned to her. She'd never meant to disrupt lives and cause hurt, yet it seemed that she had done so at every turn. "Why don't you tell me what happened while I was gone?"

Helen nodded and struggled to get her tears under control. "Th-The night after you talked to my mother, my parents had a terrible row. I know I shouldn't have, but I listened outside the door. I heard my mother telling my father—David—about your visit. He told her that she should talk to you, that she *needed* to tell you the truth about what happened, so that justice might finally be served for what Harold Purcell had done to her and the others."

Lilly's mind raced, trying to make sense of what she was hearing. She did not like the picture forming in her mind. "Go on," she encouraged, knowing she should not rush to judgment, needing to hear her wild suppositions put into words.

"Mother told him she had no intention of telling you anything more. She said you were leaving town, and that the past was dead, buried and forgotten, and she intended for it to stay that way. Then D—David—told her that the past was not dead, not buried and certainly not forgotten, that it was still there eating away at her soul. . . ." A fresh round of sobs shook the girl. "It was terrible, Miss Long. I've never heard them quarrel like that before."

"Oh, Helen! I'm so sorry. What happened then?"

"I couldn't bear it, so I went into the room to stop their arguing. Mother was beside herself that I'd overheard, and fa—David—told her to tell me the truth."

"What is the truth, Helen?" Lilly asked, though an ugly picture of the past was taking form in her mind. "What did Harold Purcell do to your mother and . . . the others?"

Helen's tears started afresh, and her anguished gaze found Lilly's. "H-He t-took advantage of them! Oh, Miss Long, D-David Holbrook isn't my father at all. Harold Purcell is."

Lilly felt no surprise. From the onset of the conversation, she'd known that what Helen was about to tell her would be disastrous. She seethed with fury. The wretched, wretched man! Harold Purcell presented himself as a man of God. A man whose duty it was to cherish souls and help guide them to Heaven. How could he have done such terrible things to innocent young girls? As usual, it was the man who'd come out unscathed, while his poor victims were left to deal with the unholy messes he'd left of their lives. Poor Helen. And poor Virginia!

"Who were the others you spoke of, Helen? Did your mother say?"

Helen dried her eyes and wiped her nose on the hem of her apron. She nodded. "She didn't want me to know about it. She said I was too young and innocent to hear such things, but David made her tell me the whole story." She drew a shuddering breath. "The others were Eloise Mercer and Rachel Townsend."

"They were *all* seduced by the preacher?" Lilly pressed,

even while something she couldn't put her finger on nagged at the back of her mind.

Another nod. "Over the course of time."

"And were they all . . . with child when the Purcells skipped town?"

Helen shook her head. "Eloise happened a year or so before Mama and Rachel."

Disgust filled Lilly. Getting three young women with child was beyond appalling, and learning that two were pregnant at once certainly explained the necessity of Harold leaving town so quickly. She ground her teeth together to keep from screaming at the unfairness of it all. It was bad enough that Purcell had been a despoiler of young girls, but how could he have been so heartless to the long-suffering wife who'd borne him a daughter and three sons who'd died? What kind of man could do that?

Just a man.

Intellectually, she knew that good men inhabited the world, but they seemed to be few and far between. After thinking it over, she thought that what she'd heard wasn't so shocking after all. Still horrendous, but perhaps not so difficult to understand. Men of the cloth were men first, and while most of them lived good and decent lives, there were bound to be a few who saw their "calling" as a way to further their own agendas. Just men, in the end.

She thought of the arrogant expression in Harold Purcell's eyes in the daguerreotype. Remembered the way Timothy had always been so certain he could charm her out of her bad moods. Recalled the way her mother's lover had been all loving and filled with good humor until she had sprung the news of the baby on him.

The pattern became clear. From her limited experience, it seemed that when some men were pushed into a corner, they suffered no qualms about sacrificing whoever was in the way of their own desires and happiness. When she'd tried to make Tim more accountable, he'd stolen her livelihood, assaulted her and Rose, and fled. When Kate's lover had been forced to face the consequences of his actions, he'd killed her rather than risk losing the life he coveted. And after the Reverend Purcell had seduced and gotten three young women with child, he'd stolen the church's money and hightailed it to another city where he probably repeated his offenses.

"I met Eloise Mercer the other day," Lilly told Helen, thinking that many of the things Eloise had said made more sense in light of this new information. Sheriff Mayhew's comments about a past misunderstanding with his daughter made more sense as well. She'd assumed that the preacher was fooling around with the women of the congregation, and that the sheriff's wife was one of them, and that he and his daughter had disagreed over the affair in some way. It had never occurred to her that he had found out about Eloise's pregnancy and placed the blame on her before learning that the true culprit was the man supposed to be the town's moral compass.

"Do you know what became of Eloise's child?"

"Mama didn't want to talk about it, but David said she should tell me so that maybe I could be better prepared in case something like that ever happened to me."

"I think David—your father—is a very wise man," Lilly told her.

Helen tried to smile through her tears and picked up the story. "Mama said when word got out about Eloise's condition she got a reputation for being a bad girl. She was sweet on Buddy Mercer at the time, and the next thing you know, they were married. I guess the sheriff thought that would help make things right. But when Buddy found out the baby wasn't his, he took to drinking real bad. They say he beat up on Eloise, and finally he took her to some quack who did something to make the baby go away. Mama said she was in a bad way, but at least Buddy had enough sympathy that he took her to Doc Ramsay. He saved Eloise's life, but she was never able to have babies after that."

"How does your mother know all this?" Lilly asked.

"Doc's nurse let the whole thing slip to her sister, and from there the news spread through town like wildfire."

"Your mother told me that Buddy died."

Helen nodded. "His horse came back to town one day without a rider and limping real bad. Sheriff Mayhew and some of his men went out to check and found Buddy's body alongside the road about three miles out of town. He must have been thrown. The sheriff said he reeked of whiskey."

Lilly closed her eyes, almost feeling Eloise Mercer's despair. Not only had she borne the shame and rejection of her family and the town, but in her desire to please her husband, who like so many others was concerned only about his own feelings, she'd forfeited her ability to ever mother a child. Then, with nothing left of her self-respect, she had sold the only commodity she had—her body. Little wonder she despised Harold Purcell.

Lilly drew in a shaky breath. "Tell me about Rachel Townsend."

"That was another scandal," Helen said, sighing. "Somehow, Rachel hid her condition several months. When she started showing, everyone began wondering who might be responsible. She'd always been such a good, God-fearing girl. Matt Travers's name was bandied about for a while, and his folks sent him off to military school real fast. His father said he wasn't about to let his son be railroaded for something he didn't do.

"Mr. Townsend's lawyering business dwindled away to almost nothing, and he was planning to move his family to St. Louis as soon as Rachel had the baby. They were scheduled to leave just days before the Purcells vanished. But before they could, Rachel left her family a note saying Reverend Purcell was responsible for her condition, and she was going away to start over."

"Let me guess," Lilly said in a dry tone. "When Mr. Townsend went to confront the reverend, he was already gone."

Helen nodded. "Mrs. Purcell said he was out of town. Then, when they all vanished, Grandfather, who is still Mr. Townsend's best friend, convinced him to stay here. He told him the town needed a good attorney and the gossip would die down."

"That's what's wrong with Mrs. Townsend," Lilly said, recalling the information that she was fragile and not to be disturbed.

Nodding again, Helen said, "Mrs. Townsend . . . well, she was so ashamed she took to her sick bed. She still never leaves the house. According to Grandfather, Rachel married, but she's never once come back in all these years. No one speaks of hearing from her. It's as if she's fallen off the face of the earth."

Sickened, yet fascinated by the sordid tale, Lilly needed to hear all the details. "How did your grandfather and Mr. Townsend find out that the reverend was the guilty party for Eloise and your mother?"

"Mama said that a couple of months after the Purcells left town my grandparents found out about her condition. Grandfather was sure the reverend was to blame. As I said, Papa was a good friend of Mr. Townsend. They started putting two and two together and took their suspicions to the sheriff. The three of them forced Mama and Eloise to tell the truth, since Rachel had already gone."

"And your mother went away to stay with relatives, married David, and lived happily ever after."

"Until you came to town, I thought so. Yes, Nana and Papa sent Mama to relatives in Memphis before she started showing, hoping to protect her from the wagging tongues that almost destroyed Rachel and Eloise. Mama had me there, and later met David, who loved her enough to tell everyone I was his child. He's been a good father," she added. "I never once suspected otherwise. No one does."

And they never should. Needing some time and quiet to think through these newest developments, Lilly felt she must first restore some small measure of contentment to the families of those who'd been used so poorly.

She took Helen's shoulders and gave her a gentle shake. "Helen, look at me."

Helen raised her tear-filled gaze. Lilly smoothed her hands up and down the girl's arms in a reassuring manner, hoping to ease her misery. "Helen, David Holbrook's actions are a true testimony of his love for your mother and for you."

Fresh tears flowed. Lilly's hands slid downward to grip Helen's. "I'm sorrier than I can express for any grief I may have caused you and your family. That was not my intent. I will apologize to your mother, if I'm given the chance, but in the meantime, please relay to her that Harold Purcell is dead, and that it is my sincere belief that God's eternal punishment will be far superior and infinitely more satisfying than what any court in this world might have given him."

For long moments, the young woman stared into Lilly's eyes. Then, as if she'd seen some sort of answer there, a glimmer of hope began to glow in her own. "I believe you're right, Miss Long," she said, giving Lilly's hands a squeeze. "I believe Mama will feel the same someday."

With her eyes dried and her composure somewhat intact, Helen went back to work while Lilly retraced her footsteps and headed to her room. At last, she understood the town's reticence to speak of the past. She would make it a point to talk to the sheriff and tell him she understood the hard feelings between him and his daughter. Or should she open that can of worms, since he had made no mention of his daughter's plight? No, there was no reason to say anything more than that she'd completed her assignment and would be leaving town. Leaving them with their secrets intact.

What about the others? Should she tell them about Purcell? No. When Helen told her mother about the preacher, Virginia was bound to tell her father, so there was no reason to contact the banker. A letter to Mr. Townsend advising him that the false shepherd was dead should suffice to put his mind at ease.

Lilly's mind was not at all at ease. In fact, now that she was in possession of the facts, a new possibility was making inroads into her thoughts. Over time, the scandal had been allowed to die, and those involved had reclaimed and rebuilt their lives, yet Rachel Townsend had made no attempt to return to Vandalia or her family. Was her refusal to return home based on the fact that she wanted no reminders of what had happened here, or could there be something more sinister at play?

The evening she and Pierce had discussed the bloody bed proving that a murder had been committed there, they'd also speculated on who might have been the killer and the victim. Pierce had asked if anyone had come up missing around that time. She'd had no idea. Now, Helen's statement that Rachel had left town a day or two before the Purcells vanished presented a new and troubling scenario: Rachel Townsend had not visited her family once in the past twenty years and hadn't been seen by anyone since she "left town to start a new life." Was it possible that *she* was the one killed in the bed at Heaven's Gate? Might she have gone to confront the preacher about her condition and been murdered for her trouble?

It made perfect sense. Helen told a harrowing tale of lies, seduction, and shame. If a man who was in the business of saving souls could consciously set out to harm the most innocent and tender of his flock, he was capable of anything.

Lilly let her mind wander further down this new path of speculation. Could the innocent-acting Prudence, who'd made the statement about women doing anything for the men they loved, have known what her husband was up to? Had she lied to protect him? Had she been there when he'd done it?

Lilly sucked in a sharp breath as an even more outrageous notion slipped into her mind. Dear sweet heaven! Was it possible that the grave with the crumbling wooden cross did *not* hold the body of Sarah Purcell, but the remains of Rachel Townsend and her unborn baby? Prudence had been a bit discombobulated when Lilly asked her about the grave. Was her uncertainty about who was buried there tied to guilt?

Theories were one thing; proving them was something else. She needed to find out if there was any truth to her wild conjecture. Or perhaps she should just let things stay as they were. Was there any sound reason she should try to prove Harold Purcell guilty? Courts could not punish the dead, and despite her reservations about some biblical teachings, Lilly did believe the preacher and his ilk would burn in a fiery hell.

Her job was finished; but for her own peace of mind, she needed to find out what had happened. Would knowing the truth bring peace to the town, or would it just resurrect old hurts and shames? After much waffling, she decided that it *was* worth the effort to try to bring justice to the innocent. She would telegraph William and tell him Purcell was dead, but that she was looking into some evil scheme connected to him. By the time William received the message and got back to her with his thoughts on the matter, she would already be searching for the truth.

She was going back to Heaven's Gate one last time, but this time she would take her derringer and a spade. Too many people had seen the bloody bed within days of the Purcell family's departure to doubt that *someone* had been killed there, and Rachel Townsend was Lilly's guess.

Still, the Pinkertons did not deal in speculation. She needed to prove the stains were blood, and to do that, she would test them as Pierce had suggested. She would check with the pharmacy to see if they had peroxide and guaiac, and if not, she would use the benzidine he'd mentioned. Then, with proof at her fingertips, she intended to dig up the bodies and notify the sheriff of her find, thus bringing decades of shame and loss into the healing brightness of sunshine.

CHAPTER 35

The next morning, dressed in her sensible olive-hued skirt and with her boots laced tightly around her ankles, Lilly readied herself for what she hoped would be her last trip to Heaven's Gate. She tucked her purchase from the apothecary into her pocket where it rested next to her derringer. She hadn't told Helen of her plans for fear she would mention it to the sheriff or her grandfather and someone might try to stop her.

Finally ready, she went to the livery, rented a buggy, and asked to borrow a shovel from Billy Bishop. Though his face took on a curious expression at her request, he asked no questions and offered no opposition, placing the shovel beneath the seat of the buggy. He'd learned that when the lady Pinkerton had a mission, she was dead set on carrying it out.

Spring was more in evidence than ever as the bay gelding trotted down the road toward Mulberry Grove. Though it had poured rain for two days previous, and the road was a muddy quagmire in places, a profusion of lavender and white wildflowers carpeted the open spaces as far as the eye could see. It was a perfect day, not at all the kind of day in keeping with the dark task at hand.

At last, she rounded the bend in the road and saw the house sitting amidst the gardens and lawn of decay. It looked just as she remembered from her previous trips, except for a few hardy crocuses that had struggled through the layers of decaying leaves and created splashes of color here and there. Like people, they fought to survive, no matter what the conditions.

She wasted no time going through things inside again, determined to get to the task at hand. Hoping against hope, she unwrapped the bottle of benzidine, unscrewed the top, and poured a bit of the contents over the stained dish towel—no doubt where Purcell had washed up after doing the terrible deed. Almost immediately, the stain began to turn blue.

Fighting back a feeling of exultation that mingled with a certain dread, she forced herself to go to the bedroom where the killing had taken place and repeated the process on the sheets. The results were the same. Though Pierce claimed other things could cause the chemical reaction and that the test didn't prove the blood was human, in her heart, Lilly knew. There was no reason for anyone to kill an animal in a bed.

Satisfied that she was on the right track, she took the shovel from the buggy and made her way through the overgrown garden to the family burial plot. Fortunately, the tallest weeds were nothing but brown sticks from the winter freeze, and the new ones were no higher than her ankles. In another month, she'd have had to hack her way through the grasses with a machete.

Since the fallen cross was near the back of the fenced-in area, there was only one way the grave would fit. A few feet from the base of the fallen cross, Lilly pushed the shovel's head into the ground and stomped on it with her booted foot. The recent rains had left the earth soft and the digging easy . . . for the first half hour. By then, the hem of her skirt was heavy with moisture and the shovel had rubbed blisters on her palms. The sun had climbed higher in the sky, and the fledgling sprouts of green leaves provided little shade.

Perspiration dripped from her face, and her labored breathing was harsh against the woodland sounds around her. Cursing the skirt that got in her way with every shovelful of dirt, she vowed that as soon as she got back to civilization, she would show her support to the Rational Dress Society. For practical reasons, the group wanted to change the number of undergarments a woman needed to wear. Better than that, she would take herself to the nearest dry goods establishment and buy herself a pair of men's breeches for such work. Using her arm to wipe the perspiration from her face, she considered the possibility of purchasing some of those denim trousers with the rivets that were so popular with men. Levi's.

She wanted to quit the thankless job, go back to town, and get on the first train to Chicago, but a compelling urge to know the whole truth drove her on.

By the time the sun was high in the sky, Lilly had excavated a hole approximately four feet long and more than thigh deep. Wearier than she ever recalled being, she decided she needed sustenance if she were to dig any farther.

She clutched huge handfuls of grass to help hoist herself upward and tried to swing her knee to the solid ground but found her skirt hindering her once more. Muttering beneath her breath, she unbuttoned it and her petticoat and stepped out of them, flinging the mud-encrusted garments onto the grass. After a moment's hesitation, she began to unbutton her blouse. What did it matter? There was no one to see her, and this was not a job that lent itself to women's garments. She tossed her shirt onto the pile. There! That was much better.

Her chemise and bloomers offered much more freedom of movement.

Reaching out, she once more grabbed great handfuls of weeds. Flinging her knee upward, she dug the toe of the opposite boot into the soft side of the cavity, pushing and pulling her way out of the hole. Halfway there, the grass came up by the roots, and she slipped back down, almost falling on her backside.

Muttering a curse, she tried again. On the third try, she found success and lay on the damp ground, breathing heavily. When she was somewhat revived, she left her skirt and blouse behind and struggled through the overgrown garden to the risqué fountain, where she eased her sore, filthy hands into the comparatively clean rain water. Its coldness stung as she gently scrubbed at her hands.

She washed away the worst of the grime and carried her lunch to the front steps of the mansion. With one elbow resting on the step behind her, she reveled in the freedom afforded her by her undergarments while devouring the sandwich she'd brought. She ate with the same gusto as a starving longshoreman, washing down the butter, ham, and fresh lettuce with great gulps of water from a jug, turning to wipe her mouth on the shoulder of her blouse. She smiled, thinking of Rose's reaction to both her mode of dress and her manners. Or lack of them.

Somewhat refreshed from the rest and the food, Lilly took stock of her raw, seeping hands with their broken nails. They hurt like the very devil. She couldn't continue without some sort of relief, and she couldn't dig any deeper without finding something to help her get out of the hole. The last thing she needed was to be stuck down there with a decaying body.

She went back to the grave and picked up her dirt-stained petticoat. She caught the bottom of the garment with her

teeth and tore several long strips. Wishing for some bag balm
or some other ointment to salve the wounds, she wrapped the
fabric around her hands, ripping the ends and tying them in
place. There! That should help.

That done, she set about looking for a board she could place
at an angle in the opening so that she would have an incline to
crawl out on. A thorough search of the barn revealed nothing.
She was about to go to the house for a chair when she saw a
small ladder leaned against the chicken house, so the fowl
could get into their raised nests at night. She carried it to the
gravesite and prayed that the wood-shingled roof had kept it
from rotting too badly. Dropping it down into the hole, she
jumped in and went back to work.

An hour passed. Another. Her mind became numb to everything but the thud of her boot on the shovel, the scrape as it cut
through the ground, the sucking sound of the wet earth as she
shoveled it up, and the soft plop as she tossed it onto the growing pile at the side of the hole.

Thud. Scrape. Plop. Thud. Scrape. Plop.

She was unaware of the black, brooding clouds that had
moved in from the west and obscured the brightness of the
sun. She paid no notice that the joyful singing of the birds had
quieted and been replaced by the mournful song of a rain crow,
or that the soft sigh of the wind rustling through the trees had
been replaced by blustery gusts. The only scent she smelled was
that of leaf mold and wet soil. She didn't feel the tears that
tracked through the dirt on her face.

Finally, when her quivering arms were unable to lift another shovelful, she fell to her knees and began to sob. By her
estimation, she'd dug to a depth of at least four feet without any
sign of a casket, or skeleton. There was not so much as a ragged
piece of rotting cloth to indicate a body had been buried
there. She faced the truth. There *was* no body buried in this
spot. No Rachel. No baby.

Lifting her tear-glazed eyes toward the bruised sky, she let out a loud scream of frustration, weariness, and disappointment. Fury. She hoped Harold Purcell was in a fiery hell. *I know you killed her, Harold. But where did you put the body?*

The unearthly cry echoed through the trees, blown there by a gust of wind that caused the horse tethered there to shift nervously. The man in the forest, who'd just dismounted, jumped and turned toward the sound. An involuntary shiver shuddered through him. There was pain akin to anguish in that cry. Anger and soul-deep sorrow. He'd heard a scream like that before. It had come from his own throat. The wind whipped the undergrowth around him. Giving a firm push to the bowler on his head, he made his way through the trees toward the house. The woman was borderline cracked, no doubt about it.

CHAPTER 36

Sick with disappointment, her limbs trembling with exhaustion, and her bloodied palms throbbing with every beat of her heart, Lilly shuffled her mud-encrusted feet to the ladder. She placed her boot on the bottom rung and put her weight on it. Simultaneously, a sharp crack of lightning split the sky and the step gave way, jarring her from the tips of her toes to the top of her head. From the front of the house she heard the terrified whinny of the rented horse. Peering over the edge of the grave, she saw the beast running hell-bent for leather down the lane toward the main road, the buggy bouncing along behind it.

Her hysterical laugh dissipated in the raging wind. What else could go wrong? *Don't worry about the horse, Lilly. What if you can't get out of this blasted hole? Won't that be a fine kettle of fish?* Then she recalled that Billy Bishop knew where she was. If the rented rig showed up at the livery by nightfall, surely he would send someone to look for her.

Gritting her teeth, she grabbed the sides of the ladder and lifted her foot to the next rung, praying that it would hold as she hoisted herself upward and onto the ground. It did. On firm ground at last, she rolled onto her back and flung her forearm over her eyes, aware finally of the absence of the sun, the thunder grumbling in the distance, and the sudden stiffness of the chilly wind. She lay still for several moments, trying to catch her breath, uncertain whether the wetness on her face was tears or raindrops.

Why hadn't she gone back to Chicago with the news that Purcell was dead and his widow had no intention of selling this godforsaken place? Why had she let her stubbornness and curiosity bring her to this?

Even as she questioned herself, she knew she'd done what she had because the innocence of three young women taken against their will insisted that the truth be revealed. Old hurts cried out for release of decades-old pain. Ruined lives demanded justice.

How could she do anything else?

"As long as justice wins out, the ends justify the means."

Allan Pinkerton's words echoed in her mind, and with them, renewed determination. Harold had killed Rachel and left her body here, or he had left and assigned Prudence, an accessory to his crime, to do the dirty deed.

Again, Lilly felt as if she were missing some vital bit of information, some clue that would tell her all she needed to know about the heinous acts committed in this place. With a sob, she rolled to her stomach and lay there for a moment with her head on her forearms, struggling to gather the last remnants of her energy.

Without warning, the hair at the nape of her neck stood on end, as it had twice before. She raised her head, her frantic gaze sweeping the woods around her. As usual, she saw nothing but shadows. Before, her watcher had been an animal. She hoped that's all it was now. Her derringer was secure in the pocket of the skirt that lay next to her, and even if her physical reserves were low, she certainly had enough strength left to pull the trigger.

The fleeting moment of panic gave way to anger. She would do what she'd come to do. Uncovering the Purcells' crime was her goal, and she intended to do it, wild animals roaming about or not. Swiping at her eyes with the back of a filthy, rag-wrapped hand, she cursed whatever was out there watching her. Pushing herself to her feet, she slipped her blouse on to protect her against a sudden chill and, grabbing her muddy clothes, flung them over her arm and stumbled toward the rear door.

How many times had she searched this place? she wondered, draping her clothing over the back of a chair and weaving like a drunken sailor through the kitchen. No hiding places here. She paused in the wide foyer, wishing for the brightness of the sun as her frenzied gaze searched every shadowy inch from ceiling to floor, looking for places that might conceal hidden hinges, or that small *something* to indicate that a undisclosed doorway might be there.

She ran her aching palms over the vertical oak boards beneath the staircase, pushing here and there in hopes a secret door might pop open. Nothing. Raw fingertips grazed the square newel post with its intricate carvings, searching for camouflaged buttons and finding none. Her feverish gaze raked the floor, moved over the dark place at the bottom of the stairs. Then, with a gasp, returned.

Before, she'd assumed wine had been spilt on the floor, staining the heart pine planks. But was it wine, as she'd thought, or was it blood? With a little cry of excitement, she rushed back to the kitchen and groped for the benzidine in her skirt pocket.

Dropping to her knees, she struggled to unscrew the top of the bottle with her sore, shaking hands and tipped the container, splashing a small amount onto the discolored boards.

She waited. The spot, at least a foot wide, was old, and either someone had made an attempt to clean it or the stain had degraded so much through the years that she feared the compound wouldn't work. She poured on more, and then, in the poor light seeping through the dirty windows, she began to see the chemical reaction as the substance that pooled in the cracks began to take on a bluish hue.

She smiled in triumph. Blood. Blood, not wine, had soaked these boards. But why would there be blood here? Had Rachel, wounded and panicked, somehow escaped Harold and fled into the hall? If so, where had she gone next? *Or where did he take her when he caught her?* Instinct told her the answer to either question was "up." Getting to her feet, she started toward the second floor, her footsteps dragging with exhaustion. Halfway up, she stumbled and fell to her knees, rapping her shin against the carpeted runner.

With her throbbing palms pressed flat against one of the steps, she closed her eyes against tears of weakness and pain. Maybe Robert Pinkerton was right. Maybe women weren't suited to detecting. A man wouldn't be brought to tears by the things she'd gone through today. Maybe she should have stayed with the troupe and forgotten about the wrongs Tim had done to her. An image of Robert Pinkerton's mocking expression materialized behind her closed eyes. No doubt he would gloat if she failed this, her first assignment. She would not grant the odious man the satisfaction. She had come this far, and would not stop now.

"Please, God," she sobbed. Not one given to prayer, she was unaware of the feverish, whispered words. Forcing her eyes open, she stared at the floral pattern of the carpet runner as she gathered the remnants of her waning resolve. Fat pink and burgundy roses and buds intertwined with yellow and white flowers she could not name against a cream background. A ribbon banner of gold swirled beneath, and a rosebud . . .

That is not a rosebud on the gold ribbon, Lilly. It's a stain. And there were other splotches mingling with the floral pattern, she noted with growing exhilaration. She had little doubt that these droplets were blood. She hadn't noticed them before, because she wasn't really looking, and because their color blended so well with the busy pattern of the runner.

New energy suffused her, and she grabbed a spindle to pull herself to her feet. Rachel had gone up the stairs, away from Harold. Keeping her gaze trained on the carpet, Lilly followed the stains to the second floor, where she lost them for a moment, only to pick them up again at the steps leading to the attic.

As she pushed open the door, a sharp crack of lightning and a cannonball boom of thunder shook the entire house. Her gaze searched the room with far more care than on her first trip.

Filled with the detritus of a family's life and a twenty-year collection of cobwebs and dust, the gloom-shrouded room mocked her. The walls were rough boards. Dusty sheeting gave ghostly shapes to unused furniture, which had been placed willy-nilly throughout the area. Wooden crates and trunks abounded. Castoff landscapes and portraits leaned against the walls. The lifeless gazes of long-dead ancestors followed Lilly as she moved deeper into the space.

Ignoring their stares and wishing for a lantern to cast off some of the darkness, she scuffed her booted feet through the powdery grime, looking for more rusty droplets. Had Harold caught Rachel outside the door? Where would he have put her, if she managed to come this far before he finished doing her in? Lilly's gaze moved past a large steamer trunk. Returned.

The gruesome notion that crept into her mind set her stomach churning. He couldn't have . . . could he? Oh, yes. He could. She was fast learning that depravity knew no bounds.

Gritting her teeth in determination, she approached the

first trunk and unhooked the latches. Then, she took a deep breath and lifted the top. To her profound relief, there was nothing but ladies' clothing inside. Moving from one trunk to another, she checked the contents and found nothing of importance. Some were even empty.

There must be a hidden room somewhere. She began a close examination of the walls, as she'd done downstairs. Against the third wall was yet another trunk topped with an assortment of crates and a large rococo mirror. She lifted the wooden boxes down one by one, and then, biting back a groan of pain, hefted the sizable mirror and leaned it next to the trunk.

As soon as she stepped aside, she saw what she'd been looking for—a narrow door. The things stacked in front of it hid a simple wood latch with a single nail that allowed the fastener to turn.

She paused, staring at the discovery. The boards that made up the door were flush to the wall and staggered in length so that the aperture became part of the partition. There was no doorframe and no hinges visible to the naked eye. Whatever lay behind the wall was meant to be a secret. This had to be the place Harold Purcell had hidden the body of the young girl he'd used in such a vile manner.

The trunk would have to be moved to open the door. The satisfaction of knowing her suspicions were right lent her new strength, and with a few tugs and pulls on the leather handles and pushing with her hips and legs, she soon shifted the trunk far enough from the wall to open the door.

She approached the narrow portal with caution, steeling herself for what she might find. Reaching out a trembling hand, she turned the makeshift latch and, taking hold of the strip of leather that served as a handle, gave the door a yank. The narrow aperture opened with a scream of unused hinges that grated on her ragged nerves.

Stepping through the door, she paused, allowing her eyes

to adjust to the deeper shadows of the windowless room. After a moment, she saw thin, faint strips of illumination on the opposite wall. There was a window, but it must have been covered with an interior shutter of some sort. Fearful of tripping over something, Lilly shuffled her way toward the sliver of light and pushed the shutters back on their hinges. Then she turned to survey the room and gave a shriek loud enough to raise the dead.

But didn't.

Chapter 37

Lilly pressed her fingertips against her lips, but the puny effort didn't stop her groan of shock as her mind registered the sight before her. Thunder rumbled toward the east, as the storm moved toward Vandalia. Watery sunlight fought its way through the sodden skies and the grime of the small window, its lackluster rays illuminating the skeletal remains of the woman sitting on a small cot. She sat on a feather tick with her back leaned against the wall, a blue quilt folded next to her. Her right hand rested inside the carpetbag sitting in her lap.

Shreds of what was once a fine lawn nightgown clung in tatters to skeletal shoulder bones. The sleeves closed at the wrists with tiny mother-of-pearl buttons. Straggles of cobweb-festooned hair hung in limp waves almost to her waist. Eyeless sockets stared out at Lilly, and small, even teeth smiled at her from a fleshless face.

Moving closer, Lilly noticed that the mattress beneath and around the woman's hips bore a large stain, which could be nothing but blood. Blood from a delivery that had gone on too long and been too hard for the young mother. Leaning nearer, she peered into the valise. There, wrapped in a tattered flannel blanket, lay the remains of a tiny infant on a bed of what looked like old letters. The bony fingertips of the female rested near a small, skeletal cheek. A dying mother trying to comfort her little one.

Comprehension and soul-deep grief washed over Lilly in cold, relentless waves. She began to tremble with horror and the certainty of her conviction. Rachel Townsend had given birth to her baby in the bed downstairs, and then, with her life's blood flowing from her, Harold Purcell had forced her up here to this secret room to hide his sin from the world. Rachel had died from loss of blood. The baby had starved to death, its mother long dead. Lilly imagined that its pitiful, mewling cries of hunger would have easily been mistaken as the howling of a ghost by two impressionable young boys playing in the woods.

Dear sweet heaven! How could anyone do such a thing to another human?

Her heart raced in sudden urgency to return to town and tell the sheriff what she'd discovered, but with her horse and buggy gone, it would take hours to walk back, and she wasn't certain she could get there before dark. Her only other option was to wait until someone came for her, and if they didn't, she would start out in the morning. A shudder ran through her at the thought of staying in the house overnight, and she rubbed her upper arms to drive it away.

"Death lies on her like an untimely frost . . ." The sadly appropriate line from *Romeo and Juliet* eased through Lilly's mind as she stared at the tiny skeleton in the valise. She found herself wondering if the baby her mother had been expecting would have been a sister or brother, and what the baby would have been like if Kate's life had not been snuffed out as prematurely as this young girl's had been.

Lilly's tear-glazed gaze shifted to the jumble of envelopes beneath the baby's remains. What was in the letters, she wondered, reaching out to retrieve one, careful not to disturb the child who slept there for all eternity. She was pulling an envelope free from the collection, when she heard a sound behind her. With a startled cry, she whirled to see a black-shrouded, rain-soaked presence standing in the doorway. The shaft of sunlight coming through the dirty window fell onto the face of the newcomer.

"Mrs. Purcell. What are you doing here?"

CHAPTER 38

Prudence Purcell tossed back the hood of the dark cape that dripped water onto the dusty floor. "I might ask you the same, Miss Long. I gave you my answer about selling the house when you came to Springfield. Why did you come back here?"

"Curiosity, I suppose," Lilly told her, still puzzled by the woman's sudden appearance. "Something didn't seem right, so I thought I'd take one more look around."

"You know what they say about curiosity."

A shiver of uneasiness slithered down Lilly's back. "It killed the cat," she said in a low voice.

"Indeed." Prudence pulled her hand from beneath the cape. In it, she clutched a small gun.

Lilly stared at the firearm in disbelief. She remembered seeing the small handgun in Harold's collection. Her mind raced, trying to make sense of what she knew and what she'd seen in this house of horrors. Why had Prudence followed her from Springfield, and why was she standing there threatening her with a gun?

Whatever Prudence's agenda could be, and despite her

own inexperience, Lilly knew she was in trouble. But how much trouble? She thought of and discarded several ways to overcome the preacher's wife and take the gun from her. Instinct told her to keep the woman talking. "Why did you follow me?"

"I didn't actually follow you, Miss Long. When you came snooping around in Springfield, I realized I needed to return here and tidy up a few loose ends."

"I believe it's called covering your tracks, not tidying up."

Prudence gave a negligent shrug. "I had no idea you would come back to Heaven's Gate after I told you I wouldn't sell, so when I got here and saw you digging in the graveyard I was shocked. It didn't take long to figure out what you were doing, but it took me a bit to figure out what to do about it. And here we are."

She smiled a bright smile, as if they were discussing the advent of spring instead of murder. "I can't let you ruin everything, Miss Long. Not after such a long time. You do understand, don't you?"

Oh, she understood perfectly. Prudence had no intention of letting Lilly go to the sheriff. No intention of letting her leave here alive. Trembling with another quiver of fear, she cursed herself for not putting her skirt back on. Why was it that her derringer was never in the article of clothing she needed it to be in? All she could do was keep Prudence talking on the off chance that she could be persuaded to put down her weapon.

"So you came back to get rid of the bodies," she said, amazed by the steadiness of her voice. She gestured toward the remains on the cot. "Why don't you tell me what happened, Mrs. Purcell? Exactly what did Harold do to Rachel Townsend?"

Prudence blinked. The surprise on her face was genuine. "Rachel? How would I know?"

It was Lilly's turn to be surprised. "This isn't Rachel Townsend and her baby?"

"Good heavens, no! That's Sarah. Sarah and my grandson."

Prudence's gaze grew vacant, as if she were staring at some inner place or thing too horrible to contemplate. When she spoke again, her voice was dull, toneless. "She was only twelve the first time, you see. Twelve and so pretty. So very pretty. He liked them pretty. And young. They were all pretty and young. I was pretty when we first married. Like Sarah. Very pretty."

Gooseflesh rose on Lilly's arms. She was looking into the eyes of insanity, hearing the voice of lunacy. How could she convince Prudence to put away the gun when it was clear that she was mad?

"Who liked them pretty and young, Prudence?" she prodded. *Keep her talking, Lilly. Keep her talking.*

The older woman's sharp, angry gaze swung to Lilly's. "Why, Harold, of course."

Perversion and madness. The Purcell legacy. "Prudence, are you telling me that your husband, a man of God, took sexual liberties with young women in town, and with his own daughter?"

"Oh, yes," Prudence said, almost flippantly. "But it wasn't just here. It happened other places, too. Everywhere the Lord's work took us."

"I hardly think seducing young women is what the Lord had in mind," Lilly snapped, her anger momentarily overcoming her fear of the madwoman with the gun.

"It was on his mind all the time," Prudence said, her wild-eyed gaze moving to the skeleton of her daughter. "Not the Lord's. Harold's. It was so easy for him. He was so handsome, you see, and had such a silver tongue. All the women thought he was so Godly, so . . . good. But they were wrong. They soon found that out."

"And you knew what he was doing all along?" Lilly asked, as horrified by that fact as with the truth about Harold.

Prudence looked at Lilly. "I knew, but I loved him. I couldn't help myself. I loved him and I hated him. I hated them, too. All of them."

Her gaze slid to her dead daughter. "Even Sarah. They shouldn't have been so pretty." She looked back at Lilly, a bright smile in her eyes, on her lips. "He liked them pretty, you know. Young and pretty," she repeated.

Her expression soured once more, and her tone of voice turned harsh, accusing. "They shouldn't have laughed at his jokes, Miss Long. They shouldn't have stolen his affection away from me."

The woman was thoroughly insane. "How could you hate your own daughter?" Lilly asked, her mind refusing to believe what she was hearing. "She was the blameless one. All those girls, all those years, they were all pure. Harold was the one in the wrong. It was his fault, not the failing of the innocent girls he led astray."

"Don't be so naïve, Miss Long," Prudence snapped. "Women have been leading men down the path to perdition ever since Eve duped Adam. The sin is passed on from generation to generation."

Fearing she had inherited her mother's nature, Lilly had discussed this topic with Rose at length. Everyone was a free moral agent, Rose had explained. Choices between right and wrong were made every day by every person. No one paid for another's sins. Lilly was comforted to know she would not bear the responsibility for anything her mother had done, since she figured she would have enough to account for with her own transgressions.

" 'The son shall not bear the iniquity of the father, neither shall the father bear the iniquity of the son,' " Lilly quoted. "Ezekiel 18:20. Regardless of Eve's sin, Sarah was innocent, Prudence, as were all the others. You should not have condoned what Harold did."

"I did not condone his actions, Miss Long!" Prudence denied in a razor-sharp tone. "I detested them."

"By not turning him over to the law you were aiding him in his wickedness!" Lilly cried, her anger once again overruling caution.

Prudence gestured toward the valise. "That's what my sister said in her letters. She'd been saying for years that I should tell the authorities, but I was trying to keep my marriage together."

"Marriage is a holy union. The marriage bed should be undefiled. What you had with Harold Purcell was an alliance with the devil."

"Who are you to judge me?" Prudence cried, the dullness in her eyes replaced with a sudden burst of anger.

"It's God's word that judges, Prudence, not I."

"Oh, yes, God's word," she said with an airy wave of her free hand. Her tone reeked of bitterness. "I certainly heard enough of that. Every time he took his pleasure elsewhere, he quoted scripture to me about a wife's duty to be submissive to her husband. And he told Sarah that children were to obey their parents. . . ."

"He was twisting the scripture to make it fit his own evil desires," Lilly said. "That's a sin, too."

"Placing blame doesn't really matter now, does it, Miss Long?"

"I suppose not," Lilly agreed, the truth of the statement draining her of her anger. "Tell me about Sarah. How did she come to this?"

Prudence drew a deep breath. "When we realized Sarah was expecting, Harold told everyone in town she had tuberculosis and had to be quarantined here at the house. That way no one would see her condition or question why she never came to town. Did I tell you he had a silver tongue?" she queried, her empty gaze drifting to Lilly's once more.

Mad.

Lilly nodded.

"There had been others in town . . ."

"Rachel Townsend, Eloise Mercer, and Virginia Reih-mann," Lilly supplied.

Prudence looked at Lilly in astonishment, as if wondering how she knew. She shrugged. "Virginia Reihmann? Well, that's a new one on me, but that Eloise always was a flirt. It was easy to see why Harold was so taken with her. Fortunately for him, she married that boy and he saw to it that the baby never saw the light of day. Of course her reputation was in tatters, and her relationship with her father was ruined, but then, these things happen, don't they?" Prudence asked.

Unfortunately.

"Harold managed to be more . . . discreet for a year or so, and then there was Rachel. She never told anyone about Harold either, until she left town, and by then, he was already gone, leaving me here with Sarah. She was getting quite far along by then."

"Who? Sarah or Rachel?" Lilly asked.

A thoughtful expression entered Prudence's eyes, tempering the madness for a moment. "Why, both of them, I suppose, since it seemed they were due to deliver near the same time. At any rate, Harold had decided it was time for us to leave town, and when Mr. Townsend came to confront Harold, he was already gone."

Her features took on an expression of exasperation. "I had to lie for Harry—not that it was the first time. I told him we should have left months before we did, but he said Rachel was keeping quiet, and no one knew about Sarah, so he thought he could handle things for a while." She frowned in thought. "I wonder if Harold made the decision to leave when he found out about Virginia?"

After a moment, she offered Lilly a bright smile. "Oh, well, it hardly matters now, does it? Anyway, I was making preparations to leave when Sarah went into labor. Perhaps it was the stress that brought it on," she said with a shrug of nonchalance. "At any rate, he left me here to clean up his mess—as usual. I truly didn't know he'd taken the money, Miss Long," she added as an afterthought.

"So Harold left by train," Lilly prompted. "And you were here with Sarah, delivering the baby."

"Yes, she had a really hard time of it. I grew so tired of hearing her scream I stuffed rags in her mouth. It took nearly sixteen hours for the baby to be born. He was fine," Prudence said with a proud smile. "So perfect. But he was big for a first baby and Sarah hemorrhaged terribly. Nothing I did stopped the bleeding."

Prudence gave a breathless little giggle that sent chills down Lilly's spine. "I was in quite a pickle, as you can imagine. I was supposed to bring Sarah by wagon to meet Harold so that no one would know we'd left town for a few days, but she was in no condition to travel. I knew she would never make the trip by wagon, and I couldn't take her by train, so I wrapped up the baby and put him in the valise where I kept the letters from my sister. I helped Sarah up the stairs to this room. My room."

"Your room?"

"Yes, mine. Harold had it built especially for me, a place where he put me while he was having relations with all those girls. No one knew it was here, of course, so I thought it would be years before anyone found it . . . or Sarah, and by then we would be nothing but a bad memory to the people in town."

Lilly swallowed back the bile rising in her throat. "So without a qualm, you just brought your daughter and grandson up here to die?"

Prudence cocked her head in a considering manner. "Actually, by the time I got myself cleaned up and drove away, I began to see that it made a certain kind of sense. We all pay for our sins, and Sarah paid for hers. Perhaps you think I acted wrongly, and perhaps to most people I did, but believe me, I've paid for my sin these past twenty years, just as Harold did. The way things have worked out is a sort of poetic justice, if you will."

"What do you mean?"

"Why, I believe that it was our penance that Harold and I have had to live together all these years with me knowing what he'd done to those young girls and our daughter, and him knowing I'd left Sarah and his incestuous baby, the son he'd always wanted, to die. It seemed . . . fitting, somehow."

"What do you mean you both had to live with that knowledge all these years? You told me Harold died."

"Of course I didn't!" Prudence scoffed. "That would have been a lie. I said that the life he loved ended. You see, Harold had a series of strokes not long after we left here, Miss Long. He's been confined to a wheelchair ever since. He doesn't walk or talk. I take care of him, and I don't have to share him any longer."

There was no brother, Lilly realized. The man in the wheelchair was Harold. "You told the neighbor he was your brother. That was a lie."

Prudence backed through the doorway, a gentle, indulgent smile on her face. "A small fib, Miss Long, since technically we are all brothers and sisters in the Lord. Besides, we do what we have to do, you know."

The ends justify the means.

There was no doubt now that Prudence intended Lilly to

die. While Lilly was weighing the wisdom of rushing the older woman, Prudence whirled and fled the room, slamming the door closed and shutting Lilly in with the ghosts of the Purcells' past. Her cry of surprise drowned out the scrape as Prudence turned the latch.

Knowing that she had just been sentenced to the same end as Sarah Purcell, Lilly stumbled to the door, kicking it with her booted foot as she pounded on it with her sore hands and screamed for Prudence to let her out.

"Don't make things worse for yourself, Prudence!" Lilly cried. "Don't repeat the wrong you did twenty years ago!"

Even over her cries for mercy, there was no mistaking the sounds of an unrepentant Prudence scooting the trunk back in front of the door, then replacing the crates and mirror on top. With a sinking heart, Lilly listened as the madwoman's footfalls faded down the stairs.

Being shot would have been a kindness.

"Prudence!" she cried once more though her throat had already gone raw from screaming. "Let me out of here!"

There was no response. Lilly didn't know how long she continued to scream and rail. She cursed Prudence and Harold and herself for being so stubbornly pigheaded. Her toes felt bruised in her heavy boots, her voice was reduced to a raw whisper, and her hands were swollen and bleeding once more. She dragged the quilt from the cot and sank down on the dusty floor. Wrapping her arms around the quilt, she rested her cheek against it while tears of exhaustion seeped from her eyes.

She must have slipped into a short sleep, because she dreamed. Dreamed of a baby sleeping in a valise while Timothy, wearing nothing but ankle boots and a signet ring, strangled a naked Kate while Lilly hid under the bed. Rose came in, hoping to help Kate, but Timothy shoved her against the fireplace and when her head hit the hearth, her skull split open and money streamed out.

Then Rose was gone and Kate was the skeleton on the bed, lying in a tangle of bloody sheets. Next to her sat the valise with the skeleton baby, but now Lilly was the baby.

She woke to the sound of herself crying and tears running down her cheeks, her heart breaking for the mother and sibling she'd lost.

Chapter 39

When Lilly first opened her eyes, she was greeted by a profound silence and a room filled with deepening shadows. For a moment, she had no idea where she was. Her sore and aching body felt as if she'd been dragged for miles behind a horse and buggy. Her hands were so swollen she could barely make a fist. Then she remembered. Though her body was beaten down, her mind was clear. The empty grave. Prudence's confession. Being locked in with Sarah and her baby.

The dead made good sleeping companions. Perhaps their blameless spirits had watched over her while she slept the deep sleep of total mental and physical exhaustion.

She thought of her theory that when men were pushed into a corner, they felt no qualms about sacrificing whoever stood in their way. Since hearing Prudence's horrific confession, Lilly had revised that opinion to include the female of the species. Evidently, some women were just as capable as their male counterparts at cunning, subterfuge, and murder. For that's exactly what Prudence had done when she left her daughter and grandson here to die. And murder was precisely what she'd intended when she locked Lilly in the attic room.

A bitter lesson learned, one that would stand her in good stead in the future. If she had a future. She glanced around the small room. There must be some way to get out. She would not die in this sepulcher without trying to escape! Instead of resorting to her earlier panic, she sat perfectly still and pondered her situation. Screaming and pounding would do her no good. Prudence was long gone, and there was no one to hear her but Sarah and her baby. Lilly had to use her mind instead of her battered body. When the sun set, she would be unable to see, and any attempt to escape would have to be postponed until morning, unless someone from town missed her and came to help. Even then, would they find her up here?

She couldn't leave salvation to chance. There must be some way to open the door from this side. She knew her arms weren't strong enough, but her legs and thighs had done a good job of moving the heavy trunk. Could she possibly use the strength of her back and legs to push out the single nail holding the latch and move aside the things blocking the doorway? How strong could one nail be?

She soon learned that with the trunk and mirror in front of it, the door refused to budge an inch. Fighting back the threat of tears, she drew in a deep breath. Oh, if Robert Pinkerton could see her now! How he would gloat. She could imagine his smug smile, could hear him say, "I told you this is no job for a woman."

Blast Robert Pinkerton! She might die here, but not for lack of trying. *Use your head, Lilly. You're a smart woman. Physical strength isn't everything.* There had to be some way to get out of this cursed place!

The only other means of escape was the window, and it was three stories aboveground. Pushing the negative thought away, she crossed the small room to see what lay below. She tried to remember what the rear of the house looked like and recalled that the back porch ran the length of the house, so the porch roof would only go to the floor level of the second story. The problem became how to get from level three to a first-floor roof.

Rubbing the grime from the panes with her bandaged hand, Lilly leaned close and cupped the sides of her face to peer out. All remnants of the rain were gone but the glistening wetness. The last light of day would soon be pushed away by the encroaching darkness, but right now there was still plenty of light, and she could see the backyard and the gaping hole she'd dug. Despite her determination to escape her prison, the sight sent a shiver of apprehension through her. Suddenly, a mockingbird's medley came through the window. The sassy song gave her a feeling of hope, and with it renewed determination.

Yes! The porch roof was there, as she'd known it would be, but even if she managed to . . . Something gave her pause. The roof below her was too small and too near to be the back porch covering. Instead, this roof was peaked and came all the way to the top of the second story, which put it within jumping distance from the window she was looking out of—if she could fit through the window.

Unable to see what lay to either side of her, she closed her eyes and tried again to picture how the back of the house looked from the cemetery. She recalled the layout of the upper rooms she'd searched earlier in the week and remembered a bedroom with two nice-size dormer windows that overlooked the rear yard. One had been used for sewing; the other boasted a window seat and a ready supply of books. This was the roof she was seeing! Below them ran the roofline of the back porch. Perhaps there was a chance.

The first thing she had to do was open the window. She soon learned that was an impossibility, which meant she had to break out the glass and wood that made up the individual panes. Sitting on the floor, she pulled off one of her muddy boots. Grabbing it across the top, she turned her face away and swung the heel at a pane. Her reward was the tinkling of glass and a slight sting as a few shards nicked her wrist and forearm.

In no more than a minute, all the glass was broken out, but the wood dividers remained. A visual search of the room revealed a small, three-legged stool in the corner. A surge of anger swept through her. Harold certainly hadn't intended for Prudence to be comfortable while he seduced the young women downstairs.

Lilly took the stool by two legs and swung it at the window with all her might, pretending she was swinging it at Harold Purcell's handsome, arrogant face. After several minutes, she found success. She blotted perspiration from her face on the shoulder of her chemise and set the stool beneath the window.

After replacing her boot, she took stock of things. Even standing on the stool, she would have to cling to the lower sill and try to give a little leap to get into position to wiggle through the opening, which was no more than two by two feet. First, she needed to pick out all the little slivers of glass around the frame and watch out for the stubborn nail that poked down from the top. She'd bent it as best she could, but it would still make a vicious gouge if she didn't stay clear of it.

Painstakingly, she plucked out the jagged pieces of glass and counted it a blessing that she only cut herself twice. Then, stepping onto the stool, she tried to hoist herself up and through the small opening. Bolts of agony shot through her raw palms. On the second try she jumped and dug the toes of her boots against the wall. The stool tipped over, but she managed to gain enough purchase to stiffen her elbows, heave upward, and get her head and shoulders through, though it felt as if the contrary nail had snagged her hair.

She hung in the window with the bottom of the frame digging in just below her ribs, staring down at the dormer roof. How could she maneuver herself to go down feetfirst? The opening didn't allow much room for manipulation, and now that she was looking directly at the dormer, she saw that it was much smaller than she remembered. There was the possibility that she would hit the peaked roof—the slippery, *wet* peaked roof—and fall all the way to the top of the porch, which meant the chance of a broken limb, or even loss of life.

While she was considering the odds of getting one leg through the opening, she heard the sound of heavy boots on the stairs. Her heart began to race. Had Prudence come to finish her off, or had she had a change of heart and come to let her out? Lilly heard the clatter of boxes being set aside and was torn between elation and fear. Should she hide in the corner and try to overpower Prudence as she came through the door? Maybe it was someone from town. . . .

She didn't hear the latch being turned for the wild beating of her heart, and when the door opened, she was still dangling in the aperture. Jerking her head to look over her shoulder, she banged her temple on the window frame and uttered a mild curse.

Squinting against the pain, she saw a large frame blocking the doorway. A sharp gasp of surprise and recognition escaped her. The boxer stood in the doorway, a grudging half smile curving his lips as he regarded her predicament.

"What are you doing here?" she asked in disbelief.

The smile died, and he gave a shake of his head. "Aren't you the grateful one?" His deep voice held a note of sarcasm. He gave a low whistle. "And aren't you a proper mess? It looks as if Mrs. Reverend rowed you up Salt River."

"She gave me hell, all right, even though she never touched me," Lilly rasped through her aching throat. "Believe it or not, other than locking me in this room, I managed to do all this to myself. Who the devil *are* you, and why have you been following me?"

With another sardonic smile, he pulled a badge from his vest pocket, and said, "Andrew Cadence McShane, Pinkerton agent, at your service, ma'am." There was no mistaking the mockery in his tone.

Lilly wondered if the self-inflicted blow to the head had affected her hearing. "You're not a boxer?"

His smile could only be described as bleak. "Believe me, though I have finally lived long enough to regret it, I have been known to crack a few heads from time to time, both in the ring and without." The expression on his face was grim. "Actually, I was assigned to be your watchdog."

"What!" Lilly jerked in surprise, knocking her head against the window frame once again.

"To the annoyance of us both, I'm sure. Since this was your first assignment, William sent me to keep an eye on you."

Irritation mingled with relief. "Then where in blazes have you been?"

Cadence McShane made a *tsking* sound as he moved toward her. He made a sketchy sign of the cross as he passed by the remains on the cot.

"Hardly the language of a lady," he said, "and a bit of an ungrateful attitude, if you don't mind me repeating myself."

He placed his hands on her waist. "Let go, and I'll lift you down. Watch that nail, now."

Still miffed, though she didn't even know why, she allowed him to lift her down and realized her midriff hurt like the very dickens. Securely on the floor, she glared up at him. "Have you followed me out here before?"

McShane wasn't in the least intimidated. "I have."

Well, that explained why she'd felt someone watching her. She balled her hand into a fist and hit his shoulder. It was like striking a rock. "You scared the devil out of me."

"Sorry."

He didn't sound sorry. He sounded as if it was all in a day's work, and she supposed for him it was.

"I've been around all along, but you're a wee bit hard to keep up with, colleen," he told her in a distracted tone as he began to remove the filthy rags wrapped around her hands.

"Don't call me colleen," Lilly commanded through teeth gritted together in pain and irritation.

The man who'd been sent to follow her looked at her with a sardonic lift of his eyebrows. Seeing the oozing abrasions and the small cuts, he pulled a pristine handkerchief from his pocket and began to dab at them, continuing his ministrations and his explanation as if he'd never been interrupted. "I had to track down where you were staying every time you moved around, and I never knew when you might be leaving town. I've been half a day behind you since you left Springfield. You told me you were leaving there the night you were almost run down, but I had no idea you'd head back to Vandalia.

"When I telegraphed William, he told me he'd neither seen nor heard from you since you'd said you were returning. I thought it was worth a shot to come back to Vandalia."

Thank goodness.

"When I didn't find you at the hotel, I figured you'd come back out here for some reason. As luck would have it, the fella at the livery told me where you'd gone when I went to rent a horse. He also told me that another woman had rented a buggy and had headed out this direction. It was a good bit later that he'd finally recognized Mrs. Purcell. He said she was acting so strangely that he was worried about you. He was getting ready to go tell the sheriff when I arrived."

Thank goodness for Billy Bishop, too.

"I was about halfway here when I saw your rig hightailing it back to town. Knowing that Mrs. Purcell was going this way, I suspected something was wrong, so I got a hustle on things. I finally saw her up ahead of me and had to hang back until we got here. God help me and my job if I'd have lost you."

Seeing the question in her eyes, his expression hardened. "Never mind."

"That must have been ages ago," Lilly complained. "Why are you just now getting here?"

"Mmm," he agreed with a little shrug, giving her palm another pat with the hanky. "I wasn't checking my watch. I'd just arrived and tied my horse in the woods when I heard you screaming."

Lilly's face grew hot with embarrassment. He must have thought she was as mad as Prudence Purcell.

"It looked as if Mrs. Purcell was still trying to figure out what to do. I had the distinct impression she hadn't expected anyone to be here. She seemed really surprised to see your buggy. She was pacing and flinging her arms around talking to herself. Finally, she followed you inside."

"Why didn't you try to stop her?"

"One of the first things you need to learn, colleen, is that in this business, you never go into a place until you've done some reconnaissance. You never know when someone is armed, or if they have others with them. You don't want to walk in blind and take a chance on getting ambushed. I looked around a bit to get the lay of things and then unhitched her horse and sent it back to town so she couldn't slip out and get away. She must have followed you up here and locked you in while I was doing that. I was watching her mare heading down the lane when she stepped out onto the porch."

"Well, what took you so long to get up here after that?" Lilly asked sharply. "Why didn't you just arrest her and come get me? I've been here for hours."

"Actually, it's only been about half an hour. I've been playing cat and mouse with the missus ever since she used that fancy little derringer on me."

"She shot you?" Lilly asked, wide eyed.

"She tried." Offering her another of those grim smiles, he poked his forefinger into a hole in the sleeve of his tweed jacket. "Ruined a perfectly good coat," he grumbled as he shoved his handkerchief in his breast pocket.

He met her gaze with a puzzled expression. "Do you have any idea how many hiding places there are in a house this size? It took me a bit to find her." Then as if he felt he'd done enough explaining, he asked, "Can you walk?"

"Of course I can walk," Lilly snapped. She took a step and stumbled.

"Of course you can," he mocked, and without another word, he swung her into his arms and carried her out of the attic room and down the stairs. Despite her ungrateful attitude, which she knew was rooted in the fact that William had sent McShane to keep an eye on her, she was thankful he'd found her. She wasn't sure she'd have had the guts to leap out that window, or even if she'd have been able to do so. His arms, the first to hold her since Timothy left her, cradled her securely; their strength inspired confidence and hope.

She stared up at his hard jaw and the nose with the bump. He must have felt her stare, since he turned his head to look at her. He scowled. Grudgingly, she admitted that she had been a bit hard on him, but this had been a day like no other.

For the first time since he'd come through the door she was aware of her state of undress. "My skirt and petticoats!" she cried. "They're in the kitchen."

"It's a bit too late for modesty," he said. "Besides, you're not the first colleen I've seen in bloomers."

The calm statement and his calling her by Timothy's harlot's name hardened Lilly's yielding heart. Of course she was not the first! With his looks and charming manner, Andrew Cadence McShane could have any woman he wanted. She'd be a fool not to remember that.

She saw that he'd tethered his mount to the back of the wagon. As he settled her into the seat, Lilly found it hard to ignore the malevolent gaze of Prudence Purcell, who was tied, gagged, and lying in the back. Turning away from the horrible woman, she watched as her rescuer drew a blanket from a wooden box beneath the seat and flung it over her shoulders. Without a word, he headed back inside and returned a few moments later with her clothing, which he tossed into the back. Then he untied the buggy and climbed in beside her. She had questions for Cadence McShane, but they could wait until she was not in so much pain and her weary mind could process his answers.

As he turned the wagon toward the lane, Lilly looked back at the house. She remembered her feelings the first time she'd seen it and how she'd sensed that the dwelling secluded in the woods held darkness and secrets. Now it was just an abandoned house. She looked up at the wrought-iron entry.

HEAVEN'S GATE

All who stepped through that entrance should have found peace and hope and love. Instead, they had crossed the threshold leading to their own private hell.

EPILOGUE

"That went better than I expected," Lilly confessed to Cadence McShane as they stepped out of Eloise Mercer's shabby little house.

The evening before, he'd taken Lilly to the Holbrook Hotel, carried her to her room, and instructed one of the Holbrook boys to bring hot water for her bath, the other to fetch the doctor. Then he told her he'd be there to buy her breakfast the next morning at eight, and bade her good night.

"Where are you going?" she'd asked.

"It crossed my mind that perhaps I should take our captive to the jail and let the sheriff know what happened." Once again, his tone held a derisive note. "I realize she tried to kill us both, but it seems wrong for a couple of Pinkerton agents to leave the poor barmy woman in the back of a buggy overnight."

"Oh," Lilly said. "I suppose you're right, though she wants a madhouse, not a jail cell."

"Which she'll probably get before this is over."

"Is the telegraph office open?" she asked. "I really need to report back to William."

"I'll see. If it is, I'll be sure'n let him know how things stand." Seeing the look on her face, he said, "Have no fear, colleen. I've no need to hang on to a woman's coattails for recognition. I'll make certain he knows this all came about because of you."

"Thank you," she'd said grudgingly. "And stop calling me colleen."

Cadence McShane had only smiled that infuriating half smile and arched one heavy eyebrow in question.

McShane had gone to the sheriff's office and watched as the sheriff put Prudence in a cell and questioned her, learning that she'd left Harold alone in their Springfield house while she'd come to dispose of the bodies of her daughter and grandson. Finding Lilly there had been a surprise, but she'd decided to deal with her as well, securing her future. McShane had asked if she knew anything about a rig that had almost run Lilly down in front of Chatterton's Opera House, and Prudence confessed that she had been the one driving the carriage.

Sheriff Mayhew had telegraphed the law officials in Springfield and told them to make certain that someone checked on Harold Purcell. If he was still alive, he would be sent to an institution somewhere until he died, as hopefully would Prudence.

After breakfast this morning, the sheriff and a group of men had ridden out to Heaven's Gate to see the evidence of the Purcells' crimes for themselves. Lilly and her associate had declined the invitation to accompany them. Though they'd said they would like to talk to Lilly before she left town, the case was closed for all intents and purposes.

While the sheriff and his men were at Heaven's Gate, Cadence and Lilly had gone to visit Virginia Holbrook, where Lilly made her apologies for disrupting her life and told her what had happened the day before at Heaven's Gate.

"I was furious with you when you first came around asking questions," Virginia said, "but after everything was out in the open, I felt really free for the first time since I was seventeen. David and the boys have been wonderful, and Helen has taken the news better than I expected. She isn't thrilled about Harold Purcell being her father, but she knows it was none of my doing."

"That's very good news," Lilly told her. "Mr. McShane and I plan to speak to Eloise and Mr. Townsend this morning."

Lilly was surprised when, upon leaving, Virginia Holbrook hugged her and once more expressed her gratitude.

To Lilly's further surprise, Eloise Mercer burst into tears when told the Purcell tale of horror. "How could they have done those terrible things to their own daughter?" she'd cried.

"I don't know," Lilly confessed.

"Sarah was kindhearted, but very quiet. Now I know why. She and her mother couldn't get close to anyone for fear of their secret getting out somehow." She dried her eyes on the hem of her scruffy dressing gown and thanked Lilly. "I know it makes no sense, and I'm sorry for what happened to Sarah, but just knowing that this is all out in the open and that the Purcells have suffered, too, makes me feel a whole lot better. Their misery these last twenty years is at least some sort of vindication for what he did to us."

Now, back out in the fresh spring air, McShane asked, "Where to next?"

"Phillip Townsend's office. His daughter, Rachel, was another victim."

As they relayed their tale for the third time that morning, Phillip Townsend just listened and nodded a time or two.

"When Helen Holbrook gave me the names of the other two victims, I thought I had everything figured out," Lilly told him. "I knew Rachel had left town late in her pregnancy and that she'd never come back. No one mentioned her—not even you, so it made sense to me that she was the one killed in that bed and her body done away with. When I found the grave empty, I felt I was missing something, and finally found the room in the attic."

She told him of Sarah's circumstance, how Prudence had known of Harold's sins and covered up for him, and of the strokes that had mercifully ended his activities.

"Knowing I would tell the truth of what happened, she locked me in the room and left me for dead. I was trying to escape when Mr. McShane found me. I'm lucky to have been spared the same fate as Sarah."

Phillip Townsend made no comments as Lilly spoke, but his face wore an enigmatic smile throughout the telling of the tale.

"It's a blessing for this town that you survived," Townsend said when she finished. He regarded Lilly for a moment, his eyes seeming to hold a secret he wished to impart, his mouth curved in a slight smile.

"It is no secret that James, Asa, and I have been upset with you for coming back and stirring up the whole sad affair. We truly meant you no harm. We just wanted you to go away so that those we loved wouldn't be hurt anymore. But now I thank you for listening to your instincts and seeing this case through. It's high time to put this whole sordid mess behind us."

Lilly smiled and nodded. "I agree."

"Since there are no Purcell heirs, it will take a while for the state to decide how to handle their assets, but it would seem that the house will be for sale after all, which will make my daughter very happy."

"Your daughter?" Lilly repeated, not understanding.

The smile he'd been holding back blossomed. "Yes, my daughter. Rachel. She and her husband are the couple who approached William Pinkerton about finding Harold Purcell."

"You knew who I was and why I was here all the time?"

"Actually, I didn't find out until a few days ago, when I received a letter from Rachel telling me of her plans. Then I put it all together. You didn't know that my Rachel was the woman looking for Purcell?"

"No," Lilly said in dazed disbelief. "I have a journal with all the case information in it, but I never made the connection that Rachel Stephens was Rachel Townsend."

"Understandable, since Rachel is a common name," Townsend said. "When she left here, she went to live with a relative in Arkansas, where she had my granddaughter, Annabelle. She met Noah there, and they've been happily married for sixteen years."

This time Lilly answered the attorney's smile with one of her own. There were at least two happy endings from this unholy mess, and at least two more good men in the world than she'd known about—David Holbrook and Noah Stephens. "If you don't mind my asking, why would Rachel ever want to move back here, and especially to Heaven's Gate?"

Phillip Townsend's face wore a look of pride. "Rachel explained in the letter that time has dimmed the horror of what happened. It's evident that my daughter has grown into a very strong woman, perhaps because she has gone through so much herself. She believes that by turning that place into one of comfort and hope, she can help heal not only herself but the community and all the young women who find themselves in a delicate position, whether they're partly responsible or not. She believes people who make mistakes need encouragement, not censure."

Lilly thought about that for a moment. It seemed right somehow. After all, it was not the house that was evil, just the people who'd lived in it. "She sounds like a wonderful woman," Lilly said at last.

"She is."

After saying their farewells, she and her companion stepped

out into the warm spring day. Lilly turned her face skyward and smiled, clutching her reticule in her clasped hands; Cadence McShane stood with his hands in his pockets, watching her. Neither spoke.

She was filled with a feeling of accomplishment for having completed her assignment so successfully. She'd done what she'd set out to do and more.

She'd remembered everything about her mother's death. Someday she would return to Springfield and visit Kate's grave, and she would query Mr. Chester Carpenter about men who might have frequented the theater there and who might possibly be her mother's killer. There would be other opportunities, other lines of investigation as well. She was equally certain that someday she would pick up Timothy's trail and find him. For now, it was enough that she had helped bring peace to three ill-treated women and justice to a dead girl and her baby.

Finally, she turned to the man standing next to her. "Thank you for coming to my rescue yesterday, Mr. McShane," she said at last, uncertain if she'd have had the courage to jump onto the steep dormer roof or not, and vowing he would never know how hard the apology was to speak.

"It was my pleasure, Miss Long," he said formally, "but I've no doubt you'd have climbed out that window somehow if I hadn't come along. Townsend's daughter isn't the only strong woman, you know."

Lilly felt a flush of pleasure at the praise. "Thank you for that." She released a deep breath. "There were times I wanted to quit, when I wondered if I could do it," she confessed and wondered why she'd done so.

"There are times we all feel that way."

There were shadows in his eyes she didn't dare ask about. "Even you?"

His smile was derisive. "Especially me."

Deciding things were getting far too personal, she asked, "Did you notify William?"

"I did."

"I imagine he was disappointed in me to say the least."

"Why?"

"Because I didn't return to Chicago when I completed the task he assigned to me."

"On the contrary. You brought justice to a killer. In fact, William said I should tell you that Allan said he was proud of you and that you'd done a fine job. An extremely fine job."

Lilly couldn't help smiling. Despite her concerns about her abilities, she'd finished her first assignment. She was a Pinkerton agent in the truest sense of the word.

"Thank you, Mr. McShane," she said again.

"My fellow workers all call me Cadence or Cade," he told her.

Cadence McShane. Cade. It was a nice name, and fit him somehow. Why not humor him? she thought. He was a fellow operative, and she'd probably never set eyes on him again. She managed a small smile. "Certainly, Cade. I'm Lilly."

"I knew that, colleen."

Before she could take him to task for calling her by that wretched name, he tipped his hat, turned, and strolled down the busy street, disappearing in the crowd.

Don't miss the next Lilly Long Mystery
by Penny Richards

THOUGH THIS BE MADNESS

coming to you in May 2017
from your favorite booksellers and e-tailers.

*Turn the page for
a quick look at
Lilly's next adventure!*

CHAPTER 1

Though this be madness, yet there is method in't.

—William Shakespeare, *Hamlet,* act 2, scene 2

89 Dearborn, Chicago
The Pinkerton Offices

"I bloody well won't do it!" The declaration came from the angry man pacing the floor of William Pinkerton's office. "I'm a Pinkerton agent, not a blasted nanny."

William Pinkerton pinned the young operative with an unrelenting look from beneath heavy brows. "You haven't any choice, McShane."

Andrew Cadence McShane faced his tormenter with defiance. "So you're saying that I haven't yet groveled enough for you and your father?"

William stifled his own irritation at the bold statement. McShane was a loose cannon, and if it were up to William, he'd fire the man on the spot. Indeed, Allan *had* fired him a year ago, for drinking and brawling and generally behaving in a way that was unacceptable to the Pinkertons' code of conduct. But, claiming that he had his life together at last, McShane had asked for his job back about the same time the young actress, Lilly Long, had applied for a position. Allan, who had always thought the young Irishman was one of his best agents, had re-hired him, on a provisional basis.

"You know exactly what I mean," William said in mea-sured tones. "No one was holding a gun to your head when you agreed to the terms of our rehiring you, which, as you no doubt recall, was probation for an undetermined length of time."

Feeling a certain amount of uneasiness over his father's decision to hire McShane and Miss Long, William had sug-gested that McShane keep an eye out for the inexperienced Miss Long on her first assignment, which would hopefully keep him too preoccupied to get into any more scrapes. Allan had agreed. So while new agent Lilly Long tried to find the lo-cation of the Reverend Harold Purcell, a preacher who had stolen from his congregation and disappeared from his home near Vandalia, Illinois, McShane had kept tabs on her by pre-tending to be part of a traveling boxing troupe.

"Until we feel confident that you will not resort to your previous unacceptable behavior, you will work closely with Miss Long."

McShane's eyes went wide with something akin to shock. "It was a barroom brawl, sir. I did not reveal any state secrets or compromise my assignment in any way."

"We've been through all this before, McShane, and I refuse to revisit it again." Smack dab in the middle of a case, McShane had gotten drunk and instigated a brawl. William's gaze shied away from McShane's, which had lost its belliger-ence and grown as bleak as the stormy April morning.

William cleared his throat. "Believe me, I understand that on a personal level you were going through an extremely rough patch at the time. For that you have my sympathy. But you must understand that the agency cannot have our opera-tives behaving in ways that make us look bad. We have a ster-ling reputation, and we must make sure it stays that way. If you continue to do well, you will soon be on your own again."

All the fiery irritation seemed to have gone out of the younger man. "Yes, sir."

"Actually, this assignment is one that will be best served by a man and woman working closely together."

Wearing a look of resignation, McShane took a seat in the chair across from William's desk. "Tell me about it."

"I prefer to explain things to you and Miss Long together," William said. "She should be here any minute. But I will tell you this much. You will be going to New Orleans."

Though the skies were still ominous with clouds, the rain had stopped shortly before Lilly's cab pulled up in front of the five-story building that housed the Pinkerton offices. She paid the driver and, careful to step around the puddles, entered the structure with a feeling of elation. Since returning from her first assignment just a week ago, she had been riding the wave of her success in bringing the case to a satisfactory conclusion, as well as basking in the knowledge that she would continue to be employed by the prestigious Pinkerton firm. She'd been more than a little surprised when she received a message that morning stating that William wanted to see her at once.

Though she knew she had a long way to go before she was a seasoned operative, the praise she'd received from both William and Allan was, to paraphrase the bard, "the stuff that dreams were made of." When her missing person assignment had evolved into a twenty-year-old murder, it had been satisfying to know that she had helped bring about justice. And Allan, who loved correcting what he perceived as social wrongdoing, had been quite satisfied that things had been made as right as humanly possible. Lilly could hardly wait to embark on her next mission.

Pausing outside the doorway to the outer office, she tucked a loose strand of dark red nape hair beneath the brim of the straw hat she'd purchased as a treat for herself the day before.

The soft green of the grosgrain ribbons of the hat was the exact hue of her new walking dress with its high stand-up collar topped with the wide, heavy white lace that marched down the front. The off-the-ground hem of her narrow skirt was trimmed with a wide band of the lace and showed the pointed toes of her shoes.

She stepped through the door to the outer office and saw Harris, William's clerk, pounding on the keyboard of the Remington typewriter, using the hunt and peck system. The morning sunshine behind him illuminated the long, thin wisps of graying hair that had been combed over to help disguise his balding pate.

Hearing her at the door, he glanced up. "Good morning, Miss Long," he said with a polite smile. "You are looking particularly chipper this morning."

"Hello, Harris," she replied. "I am chipper this morning. I'm anxious to get back to work."

Harris stood. "I'll just let them know you're here," he said.

Them. Lilly smiled. Oh, good. Allan was going to be involved in her next project. She had the feeling that the great detective supported her being hired, even though William was ambivalent, at best, about his father's insistence on hiring women operatives.

"Miss Long is here," Harris said, stepping aside for Lilly to enter.

She stepped through the aperture. William was coming around the desk, his hand extended in greeting. But it wasn't William who caught Lilly's attention. It was the man who had risen from a chair when she entered the room. It wasn't Allan Pinkerton who stood when she stepped through the doorway; it was Cadence McShane.

With her attention focused on the other man, she barely heard William's words of welcome. The last time she'd seen McShane, after the completion of the Heaven's Gate assignment, he'd made a cryptic comment and disappeared into the crowd. She supposed she'd seen the last of him, so what was he doing here?

After she shook William's hand, McShane took her hand in greeting. His hand was large, rough, and warm, and his words and smile were pleasant, but the coldness in his sapphire-blue eyes was undeniable.

What the devil was going on? she wondered again, her imagination steering her toward a deduction that was not the least bit acceptable. Seeking an answer to the questions roiling around in her head, Lilly turned her puzzled gaze to William. Allan Pinkerton's son was not noted for his slowness in assessing situations. He did not miss the query on Lilly's face or the disdain on McShane's.

"Have a seat, Miss Long," he said, gesturing toward the chair Cade had vacated at her arrival.

Lilly did his bidding, clutching her purse in her lap.

"My father and I have decided on your next assignment," William told her, wasting no time at getting to the point. "You and McShane will be going to New Orleans."

"What!" Lilly gasped, her gaze flying to Cade's. If the grim twist of his lips and the blatant annoyance in his eyes were any indication, he was no happier than she.

"Do you really feel that is necessary, sir?" she protested. "While I appreciate the fact that you were concerned about my inexperience, I thought you were happy with my work in Vandalia."

"We were extremely pleased," William assured her, "but one successful assignment does not afford you any vast field knowledge. While you were the one who discovered the truth about the Purcells, if it had not been for McShane, you might very well be dead."

Though Lilly had been in the process of trying to free herself from a very sticky situation by jumping from a small win-

dow onto a steep roof, she could not deny that there was a ker-
nel of truth in William's statement. Her plan could have gone
very wrong.

"Keeping your youth and inexperience in mind, my father
and I feel that at least for the next few assignments, you and
McShane should work together. It will give you a chance to
hone your skills."

Lilly looked askance at Cade, who was lounging with apparent indolence on the chair, though the set of his jaw and
the glittering hardness in his eyes left no doubt of his true feelings.

She made one last attempt to change the course of her
task, indeed, the course of her life, at least for the foreseeable
future. "And is Mr. McShane agreeable to this arrangement?"
she asked.

William's calm gaze flickered over the younger man. "Mc-
Shane is a professional, Miss Long," William said in a no-nonsense
tone. "He accepts his obligations and gives this agency his best."
Though he was speaking directly to her, she could not shake the
notion that his words were meant as much for her new partner
as for Lilly.

She sighed. Disappointment, anger, and frustration vied for
supremacy. Clearly, neither she nor Cadence McShane had a
choice in the matter, and to argue it further would only cause
her to appear contrary and disagreeable. As she had with her
first assignment, she would accept the situation gracefully, do
her best, and hope that soon she would be trusted to go it
alone.

With a lift of her chin, she said, "So we head for New Orleans." The statement told her employer that she had accepted
her fate and was ready to hear the details of the assignment.

"Yes. Actually, Miss Long, I believe you will embrace the
case once you hear about it," William told her, stepping from
behind the desk and handing each of them a copy of the jour-

nal they were given at the beginning of a mission. The book held the name of the Pinkerton client, the situation, and the agency's ideas for following through. As was customary, the persons seeking help would not be formally introduced to the agents or have any idea how that help might come about.

"If indeed there is a crime involved, it is against a woman, so I know you will derive a great deal of satisfaction from working it," William said to Lilly.

"A brief overview of what you'll find in the journal is this: Just days ago, we received a special delivery letter from one Mrs. Etienne Fontenot, whose given name is LaRee. She and the legitimacy of her concern have been confirmed by her long-time attorney, Mr. Armand DeMille."

William looked from Lilly to Cadence McShane. "Mrs. Fontenot believes that her deceased grandson's widow, Patricia Ducharme, has been wrongly committed to an insane asylum by her husband, Henri."

Lilly's irritation at being paired with Cade, faded as she gave her attention to William's tale. "Are you saying she believes there is nothing wrong with the granddaughter-in-law?" Lilly asked.

"That is exactly what she believes," William said.

"Why?" The question came from Cade who, like Lilly, seemed to have lost his animosity as his interest in the case grew.

"Mrs. Fontenot is convinced that the purpose of Patricia's new husband, Henri Ducharme, is to gain control of the family fortune, which, according to Mr. DeMille, is extensive."

"I don't understand," Lilly said. "Wouldn't it pass down to the remaining heirs?"

"Indeed. Louisiana operates under the Napoleonic Code, which means that the closest male relative handles the business and monetary affairs of their womenfolk, who are considered little more than chattel to their fathers and husbands."

Lilly felt herself bristling. Once again, a male-dominated world sought to keep the fairer sex under its thumb, no doubt offering the notion that they should not have to deal with matters that might be too mind-boggling for the feeble female brain to comprehend, much less deal with.

"I see you take umbrage to that notion, Miss Long, as I suspected you would," William said with a slight smile. "As you know, social injustice is one thing that infuriates my father, so he was immediately drawn to this case. It is also common knowledge that he has strong beliefs that women are very capable or he would not have hired the first female detective.

"But I digress. When Mrs. LaRee Fontenot's husband, Etienne, suffered a stroke many years ago at a relatively young age, he began to think of ways to insure the money he had amassed stayed within the family. With Mr. DeMille's help and advice, Etienne transferred all his business holdings as well as a house on Rampart Street and a plantation called River Run to his son, Grayson, in whose capabilities he had complete trust. All this before his death."

"Wouldn't everything have gone to Grayson at his father's death?" McShane asked.

"Good question, McShane, and you're right, it would have, and he would have held control of his mother's portion, which was quite generous until she remarried. By all accounts, Mrs. Fontenot was quite a lovely woman in her youth, and her husband feared that she would fall for some unscrupulous ne'er-do-well, who would gain control of her fortune. Etienne Fontenot hoped that by giving everything to his son before his own death, he could avoid the possibility of his family losing everything he'd worked so hard to gain for them if his wife married unwisely and her portion was given to her new husband to oversee. Etienne knew Grayson would be generous and fair in providing for his womenfolk, and include them in the family decisions, yet they would have no money of their own."

"It doesn't sound as if he had much faith in his wife's ability to choose a suitable husband," Lilly said.

William smiled. "Actually, according to her letter, Mrs. Fontenot took exception to that herself, claiming that it was highly unlikely that she be taken in after having such a successful marriage to her husband."

Smart woman, Lilly thought.

"According to Mrs. Fontenot, the arrangement worked well, and the same agreement was set up between Grayson and his son, Garrett, who lost no time expanding the family holdings—timber in this case—into Arkansas, where he made his home most of the year.

"When Grayson passed away, Garrett visited his grandmother in New Orleans. While he was there, he met and fell in love with Patricia Galloway. They were soon married and went back to Arkansas to make their home."

"The same Patricia who is now in the insane asylum?" Lilly asked.

"The same," William corroborated. "Garrett and Patricia had two daughters, Cassandra and Suzannah. He died four years ago with no son to inherit. Like his father, he felt that some women were as intelligent and business savvy as men, since his grandmother had regularly and successfully interjected her thoughts and ideas into the running of the various Fontenot endeavors."

"You said his grandmother *had* interjected her thoughts and ideas," Cade said. "Why isn't she still?"

"We're getting there," William said. "Bear with me.

"As a resident of Arkansas, he was not bound by Louisiana law, and in accordance with the Married Women's Property Act, Patricia became heir to all the Fontenot holdings that had been passed down from father to son. Everything the male Fontenots had amassed from Etienne's time until the present."

"Ah," Cade said with a nod. "It was Patricia, not LaRee, who fell for the unscrupulous man, this Henri Ducharme."

"That is Mrs. LaRee Fontenot's fear, yes," William told them.

"If Patricia and her daughters lived in Arkansas, how did she meet Ducharme?" Lilly asked.

"She and the doctor were introduced while visiting in New Orleans. To the dismay of the entire family, they were married as soon as her year of mourning ended."

"Ducharme is a doctor and yet Mrs. Fontenot doubts his diagnosis in Patricia's case," Cade said.

"She does. Cassandra, the older daughter, confided to Mrs. Fontenot that her mother was mere months into her new marriage when she began to suspect she had made a dreadful mistake. She felt she had unwittingly put the family fortune in her husband's grasping hands—Mrs. Fontenot's words, not mine," William clarified.

"I can certainly relate to that," Lilly said in a voice laced with bitterness. She ignored the questioning look Cade shot at her.

"According to Cassandra, it appears that her stepfather's sole intent in life is to spend them into poverty."

Lilly gave another huff of disgust.

William continued. "To further upset the family, within ten months of the marriage, Patricia found herself with child. Mrs. Fontenot says the confinement was troublesome, and that Patricia got little comfort from her husband, who constantly warned her that something could go wrong because of her age."

"Job's comforter," Cade muttered.

"Exactly," William said with a nod. "As it happened, something did go wrong. The baby, a boy, was stillborn some eighteen months ago, which naturally sent Patricia into a deep melancholy, from which, Mrs. Fontenot says, she seemed to be slowly emerging until she received another blow."

As Lilly listened, she thought of her own mother's murder

and the subsequent death of the baby she'd been carrying. She wondered if she would always be reminded of their deaths at odd times like this, with nothing but a snippet of conversation bringing back the painful memory.

"What was that?" Cade asked.

"Four months ago, in an effort to cheer her mother, Cassandra urged Patricia to attend a suffragist gathering with her and her sister, Suzannah, who somehow became separated from them in the crush. They looked for her to no avail. She was located two days later by some hobo in an alley. She had been molested and killed."

There was an apologetic expression on William's face as he looked at Lilly, but though her heart gave a lurch of sympathetic pain for Patricia Ducharme's loss, she was no shrinking violet to go into a swoon from hearing such brutal truths.

"The murder has not been solved, and the New Orleans police have little hope of ever knowing who committed the crime. Needless to say, this tragedy on top of the loss of her infant son strained Patricia Ducharme's emotions to the limit."

"It would strain anyone's emotions," Lilly said.

"Indeed," William agreed. "Henri claimed she was so overcome with grief and anger that she became physically abusive, even striking him on several occasions. Mrs. Fontenot did not witness this, nor did anyone else in the house. Ducharme further claims he had no recourse but to restrain her and administer small doses of laudanum from time to time. Fearing he would make her a fiend, he discontinued the drug after the funeral, at which time Patricia alternated between forgetfulness and belligerence. She began to imagine things that were not so, accusing her husband of everything from hiding things from her to lying."

"The poor thing," Lilly said, thinking that it certainly sounded as if the woman's sanity had fled.

"Mrs. Fontenot admits that Patricia's emotions seesawed

between bouts of deep depression, sometimes a state not far from catatonia, to a"—William referred to the letter in his hand—"'howling, screeching creature hell-bent on physical damage.' That last was Henri's description as Mrs. Fontenot recalls it."

"And so he had her committed," Cade said.

William nodded. "A month after burying Suzannah, Henri committed Patricia to the City Insane Asylum in New Orleans."

"From what you've told us, it seems Dr. Ducharme's fears are well founded," Lilly mused. "Why does Mrs. Fontenot doubt his judgment?"

"Women's intuition."

Lilly saw Cade's mouth turn upward into a derisive smile.

"She admits she has no proof that Henri is up to anything nefarious," William told them, "but with Cassandra's statement about her mother's concerns over her husband and Mrs. Fontenot's own feeling that too many disasters have befallen Patricia since marrying him, she feels she has reason to doubt."

Lilly understood LaRee Fontenot's feelings perfectly. She recalled her feeling that people were withholding the truth during her previous investigation. She also remembered the feeling of certainty that Cadence McShane was not the person who intended her harm when he had saved her from a horse and buggy intent on running her down, even though her intellect reminded her that he had been in the area with her when other dodgy things had taken place.

And then there was Timothy. She'd felt no negative vibrations from him. Nothing about him had hinted that he was a leech and a scoundrel, yet he had proved to be that and more. Oh, women definitely had an innate intuition. But was it always reliable?

"Cassandra also believes that her stepfather is somehow responsible for Patricia's mental state," William was saying. "They fear that putting her into an asylum will drive her to the very insanity from which Henri claims she already suffers."

"So our job," Cade said, glancing at Lilly, "is to try to disprove the notion of Patricia Fontenot Ducharme's insanity?"

"Yes, and to do everything in your power to find out whether or not Henri Ducharme is the villain Mrs. Fontenot and Cassandra believe he is. That done, everything else should fall into its proper place."

"Does Mrs. Fontenot know anything at all about Henri's past?" Lilly asked. "We could use someplace to start looking."

She was already feeling a bit overwhelmed by the task set before her and her clearly disgruntled partner. His dark eyebrows drawn together in a frown, Cade was looking over the notes he had been taking as William explained the situation in New Orleans.

"The doctor is, by Mrs. Fontenot's grudging admission, an attractive and charming man, forty-five years old, and has been married before. She has no idea to whom he was married," William supplied. "She believes the first wife died."

"Am I correct in assuming that we will be employed by Mrs. Fontenot at the house on Rampart Street?" Lilly asked.

William nodded. "You will be hired as a married couple."

Cade and Lilly shared a stunned look.

"We have tried to arrange things so that it is almost a given that you both will be hired."

Connect with U s

Visit us online at
KensingtonBooks.com
to read more from your favorite authors, see books
by series, view reading group guides, and more.

Join us on social media

for sneak peeks, chances to win books and prize packs,
and to share your thoughts with other readers.

facebook.com/kensingtonpublishing
twitter.com/kensingtonbooks

Tell us what you think!

To share your thoughts, submit a review,
or sign up for our eNewsletters, please visit:
KensingtonBooks.com/TellUs.